Murder in Los Lobos

Murder in Los Lobos

A Bella Kowalski Mystery

Sue McGinty

2008 · FITHIAN PRESS, MCKINLEYVILLE, CALIFORNIA

Published by Fithian Press
A division of Daniel and Daniel, Publishers, Inc.
Post Office Box 2790
McKinleyville, CA 95519
www.danielpublishing.com

Distributed by SCB Distributors (800) 729-6423

LIBRARY OF CONGRESS CATALOGING-IN-PUBLICATION DATA
McGinty, Sue, date
Murder in Los Lobos : a bella kowalski mystery / by Sue McGinty.
   p. cm.
ISBN-13: 978-1-56474-477-7 (pbk. : alk. paper)
ISBN-10: 1-56474-477-9 (pbk. : alk. paper)
 1. Women—Crimes against—Fiction. 2. Women journalists—Fiction.
3. Environmental protection—California—Fiction. 4. Political corruption—
Fiction. 5. Family secrets—Fiction. I. Title.
PS3613.C4835M87 2008
813'.6—dc22
                    2008007494

For Katie and Julie, Jordon and Austin, Kyle and Kaitlyn.
You are my heroes. And for Jerry, who always finds the right words.

* * *

This is a work of fiction. While inspired by a real situation,
the characters and story live only in the writer's imagination.

A tip of the writer's cap to former San Luis Obispo County Supervisor Evelyn Delaney and retired SLO County District Attorney Homicide Investigator Larry Hobson, who now owns Hobson's Polygraph Service. Both gave generously of their time and expertise.
Any errors are mine alone.

Special thanks to Terre Dunivant of Gaia Graphics.
You listened to my cover ideas and turned them into magic.

1

Ring, ring. "Good morning, *Central Coast Chronicle*, obituary desk. How may I help you?"

"This Bella Kowalski?"

"It is. Have you lost a loved one, sir?"

"No, I have infor…"

"Would you repeat that please? You seem to be breaking up."

"I *said* I have information."

"Okay, sir, no need to shout. What kind of information?"

"Impor…"

"Did you say important?"

"That's right."

"Let me connect you with our managing editor."

"No, I want to talk to you."

(Sigh) "All right. Please go ahead when you're ready."

"The sons-a-bitches running this town are planning to buy the Mercado property for the sewer plant."

"Uh…"

"Did you hear me?"

"I did, sir, but that can't be right. That property is supposed to be donated to the Land Conservancy."

"Well, things change when you live in Los Lobos. Bye."

"Sir? *Sir?* Please don't hang up."

(Ring, ring) "Managing Editor, Amy Goodheart here."

"Amy, it's Bella. I've just had the most disturbing phone call."

2

Monday morning, three weeks later:

"Hey Sam, ready for a hike?"

Already settled into the worn passenger seat, Sam rattled the links of his collar. I took that as a yes. "Hike" and "dinner" are magic words for my Golden Lab.

"Great. Let's go."

I buckled the seatbelt across his considerable girth and he gazed at my hands, the ritual seeming to puzzle him. But he accepted the restraint with his usual good grace. Soon we were rocketing west along Los Lobos Road. Well, more like crawling. One can expect only so much from an '84 Subaru.

Didn't matter. Morning rays streamed through the hatchback window. Almost giddy from the sun's touch on my back and shoulders, I decided to forget the sewer project and seize the day. The morning anyway. My shift at the paper began at two.

A mile from home the two-lane highway veered sharply left, narrowing into the stretch that led to *Escarpa el Dorado*, Bluffs of Gold, our hiking destination. Called simply "the bluffs," by locals, they were—and are—my refuge and my escape.

Just before the turn, on our right overlooking the bay, sat the Mercado estate. Both the mansion and its surrounding twenty acres have drop-dead views of the bay and open ocean beyond.

"Downright criminal to ruin that fragile land with a wastewater treatment plant," I muttered to no one in particular.

Sam gave me a "give it a rest, Bella" look, then returned to gazing out the side window of the Subaru. He fidgeted in the seat, and an odor both sweet and foul filled the car.

"Sam, did you fart?" He pretended not to hear.

"Okay, be like that. Let's get some air in here." I tried to open the window on my side. Handle refused to budge. Damned old junk pile. At least twenty years past its prime.

I slowed, and seeing no other place to pull off, wheeled onto the broad expanse of the Mercado driveway. I stopped, leaned over and cracked open the passenger window. Sam's tail wagged his thanks and he pushed his nose through the opening. "What's the matter, boy? Can't stand the smell yourself?"

Hello. What was this?

I glanced past Sam's bulk to see that the imposing wrought iron gates stood ajar. To my knowledge, they hadn't been unlocked since the elder Mercados died in a plane crash last year. "Something going on?"

No response from Sam. He was too busy licking something off the glass.

My eyes moved past the gate, up the sloping drive to the house itself. Surrounded by giant eucalypti, the mission style *hacienda* looked much as it always had, timeless and permanent. The house seemed so uniquely at one with its land. It would be a sin to tear it down.

The Mercados were the closest thing Los Lobos had to a First Family, even though their businesses were rather mundane: heavy and light construction, real estate, real estate, real estate, a car dealership or two, even a glorified thrift store. One son, Rik, was a household name if your house included a teen. Rik was a rock star.

Other than Rik, who lived in Las Vegas or some such place, the others kept a pretty low profile. Raymond, Rik's twin, continued to run the father's construction company. The oldest, Connie, did her own thing, selling second-hand "treasures" and performing weddings in a chapel attached to her store. Neither chose to live in the family home.

Unable to resist a quick snoop, I studied the house. The massive oak door stood closed, locked no doubt, against intruders. Not that it mattered. If the sewer deal went through, a thousand locks wouldn't stop the wrecking ball.

Sam turned to me with one eyebrow cocked. I stroked the silky yellow head. A wastewater treatment plant would blight this unique land forever. This would happen even if the Coast Regional Utilities District (CRUD to the locals) made good on their promise to add a park with a footbridge over the pond and winding footpaths to Los Lobos Bay.

What were they thinking?

In the three weeks since my paper leaked the news of the proposed sale in its "Slice and Dice" column, Sam was about the only one in Los Lobos who hadn't offered an opinion on what everyone called "the sewer," though technically it was a wastewater treatment plant.

Like a love affair that neither party can end, the sewer issue had dragged on for years. Half the residents wanted the plant built anywhere to avoid looming state fines; most of the others were hanging tough for an out-of-town location. A few wild-eyed characters advocated for a more "natural" solution, whatever that meant. I shuddered to think.

"Okay, time to go." I put the car in reverse and wouldn't you know, popped the clutch. The car lurched forward a few feet and died. My view shifted. A man stood between a garage big enough for maybe six cars and a Hummer, one of the monster ones that looks like a rhino. He had a shaved head and a cell phone attached to one ear.

I sighed. So twenty-first century.

No indication that he'd seen me. But something about the guy froze the roots of my hair. "Come on, Sam, let's go." I coasted out of the driveway onto Los Lobos Road and started the car, veering left on the narrow, winding road that led to the bluffs.

Inhaling a whiff of crisp air through Sam's half-open window, I felt a warm breeze on my arms. A rare day for June on

California's Central Coast, with just a hint of fog far out to sea. Above the engine noise I heard sea lions on the rocks offshore. Native people called them "sea wolves" because of their mournful cries, and this area became known as *Los Lobos*—not to be confused with Point Lobos, three hours to the north. According to its Chamber of Commerce, they had even more sea lions. They're welcome to them.

When we'd gone maybe half a mile, daytime headlights flashed in my rearview mirror. A gray Hummer. The same guy? I sucked in my breath. If he was your typical aggressive driver, he'd pull up behind and tailgate me the entire three miles to the bluffs. I didn't learn to drive until I was forty-one. Even after eight years behind the wheel, I'm hardly NASCAR material.

The man advanced relentlessly. I looked for a place to pull off among the eucalyptus trees that bordered the road. Not a chance, no shoulder on this stretch. Clamping my teeth together, I determined to set the pace. The Hummer sat on my tail. "Hey," I called, even though he couldn't hear, "what's your problem?" My heart beat wildly and a voice from another life whispered, *"Hail Mary, full of grace…"*

Once a nun, always a nun.

Sam whined and began to fidget. I turned too sharply and over-corrected. With a heart-stopping shriek, the Hummer nailed my rear bumper and then the left rear fender. This was crazy.

We approached the bluffs and a steep drop to the cliffs below. I slowed, despite my shadow. Blasts from the guy's horn shattered the stillness. Why didn't he just pass?

Disturbed from its perch, a crow took flight. I ducked as it barely cleared my windshield. The Subaru rocked dangerously. My breathing became shallow and my legs shook so hard I could hardly keep my feet on the pedals.

I forced a deep breath that I hoped would be calming. It wasn't. "Come on, Bella, you can do it." I knew every inch of this road, and we were fast approaching the worst part—a series of tight S-curves, all uphill, with a vertical drop-off on our right.

I kept my hands at 10 and 2, finished my Hail Mary and began another.

All of a sudden I felt a strong vibration on my left. The guy was passing me!

No, he was trying to run me off the road! Closer and closer he inched, creating a suction between us that threatened to pull me into his side. Sun shot through the trees. Instinctively, I took one hand off the wheel to shield my eyes. Oh no. Through splayed fingers I glimpsed a car in the opposite lane. He was going to hit the Hummer head-on!

I gripped the wheel and prepared to die. The Hummer dropped back across the double yellow line with seconds to spare. The other car shot past, heading toward town. It's over, I thought.

But it wasn't over. Like the bully he was, my stalker-on-wheels kept his distance until the other car disappeared, then came at me again. This time I was ready. Praying I had enough time, I jerked the wheel to the left, careened across the oncoming lane, and bumped to a halt in a patch of scrub on the other side of the road.

Winded and sick, I slumped over the steering wheel and watched his tail lights recede. The bluffs were still a mile away. Sam whimpered. We were both shaking as I patted his back. "It's okay, boy, it's okay. The guy's gone."

He sneezed, once again rattling his collar. I pulled him close, both of us taking comfort in each other. Sam and I go back to my days in inner-city Detroit. No one was going to hurt him while there was life in my body.

Let the sheriff handle the Hummer. I pulled my cell phone from my day pack and snapped it open.

"No Service." Swell.

Despite Sam's presence, I felt vulnerable and very much alone. What if the guy came back?

"Sam, we need to get out of here, and fast."

I wheeled the car onto the road and hightailed it toward town, checking my rearview mirror every few seconds. About a mile from the S-curves, I ducked as dark shadows whooshed across my side mirror. Just blowing leaves, but the scare kicked my emotions into high alert. What if the guy caught up as we approached the most dangerous part of the road?

"Come on Bella, most likely he's surfing." Or doing whatever guys in Hummers do, having had his bit of fun with a local.

Mike, my husband, was always on me about what he saw as my irrational anxiety. But he's a retired cop—and a guy—and his sensibilities are different. His motto: "Feel the fear and do it anyway."

That didn't work for me. Bea, my sister, older by eleven months, was murdered outside my Detroit apartment. I still have dreams where she reaches from her grave and snatches me inside.

Why dwell on such dark thoughts? The morning offered sunshine and warmth, we were in a beautiful place and I would not give in to fear. "What do you think, Sam? Our friend seems to have disappeared. Still up for a hike?"

His tail thumped on the cracked leather seat.

I wheeled the Subaru around and headed back, deciding to stay well north of the visitor's center and parking area. My trusty Timex said a little after eight. We'd have the trail to ourselves. Good. I needed time alone.

Sam's tail thumped again as I reached into the back seat for his leash and snapped it to his collar. The driver's side door creaked open on time-worn hinges. No damage there, thank God.

I ran my hand along the left rear fender, finding little damage to the faded red paint. The back bumper sported a new ding, but no transfer of paint. That's the neat thing about driving an old car; no matter what happens it doesn't look that much worse.

Sam and I started up the trail. About a mile in, I veered east onto one that climbed straight up Mercado Peak, the highest point of the bluffs. I needed to work up a sweat and get my strength back.

I gazed around as we climbed. Even though the state owned it now, this land still bore the Mercado name. The family's history goes back to Spanish land grant time, and even today, no one messes with a Mercado.

Five hundred yards up the trail, I stopped to catch my breath. The experience on the road had left me badly shaken. I leaned over, clamped my hands on my knees, inhaled, then straightened up. My senses filled with the aroma of the sea, a unique mix of salt, fish and something primal I could never define.

So far so good. I reached into my backpack for my water bottle and took a healthy swig. What I really needed was a cup of black tea with lots of sugar. That was my English grandmother's cure for all ills of body and spirit. What was it she used to say? "No matter what the problem, the answer can always be found in a nice cup of tea."

Maybe so, but water would have to do. I poured some into my cupped hand and Sam drank in great slurps. Wiping my palm on the side of my jeans, I scanned the hills, carpeted with California poppies of rich orange-gold. No wonder the Spanish called this place "El Dorado."

Sam picked up a scent, probably a rabbit, and pulled me along a narrow trail lined with gray-green scrub oak. Other than a lone gull who screamed overhead, we walked in silence.

We climbed hard for several minutes and I mulled over the complications the proposed sewer location had created in our lives. Why had the person I now thought of as "Deep Throat" called me three weeks ago? I was the obituary editor for cripes sake. And he (I think it was a he) called several more times, hanging up when I pressed for his name.

Of course the state was pushing hard for a sewer, but these things didn't happen in a vacuum. What about the master plan that laid out the growth pattern for our area? The plan would have to be changed to allow the wastewater treatment plant to be built on the Mercado property. Surely CRUD could find a more suitable location.

The sewer system had been opposed for years by a vigorous

contingent of no-growthers. But many of them had died off, and while residents like Mike and I saw the need for a sewer, we were concerned about cost and location.

Residents had been warned that bills could run to over a hundred dollars per month, something few of us could afford. Our property sat far back from Los Lobos Road and hook-up costs alone would require a second mortgage. Add that to an astronomical monthly tab and you had a nightmare scenario.

Also, location of the wastewater plant was a huge issue. Our economy depended heavily on tourists. Would visitors want to see—and perhaps smell—a sewage treatment plant as they drove out to the bluffs, our main tourist attraction?

Location represented a quality-of-life issue for us. We both came from gritty Midwestern cities and hated to see urban blight imposed upon our perfect little hamlet. I had joined those against the Mercado purchase, and was even featured in a *Los Angeles Times* article detailing our "tempest in a chamber pot," as they smugly called it.

While I whined to the *Times* reporter and handed out flyers at the local market on Saturday mornings, my husband Mike adopted a neutral stance, at least in public. Anything else might be perceived as self-serving. He ran the only septic tank pumping service in town.

Despite flak from Mike—he's a hard person to say no to—I'd continued to wage an impassioned campaign against the Mercado purchase. My activism, and that of others, had forced the nefarious plan into the open. A town hall meeting was scheduled for Wednesday, two days from now, to get input from residents.

Unanswered questions rattled around in my mind like Lotto balls. Why the Mercado homestead? If the powers-that-be were so determined to grease that family's palms, why not set their sights on the tract of land where Raymond Mercado ran his construction business? It was off the main road east of town, a distinct advantage because our prevailing west wind would keep the town odor free.

Maybe Raymond Mercado thought I was snooping. Maybe

he'd sent the Hummer guy to intimidate me. Wouldn't be the first time that creep had resorted to strong-arm tactics. Could Mike be right? Had my high-profile stance against the project put me in jeopardy? I shivered at the thought.

Finally, Sam and I reached the summit. I gulped several deep breaths, turned and gazed out at a vista of rolling hills and deep gullies covered with wind-sculpted oaks and wildflowers. Beyond, sandstone bluffs held back an indigo ocean that boiled white as it reached the outcrop of rocks below. The largest, called *Las Tablas* because of its flat surface, stood well above the rest.

I looked, and looked again.

Something clung to the rock, something that didn't belong. My mind tried to make sense of the nebulous shape. A dead sea lion perhaps, or a pile of seaweed washed up by one of our in-famous rogue waves. "We'll check it out after lunch," I promised Sam, whose look said he couldn't care less.

We retreated from the summit to the trail's only picnic table. Sam and I shared a bagel spread with peanut butter and drank the remaining water. Sam wolfed down his bagel half. He'd eat just about anything—and often did. Last week he'd shoveled his way through a plate of Mike's special *golumpki*, stuffed cabbage rolls, left on the counter. While Mike was apoplectic, Sam didn't seem the worse for his gastronomic adventure.

At ten, old for a Lab, he'd been hardly out of breath when we reached the summit. "You're going to be with us for a long time, fella," I said now, patting his huge yellow head. "Let's get going."

Aware of a sudden chill, I reached into my pack for the wind-breaker I kept at the ready. The weather changed so fast here on the Central Coast—mostly leaning toward San Francisco soggy. I looked out to sea; fog rolled in like charcoal smoke, obliterating the view, if not the cries, of the sea wolves offshore. Soon we'd be socked in. Another squint told me the dark shape still clung to *Las Tablas*. "Come on, Sam. Let's check it out."

Shifting my backpack, I struggled into the windbreaker as we scrambled down a different path. This one didn't afford a view, but led directly to the bluffs. As we got closer, fingers of fog snaked around and across the rock, caressing and then retreating from the alien thing on its surface. Gradually the mist cleared and the thing began to take shape.

Something from the human world.

Now I ran, with Sam hard on my heels. We reached the end of the path, crossed the road and peered over the bluff. "Stay back, Sam," I warned when he moved too close to the edge. Below us, a body lay face down on the rock, arms flung out. Impossible to tell if it was male or female. A lone seagull, that ancient harbinger of death, hovered overhead.

Horrified and yet attracted by the macabre scene, I edged closer to the drop-off. Big mistake. Waves of vertigo washed over me. Like a blind person I groped for something to steady myself and found only a yawning cavern of empty space.

A sense of déjà vu overwhelmed me, and I heard Bea's childhood taunt: "Jump, Bella. You can do it. Don't be afraid. *Jump.* I'll catch you."

So easy.

Sam moved forward and stood barely touching my leg. It was like a blessing, and it was enough. I put my hand on his head, planted both feet, forced myself to look down.

Wedged vertically to the bluff, was a car on its nose. The driver's side door was missing. A car like mine, dull brown instead of faded red. Connie, the only Mercado daughter, drove a brown Subaru.

I stepped back from the edge, fumbled for my cell and gave silent thanks for the "Service available" message. With shaking fingers I pressed 911.

Overhead, the gull screeched and flew away.

3

Monday noon:

Amy Goodheart sailed out of the Managing Editor's office, moving across the newsroom on feet that seemed too small to support her weight. A tsunami of Obsession preceded her. From a distance she appeared the same as always—a large capable woman in her mid-thirties. Up close her face showed traces of smeared mascara and tear-stained foundation. Cheek muscles sagged over a strong jaw, adding ten years to her face. Someone who'd lost her best friend.

I jumped from my seat and hugged her, trying without success to keep her big, teased hair out of my nose. "I'm so sorry about Connie," I said, struggling not to sneeze.

She gave a wrenching sob, reached across my desk for a Kleenex and poked it under her tortoise shell glasses. "This is just the worst thing that ever happened. I still can't believe it."

"When did you find out?"

"The sheriff called after I got back to the office. He'd been trying to reach me all morning, but I had my cell off." She pointed to one swollen cheek. "First a root canal and now…this." Once again she mopped her eyes.

"Tough day," I agreed, brushing her cheek with my fingers. Hot to the touch. "Hurt much?"

She grimaced. "Like a son-of-a-bitch." A plump freckled hand flew to her mouth. "Sorry."

"That's okay. I've heard it before. Amy, why don't you go home for the rest of the day?"

She held up both palms in a don't-go-there sign. "No way, I'm a professional and I'm better off here than moping at home. Besides, I need to hear everything that happened this morning. Come on." She turned and waggled her fingers over her shoulder.

Oh dear, I really didn't want to have this conversation.

We sat on opposite sides of an enormous desk heaped with papers. Amy rummaged in the drawer, leaned across and thrust a snapshot at me. "This is from our high school graduation party."

I studied the washed-out, Reagan-era photo. Two girls in cap and gown beamed into the camera with the confidence of youth and the expectation of long and happy lives. A tall, reed-slim Amy, her hair platinum and straight, stood shoulder to shoulder with her equally tall, dark-haired pal. They toasted the person behind the camera with bottles of Coors in a classic pose that proclaimed "Hey, we made it!"

"I didn't know you drank," I said, surprised. I studied Amy and the photo, trying to reconcile this image with the woman who now refused anything stronger than Diet Pepsi.

Amy stiffened. "I don't, not now. Connie, on the other hand…" She let the sentence dangle and I wondered why, but did not ask.

I studied the photo more closely. Connie's eyes seemed too sad for such a happy occasion, like she knew her life would end tragically, even then. Maybe I was reading too much into a simple snapshot. "Have you known her all your life?"

Amy's ample bosom rose in a sigh. "Since first grade. Connie's parents lived in Mexico City for several years before she started school." She grimaced. "The Evil Twins were born there."

"'Evil twins?' Why do you say that? I know Raymond's a jerk, but I've never met Rik."

"Haven't missed much." She shook her head. "Those nasty little boys made Connie's life a living hell."

"Brothers can be a trial, I'm sure."

"You don't know the half of it. And," here she paused, "you don't want to."

"Okay." I returned the photo without further comment and slumped in my chair, sorry for a life snuffed out so soon. Connie was the oldest Mercado sibling and only daughter. A simple person and a free spirit who loved to party, she'd turned her back on the lifestyle her family's wealth made possible. Why else would she drive an old Subaru like mine and run a thrift store?

"Were you still there when they retrieved her body?" Amy twisted an oversize topaz ring on her pinkie.

"Yes, but I didn't see much. I was at the visitor's center across the road giving my statement to the deputy."

Amy blinked a bit. "On the phone earlier, Sheriff Whitley said he was in Sacramento for a conference but that he wanted to break the bad news himself. "

"That was nice of him."

She tapped a pencil on the desk. "It was."

"I don't know if I should say this—"

The pencil paused mid-tap. "Bella, I want to know *every-thing.*"

"Well, it looked like she went straight off the bluff. The car got wedged between it and the rocks. Connie was thrown clear."

"Oh my God." Amy cradled her head in her hands for a few seconds, then took a sip of water through a straw, wincing when it hit her tooth. She pulled the straw out of the glass, looked at it with distaste and tossed it in the wastebasket. "Where did she go over?"

"In that spot where the surfers and hikers park, on the ocean side of the visitor's center. Her body was on *Las Tablas.*"

She shivered. "The way they pull up so close there, I've always thought a car would take a nose-dive someday. Did anyone see her? There must have been other people around."

"There were two cars, both empty. Probably surfers."

"Well, she didn't commit suicide, that's for sure." She added as though to herself, "Not now."

Like her earlier comment about Connie's drinking, this seemed like a private thought and I didn't pursue it. "She may have been the victim of"—how could I say this?—"of foul play."

Amy's blue eyes widened behind her designer frames. "Foul play? You sound like *Law and Order.* If you're talking murder, say so in plain English."

Amy always spoke her mind. I gulped, trying to swallow the memory of this morning's terror. "When I was driving out there, a guy in a Hummer tried to run me off the road. I think he may have mistaken me for her. He was on a cell phone in the Mercado driveway."

"No shit?" Amy grimaced, I assumed at her accidental use of the expletive. "What did the deputy say? Did he find paint on your car?"

"No. He said they'd look into the matter."

"That's *it?*"

"For the moment."

She focused on a spot over my left shoulder. "Why am I not surprised."

"Do you think Connie was murdered?"

"God, I hate to say this, but it sure looks like it. I just hope law enforcement gets on the stick." A sigh. "Honestly, don't they watch cop shows? If a murder isn't solved in the first forty-eight hours…"

"Maybe you should remind Sheriff Whitley of that."

Amy peered at me over the top of her glasses. "No wonder they kicked you out of the convent. You're too sassy to be a nun."

"I didn't get kicked out. I left."

Gazing into space, she didn't reply. Finally, her red-rimmed eyes came back to me. "Do you think the guy in the Hummer was the one who tipped you off about the sewer plan?"

"Amy, why would you even ask that? I have no idea." My voice sounded sharp and angry. "I do think the caller three weeks ago must have been on a cell. He kept breaking up. But today I was trying to *avoid* Hummer Man, not have a conversation with him for cripes sake."

"Don't get huffy. I just asked for an opinion." Another long silence then, "Bella, it's over."

My heart knocked against my ribs. It does that sometimes. Warns me when something's not right. "What's over?"

"Leaks, protests, editorials. They're part of the newspaper

game, but possible murder sends this thing into a whole new league." Her eyes darted to the thin side walls, and she leaned forward. "You don't know the pressure I've been under. Powerful people want the sewer on the Mercado land."

"Including Raymond Mercado? Mr. Money Bags himself?"

She shrugged like it was too much to think about. "Could be, I don't know. Advertisers have threatened to cancel accounts. I don't have to tell you I can't let that happen. Especially with all this talk of a merger between our parent company and that other news organization, whose name I can't bear to think about, much less mention."

"What are you saying exactly?"

"From now on the paper's going to remain neutral on the sewer issue. And I want you to back off your soapbox."

I felt the heat in my cheeks. "Back off? And if I don't?"

Her eyebrows went up a notch. "Then things would become awkward between us."

"Seems like what I do on my own time is my business."

"Normally it would be, but this is a real hot button issue. Look, promise me you'll at least talk it over with Mike. Looks to the world like you have a conflict of interest, with his business and all."

I nodded. My husband would be looking for a job after everyone hooked up to the sewer. For that reason alone I needed *my* job. "Okay, I'll talk it over with Mike."

"Good." Amy stood up to signal the end of our meeting. "I want you to give Ben a statement, but only about Connie and the incident itself. Don't mention the guy in the Hummer."

Ben Adams was a new hire whose journalistic skills left me cold. He'd been covering the Los Lobos sewer debacle and couldn't seem to get a handle on either the technology or the political situation. After reading one of his articles, I'd think: What was *that* all about?

Amy thought he was Pulitzer material. "Thought maybe you'd let me write the story," I sniffed.

Amy shook her head, releasing a fresh wave of Obsession. "I need experienced writers on a story like this."

"Okay fine. Whatever."

"Bella, act like a grownup. I hired you because I thought after twenty-five years in social work you'd bring a compassionate voice and some maturity to the obituary desk. People, especially people with problems, feel comfortable talking to you."

"I see." I wasn't about to be swayed by the compliment.

"Do you?" Another head shake, more Obsession perfume. "You are aware that your predecessor was just nineteen?"

I nodded, wondering where this was leading. "She was a disaster. The last straw was when she added, 'You go girl!' to the obituary of a lady who passed at a hundred and five. The family was not amused."

I giggled in spite of myself. "At least she had imagination." Editing the tortured prose that relatives wrote for departed loved ones—or writing it myself—had been a challenge at first. After a year and a half I was running out of clever ways to say "went to his/her eternal reward."

"I'd like to work into a reporter job."

"We'll see." Amy walked around the desk and lifted the ends of my cropped hair. "First we need to make your image as sharp as your tongue."

"*Mine?*" I placed a hand on my chest.

She laughed. "Yours. Why don't you let me send you to my hairdresser? A little color to cover the gray, a good razor cut and you'd look less like a…" She stopped.

"A nun?"

She grinned, warming to her task. At least it took her mind off her friend. "Some Gucci frames would set off those big brown eyes." Her glance moved to my feet. "I don't believe in dress codes, but those Birkenstocks are way too hippie looking. And a pair of heels would make you seem taller."

She had a point. At Holy Name, they called me Sister Munchkin.

"Mike prefers me the way I am. He finds nuns sexy."

"You're *sure?*"

I gave her a smile that I'm sure was a bit smug. Mike's love was one thing I could count on. "Absolutely."

4

Late Monday afternoon:

As I drove the twelve miles from the Tolosa newspaper office to our home in Los Lobos, I gripped the wheel and kept one anxious eye on the rearview mirror. The whole day had left me with an unsettled feeling, like something basic in my life was about to shift.

Near the western edge of town, I pulled off the highway onto the short access road we share with two other homeowners whom we rarely see. Crunching onto the gravel of our gently sloping driveway, my hands relaxed on the wheel and my breathing slowed. Our home, a converted windmill, is our refuge, a place where we leave trouble at the gate.

Towering over a grove of oaks, the four paddles atop the mill slashed a huge black X into the azure sky. The place hasn't been a working mill since the 1930's, after the last miller tied down the paddles to secure them against the relentless ocean wind.

I parked, hopped out and creaked open the gate, noting with a shiver of pleasure the classy black and gold sign that read: Divina Mill, est. 1888. Mike wanted to change the sign to "Kowalski Mill." I'd vetoed the idea, saying it didn't have the same ring. We were lucky to own a piece of history. Here wheat grown in the Midwest and shipped to California on the new Iron Horse was ground into flour for the nearby ranchers. Mike had backed down, but our disagreements were rarely settled. They just went into remission.

Sam heard the squeak of the gate and trotted out to meet me, head down, upper lip folded back in a smile, tail wagging the whole dog. I'd dropped him off on my way to work, disappointed that Mike wasn't there. We'd talked briefly by phone and he knew what happened. He'd said little. Usually he had an opinion on everything and didn't hesitate to share it.

"Come on, boy. Had enough of your own company?" Sam jumped into the car and we rode companionably up the rest of the driveway. Smelling only slightly doggy, he leaned into me as I swung left into the area in front of the house. Mike and I parked there for convenience, even though we had a perfectly good barn on the lower lot, a hundred yards from the house.

I turned off the ignition and took my usual moment to admire our funky find. The main house was connected by a short breezeway to the mill on the west side of the house. Actually, the paddles and exterior structure were all that remained of the original mill. The ground floor that once housed the old grinding wheel became a storage area, now littered with our bikes and camping gear.

On the east side of the house, a medieval-looking turret protruded like an misplaced mushroom above the living room. Talk about eclectic architecture!

We'd dubbed the mill and this strange turret the West and East Wings, though in the latter case it wasn't a wing at all. Since we both needed our space, we used them as separate "nests." (Mike's term.) We'd drawn straws for the West Wing, and I won, throwing Mike into a royal funk. Too bad, I won fair and square.

He's still not above making remarks about my nest, insisting the widow's walk is technically a catwalk, once used for maintaining the paddles. So what? Widow's walk sounds more romantic. Anytime it suits me, I step outside the sliding doors and marvel at the ever-changing blues and grays of Los Lobos Bay and the open ocean. Halfway round and I'm in another world, savoring a green and gold tapestry of mounded hills to the east.

The Divina Mill even comes with its own ghost. According

to local lore, Emily Divina killed herself by jumping from the widow's walk after her lover, a fisherman, failed to return from the sea. In a jealous snit, her miller husband, who was no doubt dull as a doorknob, turned her portrait to the wall. The first thing I did when we moved in was to turn Emily's face back to the world.

I even planted a small prayer garden on the spot where she fell. Emily was a knitter like me, and I keep hoping she'll reveal herself as I knit and purl my way through the evening. After five years and the completion of more blankets for foster kids than I can count, there's been nary a peep or knock from Emily.

Enough wool gathering. I opened the car door.

As I pulled a bag of groceries from the hatchback, I heard the rumble of a pickup and Mike's F-250 rolled into the driveway. He parked The Beast next to me, shut off the motor and slid out. "Damn, what a day."

I set my groceries down and put my arms around him. "You're not just a-kidding." We held each other and I tried to ignore the odor of the job which clung to him like a second skin. We usually deferred hugs until he'd showered, but today was different. I squeezed harder and felt him tremble.

"You okay?" I held him away and noted that his face sagged the way Amy's had this afternoon. Pale, too. My heart did its fluttery thing. "Well, are you? Did you hear any more about Connie?"

His steely eyes shot sparks. "Bella, can we talk about that later? I just got home for chrisssake."

"Sorry. I just thought—"

"Later." He leaned down, picked up the bag and peered inside. "What's for supper?"

"Uh, frozen *pierogi*. Thought they'd be quick."

My husband is a connoisseur of Polish food and I expected mild grousing. Instead, he shrugged. "Whatever. I'm not hungry anyway. I'll take a shower."

When I heard water running, I threw several cut-up onions

into sizzling butter and popped a bottle of the wine Mike called "the two buck fuck" into the freezer. We could both use a glass. Maybe two. I was nestling the little pillows of cheese-filled dough into their bed of sweet-smelling browned onions when I heard footsteps.

"Smells good." He came up behind me and put his hands on my shoulders. His chin rested atop my head and I could feel the movement of his strong jaw. We stood that way for a few moments. Despite the closeness, I sensed that his mind was elsewhere. Sure enough, when I turned my head, he was staring at the picture of his son.

Ethan had died along with his mother after she'd driven the family car into an Illinois lake. Grace's body showed no traces of alcohol or drugs and her death was ruled an accident. Ethan's body had never been recovered.

His picture sat in a small frame next to our kitchen message center. Mike often gazed at it as he talked on the phone. The photo, one of those awful school shots, showed a typical seven-year-old, all eyes and hair and brand new teeth that he hadn't grown into. He never got the chance.

My heart ached for my husband, as it always did when I caught him looking at the picture. I put my hand on his arm. He allowed my fingers to rest there a moment, then gently removed them. "Ready for a glass of wine?"

"Always." I pulled a salad from the fridge while Mike uncorked the bottle and set it on the small glass table that overlooked my kitchen herb garden.

We observed a moment of silence and clinked glasses. Despite, or maybe because of, the guy in the Hummer and Connie's body on the rocks, I was starving. What was it about food and death?

After I'd wolfed down a few forkfuls of *pierogi*, Mike allowed me to fill him in on what happened, starting with the Hummer.

Mike ate little, said less. I came to the part about Connie and his eyes filled. "Poor kid. She deserved better."

For some reason, perhaps the pressures and pure terror of the day, this hit me wrong. I set my fork down. "What about me?" I said, slapping my hand against my chest. "When I called, you didn't even ask how I felt. Didn't you realize I'd be upset? Seeing Connie on the rocks was almost like finding Bea dead in the street. In fact…"

I didn't tell him about hearing my sister's voice. Mike pretty much lived in the moment. He'd think it was silly, or that my anxiety got the better of me again. Hell, anybody would be anxious. Except apparently, my husband.

Mike scratched at a spot on his neck, which was starting to sprout blotches the size of cranberries.

"Bella," he said with quiet seriousness, "it's worse than you think."

"How could it be any worse?"

He inhaled deeply. "Connie was shot." He paused. "In the temple."

"Shot? What kind of sick pervert—" All of a sudden I couldn't just sit there. Amy was right. Connie's death was murder. I struggled to my feet, almost upsetting my wine. "How come the sheriff's deputy didn't tell me when I gave my statement?"

"He probably didn't know. Or maybe he thought you didn't have a need to know. Please sit down."

Hot tears stung my eyes. I sank back into the chair and gulped wine, letting it burn all the way down. "Sheriff Whitley called Amy around noon. He didn't say anything about her being shot."

Mike shook his head. "Maybe the sheriff thought it would be too much for Amy at that point, Connie being a friend and all."

"Amy's the managing editor of the newspaper. It's her business to know."

"For sure she's heard the news by now because of the paper's deadline. Maybe you should call her later." I nodded and he reached across the table and covered my hand with his own. "Bella, I'm a jerk. Of course I should have realized you'd be upset.

It's…" his eyes filled again "…it's just that she was a human being and she was killed in such a brutal way. I guess I knew her better than you did."

"So, do…" I corrected myself, "did…you still meet her for coffee?"

He smoothed his salt-and-pepper crew cut, not that there was much to smooth. "We don't…uh, didn't…*meet* for coffee. I sat with other working stiffs at the tables in front of the store. If the thrift-store business was slow, which it usually was, she joined us. Christ, Bella, you know all this. Why the third degree?"

"I don't know. I just feel like you should be more concerned about me than you seem to be."

"I am concerned about you. That should be obvious. Why do I have to keep *saying* it?" Cop eyes assessed me. "You know, Connie mentioned once that you avoided her."

"Oh great. You *discussed* me with her?"

"Well, no, we didn't discuss you, but she did mention it in passing. You certainly never went out of your way to be friendly."

"Excuse me, I didn't know that was a requirement."

"It wasn't. It's just that—"

"And where would I have struck up this friendship? I know she was a good Catholic, but we rarely go to Mass and never here in Los Lobos. And she was a Mercado. We moved in different circles."

"Oh for Christ sake, Connie is—was—as plain as an old shoe. Not like that jerk-off brother of hers."

"Raymond might be a jerk-off, but they can't all be bad. His Uncle Stan is a sweetie."

"How do you know Stan?" Again, cop eyes.

"Don't you remember? He helped me write the obituaries after Mr. and Mrs. Mercado died in that plane crash."

A curt nod. "That's right. What about Raymond's twin, what's his name?" Mike's brow furrowed. "Isn't he a female impersonator or something?"

"His name is Rik and his group plays heavy metal."

Mike looked at me as though I'd spoken in Chinese.

"Rock that uses heavily amplified guitars," I explained, having checked the Internet that afternoon. "Rik lives in Las Vegas."

"Strange home for a rock star. Vegas is a place I associate with old farts like Wayne Newton."

"I have no idea why he lives there, or even if he really does."

"We'll know soon enough," Mike said. "Wonder if the asshole will lower himself to come to Connie's funeral. Couldn't be bothered when his own parents died as I recall."

"Mike?"

"Huh?"

"Why are we fighting about the Mercados?"

"Beats me." Once again his hand found its way across the table. "Truce?"

"Truce." I squeezed his knuckles with one hand and reached for the bottle with the other. "More wine?"

5

Monday evening:

After we killed the Cabernet, Mike helped me with the dishes. Then I picked up the throw I was knitting for the Linus Project. We sat in our recliners in front of the TV, another middle-aged couple having a scintillating evening at home. That was okay. The day had been exciting enough.

Silently, we watched *CSI* reruns, the set of DVDs a Christmas gift from my mother, her attempt to get back in Mike's good graces. It was the least she could do after the way she acted when we got engaged. You'd have thought he kidnapped me from the convent, which he most certainly did not. Since my dad died, she traveled constantly and we seldom heard from her.

Knit one, slip one, knit one, pass slipped stitch over knit stitch, repeat to end of row, knit one and turn.

I examined my work, seeing a small flaw two rows down. I began to rip it out. These throws I made for kids entering foster care took so much time and energy, I sometimes wondered if they were worth the effort. I could go to the Tolosa K-Mart and buy throws almost as cuddly and soft.

Still, I'd received enough carefully lettered notes over the years to know that a mass-produced blanket wouldn't be the same. A kid in foster care needed something special made by someone who cared. I had no children of my own to lavish with love and attention and it gave me satisfaction to do this small thing. I buried my nose in the yarn, taking comfort in its fresh fragrance.

Lost in my own thoughts, I failed to notice that Mike had grabbed a pencil and was drawing rows and columns on a sheet of notebook paper resting on an old *Scientific American*. When I saw what he was doing, I reached over to the arm of his recliner for the remote and snapped off the TV.

"Hey, I was watching that."

"You weren't either. What are you working on?"

He smoothed the paper. "I'm just doing a matrix to see who might be the most likely suspect."

Uh-oh, he was in cop mode.

He rubbed the back of his neck, then lifted a stack of magazines off the ottoman and pulled it over by him. "Come help."

I groused some, but scooted over.

He laid his hand on my knee. The warmth of him flowed up my leg. "Let's look at the cast of characters and see if we can find a pattern. We'll start with the Mercado family, or what's left of them."

I shivered, despite the heat of Mike's hand. In little over a year, the five-member family had been reduced by more than half, first the parents and now their only daughter.

"Let's start with the brothers." He licked the tip of the pencil and wrote "Raymond" in the first column.

"Why do you do that?"

He looked up. "Do what?"

"Lick the pencil lead."

He shrugged. "I dunno. Old cop habit."

"If you smell like lead, I won't want to kiss you later."

He rubbed his neck once again.

"Do you have a headache?" I asked.

"No," he said, "just old."

"Let me give you a neck message."

"Later. Work first." He jabbed at Raymond's name with the pencil point. Raymond was in his early thirties, young to be running the area's largest construction company. He and Mike worked together sometimes, and not amicably. Each found the other testy. In my experience Raymond had the social skills of a wild boar.

"No doubt, he'd be all for the sale," Mike said and I agreed. "Not only that, his company will get a major piece of the construction pie."

"Wouldn't it be a conflict of interest to sell the land to the county and then get the construction bid?"

Mike gave me a "be serious" look. "This is Los Lobos and Raymond's a Mercado."

"Silly me."

Mike gave his pencil another lick. "Who's Raymond's twin? I've forgotten the guy's name already."

"Rik," I said. "Three letters, no c. Unless he and Raymond are identical twins, I wouldn't know him if I saw him on the street. He probably doesn't need money."

"Don't be too sure. Celebrities often have nasty, and expensive, habits. Drugs, alcohol, gambling." A pause while he added a question mark next to Rik's name. "Okay, let's review some basic facts. Has the estate of the elder Mercados been settled yet? In other words, are the Mercado siblings the legal owners of the land?"

"What am I, a walking records bureau?" I glanced at our bedroom down the hall. Surely this could wait until tomorrow.

"Amy will know," Mike said. "A newspaper editor knows everything. Ask her tomorrow."

"She'll wonder why."

"Say you need background information for the obituary. Let's move on."

I groaned as Mike said, "Okay, Stan. Do you know where he stands?"

Stan Mercado was their father's younger brother. He was perhaps fifty-five, a gray-bearded biology professor at the local university, your typical pipe and slippers guy. "I haven't a clue, but he leads nature walks on the bluffs every third Saturday."

Mike nodded. "So our biologist is probably a quality-of-life person and not thrilled to have the Mercado land become a wastewater-treatment plant."

"He probably doesn't inherit unless all the siblings die. And maybe not even then."

"True." Mike scratched his chin. "But let's leave him on the list. Connie complained that his new bride is a big spender." He pretended not to see the face I made at the mention of Connie's name and added a question mark next to Stan.

"Um…," I fiddled with a loose thread on Mike's chair arm… "what about Connie? Did she want to sell?"

"Don't know," Mike mumbled.

"*What?* No one in town has talked about anything else for three weeks. It must have come up when you and the guys were having coffee with her."

"I'm telling you, I don't know." Once again he stabbed at Raymond's name. "Looks like he's the only yes-for-sure person."

"And knowing Raymond, he probably pushed his brother and sister hard to sell. True?"

"Don't know," he repeated. "This is just a first step."

"What about Charles Cantor and Paisley Potter, those two CRUD members who are always at each other's throats over the sewer plant?" I asked. "Paisley is violently opposed to the Mercado site."

"It's hard to imagine Paisley would kill a Mercado just to

delay the sale," Mike said. "Remember, most murder victims are killed by people close to them. And when there's money involved, you usually can follow the trail right to the killer's door."

"So who else is on the money trail?"

Slowly, "We are."

"You're kidding." My heart turned a somersault in my chest.

"Nope. It's bye-bye for our business the day the sewer goes online."

"That will happen no matter where it's located," I mumbled.

"True, but any delay is money in our pockets. And Bella, you've been really out there opposing the Mercado site."

"That's what Amy said."

"She's right. If I were the sheriff, I'd consider us people of interest in the case."

"You're kidding."

"You just said that." Mike stood up and stretched. "Ready?"

"You bet." I reached up and touched his bare arm, feeling lucky in spite of everything to have him in my life. We'd gone through hell to get to this point, but it had been worth it.

Later, after I'd declared his kisses sufficiently lead-free to want more, Mike mumbled into his pillow, "I cleaned out the e-mail. There's one from your nephew."

"What's Chris up to? Are things better between him and Janet?" I always thought of Janet as "that woman." She got her hooks into my brother-in-law Ed Jensen seven months after Bea died. The ink had hardly dried on the license when the newlyweds sold Bea and Ed's house, and the reconstituted family up and moved to Cleveland, Janet's home town.

I suppose one, *one* being my mother, could make the case that Ed deserved a new life, but what about his nine-year-old son? Less than a year after his mom died, Chris found himself in a new school in a new city, with a new stepmother.

Their relationship had been testy from day one, and no wonder. Apparently she didn't realize that family ties were delicate tapestries that needed to be woven one thread at a time. I'd never been a mom, but even I knew that. "Well, what did Chris say?" I asked the lump of mashed potatoes lying next to me.

"Read the e-mail." Mike worried his pillow into a better position.

Long after Mike dropped off I lay awake thinking about the day and how much trouble we could be in. Finally I got up, logged onto the Internet from the laptop in the kitchen and opened Chris's e-mail:

> dear auntie bella,
> how are u? i'm fine, except that i didn't get such good grades. dad and janet are mad as hell. i was thinking, could i come and stay with you guys? till things chill here. janet can't seem to stop talking about my "issues" and dad won't even listen to my side.
>   love u,
>   *chris*

6

───

Tuesday morning:

The beginnings of a headache gnawed at my temples, the legacy of too much wine and too little sleep. The pain wasn't helped by a headline that shouted across the kitchen, "Mercado heir dies in crash!" The lead article went on to say that an unnamed person (me) found the body and the sheriff's office was asking other witnesses to come forward.

While Mike hid himself behind the paper, I added leaded grounds to the June Cleaver percolator he preferred and set the teakettle on to boil. No wimpy decaf for us this morning;

we needed the real thing and don't hold the sugar. With the first whiff of coffee, I marveled that the stuff always smelled so much better than it tasted. But then it would to a tea drinker. I tiptoed across the terra cotta tile so as not to jar my head, set the sugar bowl on the table and leaned over Mike's shoulder.

Mike swung sideways, pulling the paper with him. "I'll be done in a minute."

"Okay fine." I sat opposite and gazed out the window at my kitchen garden while I waited for tea water. The capillaries in my temples relaxed as I noted the little green herbs poking their way through the spot which, a few days ago held only black soil. "*Parsley, sage, rosemary and thyme.*"

Rustle of paper. "Would you mind not singing?" Little white lines formed a parenthesis around Mike's mouth.

"Look," I said, "I hate to have a serious discussion before we've had caffeine, but what is your problem?"

"It's *our* problem and there's more than one." Brief pause. "Did you read Chris's e-mail?"

"I did."

"*Aaand?*" He stretched out the word, letting me know what was expected. The teakettle shrieked like a blue jay whose peanut had been stolen.

I winced and moved to the stove. "And…I want him to come." I killed the flame.

"Hmm," was all he said until I set a mug before him. He spooned three sugars into the coffee and stirred noisily. "It's just that with all the problems we've got right now, I don't think we need a kid around."

I sat down, added milk and sugar to my tea and messaged my temples. "He'll keep our minds off our problems." A tentative sip announced the need for more sugar and I added another spoonful. "You and Chris got along great at the wedding."

"Chris was"—Mike counted on his fingers—"nine. Now he's another teenager with problems—"

"He's not just another teenager, he's my nephew! His mother

was murdered in case you've forgotten. And Ed and that…that *woman* he married think if Chris just knuckles under when she snaps her fingers, his problems will disappear. I know it's not that simple." I didn't need to remind Mike I'd experienced plenty of mindless authority in religious life.

Mike banged his cup down, spilling coffee on the glass table top. He grabbed a napkin from the holder and scrubbed at the spill, mostly just spreading it around. "That's exactly the point. You spent most of your adult life dealing with problem kids. Bella, do you need more of that right now?"

I sipped my tea and stared out the window, not answering his question because I had none to give. Having a teen around wouldn't be easy. "It's only for a few weeks."

"Could easily stretch into the whole summer," he groused. "And if this sewer thing goes the way I think it's going, I'll have to figure out what I want to be when I grow up."

I smiled grimly. "You said it, not me."

Mike pushed his cup away. "Dammit, I know it's selfish but I want us to be alone this summer." He sighed. "Especially now."

"You always want me all to yourself. Is that why you dragged me all the way out here, away from my family?"

"*What?* Away from your family? Give me a break. You wanted to get away from Detroit—and your mother."

Silently I acknowledged the truth of his words. My mother gave me a hard time after Bea died and I left Holy Name. I just couldn't stay after that. I'd been thinking of leaving for some time and murder was the catalyst that drove me from the order

When I told Mother I was thinking of leaving, she said it would kill my father. The classic parent guilt trip. Perhaps she was right; Pop died six months later, of a broken heart, Mother said, from losing one daughter to a bullet and one to a crisis of faith.

But it was more than a crisis of faith. What Mother didn't know to this day, was that Mike and I were an item before I left. Not in the physical sense, but certainly in the emotional one. He'd showed up at Holy Name House one day as a volunteer.

One glance and we dropped into a senior version of *When Harry Met Sally*. I'd struggled with my physical cravings for years, and when he smiled at me I knew it was just a matter of time until I let him satisfy them.

Mike, who'd been silent for several seconds, said, "Still don't want a pain-in-the-ass kid around."

"How would you know what it's like to raise a kid?"

Seeing his stricken look, I stopped. Why, oh why, was I such a bitch? After twenty-five years as a nun wouldn't you think I'd have learned some compassion? Or at least to keep my mouth shut. My eyes darted to the small picture of Mike's son by the phone.

"Neither have you raised a kid, so don't give me that," he shot back, giving as good as he got.

My temple throbbed as I studied my husband, the strong, cop demeanor. All these years and I still didn't know what bubbled beneath the surface. He was alone in the world with no nosy, interfering family like mine. If I never laid eyes on the rest of them again it wouldn't bother me, but I needed to see Chris, to get to know the young man he'd become. He was Bea's legacy, and maybe I could lay some of my own demons to rest if I got to know him.

My eyes were again drawn to the picture of Ethan. With a start I realized he'd be fifteen now, two years younger than my nephew. "Mike, I'm sorry for what I said. But you're a stubborn Pole and it seems like I always give in to you. This time, I'm sorry, but I just can't. I want this too much and I'm going to tell Chris it's okay."

"Okay, fine," Mike said, and we left it at that.

7

Wednesday evening:

After a hectic day at the paper with seven obituaries to write and six more due on Thursday, I arrived for the eight o'clock CRUD meeting tired, hungry and in pain. On the drive over, the tension headache I'd had on and off for two days returned with a vengeance.

The lot in front of the Community Center was jammed and I had to park by the library, half a block away. Each step up the sloping drive made my head pound. Halfway up the walk, I heard angry voices through the open double doors and sighed. Like all CRUD meetings, this one would be contentious.

Nearby, stragglers gathered into tight little knots. They stood with their heads bent toward each other, darting occasional sideways glances at other groups. The sewer issue had pitted friend against friend, neighbor against neighbor, and sadly in some cases, family against family.

As I passed among the groups, some of them drew closer together, body language for "you're not with us." My opposition to the project location was well known thanks to the *LA Times* article and I'd decided to make an additional statement tonight, hopefully something conciliatory that would help bring the two sides together.

Maybe not. No matter what I said, someone would take issue with it. I stopped and massaged my aching temples. With Connie's death, work, and the situation with Mike, I had more than enough conflict in my life. In the convent we were taught to never speak up, never offer an opinion, and I'd never totally overcome that indoctrination. Except with Mike, of course. With him I overcompensated.

It had been a crazy couple of days. Yesterday morning, before I could change my mind, I'd e-mailed my nephew and told him to book a flight. Last night we'd retreated behind separate, silent walls, Mike with his *Scientific American*, me with my knitting. I knew Chris's visit would further complicate our lives, but I'd heard a cry for help in his e-mail. Seventeen is such a vulnerable age.

And it might be good for Mike to be around a teen for a while. He seemed to shy away from teenagers; maybe a good experience with Chris would make them seem less like an alien species. At least that's what I told myself.

I stepped through the doorway and surveyed the main room of the Community Center. Normally used for social gatherings, it was a bit small for CRUD committee meetings. But it was the best we had. Tonight the seats were filled, with the spillover crowd milling around the entrance and in the aisles. I stepped to the left and immediately tripped over a pile of signs. CRUD president Noah Bullard forbade them, and with good reason. If things got hot, they could be used as weapons.

Cell phones chirped or rang or played Beethoven's Fifth and the air buzzed with chatter. Like most places on the Central Coast, the Community Center had no air conditioning and the room stank of tension and too many bodies crammed into too tight a place. I struggled for breath. After the silence of religious life, noise made me anxious.

Rubbing my ankle where it made contact with the sign, I considered hightailing it out of there to someplace cool and safe. Then I spotted Amy at the end of the front row. The chair next to her was empty, perhaps a sign I should stay. I fought my way down the aisle. "Hi, Amy."

She looked up from her notebook. "Oh hi. Figured you'd be here." She patted the empty seat. "Park it. I saved this despite several death threats."

"Thanks. Appreciate it." I crawled over her legs and sank down. "I'm surprised to see you here. Where's Ben?"

"Even stars have to rest sometime." A wicked grin lit up her face as I stuck out my tongue. "Gave him the night off. Besides, I need to keep busy, you know?" I nodded my understanding, then slipped out of my Birkenstocks and wiggled my toes. She frowned at my white anklets, started to say something, then apparently thought better of it. "Are you going to speak tonight?"

"I was, but I'm not sure I'm up to it."

"Good. You've said too much already."

"Now just a minute."

She looked at me as though debating whether to say more, then whispered in my ear, "New information."

My heart shifted a little inside my chest. "What? Tell me."

"I'm not supposed to say anything, but you don't count, I guess."

"Thanks."

She consulted a scribbled Post-it. "What color did you say that Hummer was?"

"Gray, why?"

"They found traces of gray paint on the back of Connie's car."

"Like maybe the killer used his vehicle to push her over the cliff after he shot her?"

Amy's eyes filled. "Sick bastard." Mike was right. She had a tough time accepting Connie's death from a bullet wound.

"Oh my God." The enormity of what had happened only two days ago washed over me. My knees began to shake and my upper lip broke out in a sweat. That could be my body lying in the morgue. "Witnesses?"

She considered. "If so, they're probably too scared to come forward. But maybe we'll still get lucky." Suddenly she looked over her right shoulder. "Speaking of coming forward, don't look now. We have a Mercado sighting at five o'clock."

"Just what I need."

Raymond stopped at the end of our row. With his thatch of dark hair, close-set eyes and beaky nose, he reminded me of a crow. He gave me a heavy-lidded, opaque stare.

"Miz Kowalski." He ignored Amy and drew out the "miz"

in a way that sounded vaguely threatening. "What y'all doin' here?" Raymond always sounded like he'd be more at home in west Texas.

"And hello to you, Raymond," Amy said, while I searched for my voice. "Bella's here because, like all of us, she wants to find out what's going on with the sewer."

Raymond's eyes roamed over me, lingering a second too long on my breasts.

Idiot. I hugged my arms.

"Hope you're not thinkin' a' makin' a stink, Miz Kowalski. That wouldn't set well with me. Not a'tall." He cocked an index finger at me. "Connie's dead and you and your friends prob'ly caused her death with your meddlin' ways."

"Now just a minute!" As I came off the chair, I heard pounding in my ears. Finally I realized it was Noah Bullard's gavel. He threw it down and yelled, "Will you people just shut the hell up so we can get started?"

Amy pulled me back into my seat as Raymond said, "Don't y'all forget now." He gave me a smirk that sat uneasily on his crow's face. Then he moved forward and eased his lanky frame into a chair opposite the state water representative.

"What's with him?" I asked Amy.

She shrugged. "Just Raymond being Raymond."

"I suppose." A shiver of unease ran down my spine.

The gavel banged and Amy whispered, "We'll talk later."

Heads turned toward the speakers' table and the five committee members. The state water rep, a real in-your-face guy whose name I'd forgotten, and Raymond shared a microphone on a small table in front of the dais. Despite the small space, mikes were used so meetings could be recorded. The water guy leaned over and whispered something to Raymond, who smiled, and whispered back.

Hmm. Mighty cozy.

Another thing, Raymond didn't seem sad enough for someone who'd lost his only sister. Perhaps they were estranged. But half your family dead within a year should give anyone pause.

After a desultory pledge of allegiance, Noah Bullard spoke into his mike. "The first thing on the agenda this evening is a discussion of the changes needed to the General Plan for the wastewater project to go forward." The words "General Plan" and "changes" sent the audience into a tizzy. Folks looked at each other and rolled their eyes. The plan laid out the county's high level blueprint for the area in matters of housing, light industry, major roads, parks, and yes, even wastewater treatment.

Changing the plan was a big deal that could lead to all sorts of unintended consequences. Revisions had to be done at the county level and CRUD would only be involved in an advisory capacity. Beside me, Amy scribbled.

Once again Noah used his gavel to silence the crowd. His hand shook as he reached for his water bottle. I'd be nervous too, in his job. He took a sip of water and sloshed it around in his mouth. He swallowed and his Adam's apple moved up and down like a small animal. "Ahem, as I was saying, we'll discuss changes to the General Plan, then hear *brief*, and I do mean *brief*, comments from the community. After that, Jackson Ripper"—he gestured to the water rep guy—"would like to say a few words."

"First, let's bow our heads in a moment of silence for our friend and neighbor, Connie Mercado, tragically taken from us two days ago." He bobbed his head toward Raymond. "Our hearts go out to you at this time."

During the moment of silence Raymond and the water guy leaned toward each other in whispered conversation. What was with those two? Even Noah, who usually fawned all over Raymond, gave him a dirty look, and he wasn't the only one. Had they no respect? Amy saw it too. She and I exchanged glances. She leaned close to my ear. "What an idiot. Good thing Brenda's up next or I'd have to go up there and punch Raymond's lights out."

"Amen to that."

Noah introduced wastewater spokesperson Brenda Livingston to outline the proposed changes. Layered reddish hair fell into her face as she leaned forward and gripped the mike in both hands. "Uh, tonight…" She paused as though she'd forgotten her lines and studied the papers before her. "Tonight, we'll…" A hand went to her mouth and she turned to Noah. "Connie was my friend, and…and, I just can't do this right now."

Beside me, Amy shed tears onto her notes. The three of them, Brenda, Connie and Amy, friends since kindergarten. Brenda had probably taken the graduation photo. I handed Amy a Kleenex, wishing I could do more.

Noah squeezed Brenda's shoulder. "Brenda my dear, we don't have to do this. I'm going to move that we continue this discussion at the next meeting."

The motion was made and seconded to a general murmur of assent. I thought maybe that signaled the end of the meeting, but Noah beavered through the agenda, introducing the water rep. Jackson Ripper claimed the mike he and Raymond shared and tapped it, producing an electronic thump a rock band would envy.

"Get it together, Ripper," someone yelled from the audience, earning a gavel rap from Noah.

Ripper cleared his throat. "My statement tonight will be brief." He paused. "Uh, we at the state realize you've had an unfortunate turn of events here, and we're willing to wait a reasonable time for things to go forward. Our lawyers tell us it takes time to probate a will."

"You need lawyers to tell you that?" someone shouted.

Ripper gave the man a look that would stop a truck. "For years and years it's been one thing after another with *you people*." Shocked silence at the utter scorn in those two words. One man began to stamp his feet. Others joined in. The sound stretched and swelled, resounding off the walls and ceiling with the timbre of an advancing army.

Ripper clutched the mike, his face the color of a boiled beet. "Unless *you people,*" he shouted, "want to start paying thousands of dollars in fines for noncompliance, you'd better not use this as an excuse for another delay." He soldiered on, but the more he shouted, the louder they stomped. Finally, he pushed aside the mike and cast Raymond a look of desperation. Raymond gave him an almost imperceptible nod.

Silence for at least fifteen seconds, then someone shouted, "Where's your heart, Ripper?"

"He's sittin' on it," someone else answered.

Ripper leaned into the mike. "It's not me. It's the lawyers," he bleated.

"Then we're all in trouble," shouted a third someone. The audience howled.

Noah almost wore out his gavel getting the crowd, which now resembled a mob, to settle down. This could really get nasty, I thought and glanced over my shoulder. If I headed straight up the aisle, I'd have a clear shot at the door.

The crowd quieted and I became aware of an intense whispered discussion between board members Charles Cantor and Paisley Potter. They sat next to each other and disagreed about almost everything. They must not realize their mikes were live. I glanced sideways at the audience. All eyes had now shifted to the couple.

"See what your environmental activist bullshit's done, Paisley? We could all lose our homes because of fines."

Paisley turned to Charles, who seemed more nervous than usual, fidgeting with papers, rearranging pens. "Oh no, you're not laying this one on me. You're just so determined to shove this deal down our throats no matter what anyone thinks." She thumped her mike and looked shocked when it thumped back.

Meanwhile, without knowing quite how I got there, I found myself on my feet. "See what's happening to our community over this?" I shouted. "We need to find a better site for the wastewater-treatment plant. This is insanity. Why can't this town get it together? As an ordinary citizen, I feel like a person trapped between two speeding freight trains."

Noah stared straight ahead as though having an out-of-body experience.

"Sit down, Sister Do-Gooder," someone yelled. "You're just trying to save your own hide."

"Let her speak," someone else shouted as Noah came to life and reached for the gavel.

Apparently emboldened by my words, Paisley jumped up. "Wouldn't you just love to know why Charles and some of our other board members are willing to consider only this one location?" She rubbed her thumbs against her fingertips in the time-honored gesture for "money."

The crowd erupted in a melee that no amount of gaveling could quell. Once again Amy scribbled furiously. Expecting flying chairs, I ducked as Raymond rose and turned. Before God and everybody, he cocked his finger at me. *Again.* Red spots of anger swam before my eyes.

Amy pulled me into my seat. Cool as you please, Raymond hooked his thumbs into the waistband of perfectly pressed Levi's. The audience was slammed into silence as though someone had punched the Off button. He waved aside Noah's offer of the portable mike and said in a soft, earnest drawl, "Despite what y'all just heard, I wanna say that we're movin' ahead. It's the right thing to do." He paused for effect, like a politician, or a preacher. "For Connie, for Los Lobos." He bowed his head. "She would have wanted this."

"Amen," someone said, and heads nodded. I couldn't believe it. By all accounts Connie was very close to her parents. Surely a wastewater-treatment plant on their property would seem like a desecration of all they held dear. Now good ol' brother Raymond, using the power of the Mercado name, had convinced a lot of people that going ahead with the project would honor her memory. I felt like throwing up. How could these folks be so gullible?

The next few minutes went by in a blur as Noah adjourned the meeting and people rose to gather into tight little knots. Amy and I stood in the aisle with our backs to the door. "Do you think Raymond and 'Rip' are playing good-cop, bad-cop?" she asked.

"I don't know, but Raymond sure knows how make nice when it suits his purpose. Let's leave. I've had enough."

The words were no sooner out of my mouth when someone tapped me on the shoulder. "Bella?"

Turning, it took me a second to recognize Stan, Raymond's uncle and unofficial family spokesperson. We worked together last year on the obituary for Raymond's parents. "Stan, I'm so sorry about Connie." I put out my hand, and then because he looked so sad and miserable, I leaned forward and hugged him. "And congratulations on your marriage." He'd married one of his students a couple of months ago.

"Thanks, and thanks," he said with a sweet, sad smile. A stunning blonde stood next to him. Must be the wife/student. Stan reached over to take her hand. She pulled away with a glare of annoyance. Trouble already?

Stan looked to see if anyone had noticed, then continued gamely, "Lana, this is Bella Kowalski. She works at the paper."

Lana flicked her dark eyes over me. I reached out to shake her hand, but she shifted so it would have been awkward to grab her manicured paw. Maybe she had a thing about touch.

I introduced the couple to Amy and three of us made awkward small talk while Lana stared at the ceiling. "Stan, when's the funeral?" I asked, to fill dead air space. Oops. Sounded too flippant. "Er, what are the arrangements?"

Another smile, bigger this time, took five years off his face. "'Arrangements' are still being made. There's the autopsy and we're waiting for my nephew Rik to get back from Sweden or wherever the hell he's performing. I'll come see you after I know more. I really appreciate you writing another obituary for the family."

"Don't worry about it. Are you okay?"

He shrugged. "Well as can be expected." The sweep of his arm took in CRUD members, Raymond and the water rep guy, still acting tight as ticks. "My niece Connie was such a sweetie. She didn't deserve to have Raymond's ideas put into her mouth."

Wow! I stared, first at him, then at Amy, whose eyes registered her own surprise. Lana's expression didn't change. Mike was right again; the family was divided over the sale. I wanted to know more, but this wasn't the time to ask. "We'll write something that will do her proud." I gave him another little squeeze.

The couple moved off, grief apparent in Stan's every step. Poor guy. Stuck with a bitch. Maybe she just had PMS. Gradually I became aware that Amy's eyes were fixed at a point over my left shoulder. "What's wrong?"

"Don't look now, but that woman is staring at you."

Of course, I looked. A woman in her mid- to late-thirties sat tall and straight two rows behind us. She wasn't there a few minutes ago. Too-red-for-real hair fell to slim but wide shoulders. Our eyes locked for a single second; time to send a shiver down my spine. Then she looked down to her lap and began to comb a small dog's long, pale coat with restless fingers.

The woman looked familiar, like a character in a half-remembered movie. The dog barked and her hand came down over its tiny snout. It struggled to get away and she smacked its rear end.

I turned to Amy. "Must be new in town"

"Do you know her?"

"No, and I don't want to."

8

Several people anxious to air their views cornered us after the meeting. It was after ten when Amy and I emerged from the Community Center. The parking lot lay blanketed in fog, relieved only by the amber fuzz of a single streetlight. I glanced around. The mysterious redhead had vanished. Thank goodness. She was creepy.

Amy rummaged in her purse, tugged out a janitor's ring of keys and chirped open the lock of her Murano SUV. "Where you parked?"

I pointed over several straggler cars to the deserted street. "Up by the library."

"Get in. I don't want you walking by yourself."

I started to protest and then gazed into the black hole where the street curved beyond the library. "Okay."

She drew up behind the Subaru, killed the engine and gave me a worried look. "You all right? Want me to follow you home?"

"I appreciate your concern, but yes I'm fine, and no, I need to stop at the market." My hand groped for the door handle. I hadn't noticed her perfume so much at the meeting, but within the cocoon of the SUV, her Obsession was giving me another headache.

"Bella?"

I gripped the door handle. "Yes?"

"Want to talk now?"

"*Now?*"

Amy ignored the edge in my voice. "What possessed you to stand up tonight before that crowd? Everyone knows your position. What were you planning to say that you haven't already said a dozen times?"

My eyes tracked the shadows Amy's headlights made on the Subaru's rear window. "Well, I had to support Paisley for starters."

Amy sniffed. "I think you were in the business of saving souls too long. You might want to think about saving your own neck."

"I'm not sure what you mean," I said, though I had an idea.

She tapped Revlon-red nails, one at a time, on the wheel, as though playing scales. *Do, re, mi.* "I'm not trying to change your position. Think what you like, just quit preaching against the sewer plant location every chance you get. We had this conversation the day Connie died. I told you then I was under pressure from advertisers to maintain a neutral position."

"Which advertisers?"

Her hand flew off the wheel and waved impatiently. "That's not important. It looks bad if a staff member takes a public anti-sewer stand when the paper comes out as neutral on the issue." She paused. "At least until more study's been done."

I clamped my own hands on my knees to keep both of them from shaking. "So, do you still say you can't keep me if I continue to say what I think?"

Silence then, "That's right, Bella."

I gazed into the blackness outside. I couldn't lose my job, not with Mike's business about to go south. Something was definitely rotten in our own little hamlet, and it wasn't sewage. "But I have to keep up the fight. Paisley is right. Some members of the CRUD board are being bribed. Why else would they pick prime land like the Mercados' for a wastewater treatment site?"

Amy heaved a sigh of exasperation. "Bribe is a pretty strong word, Bella. Could get you sued for defamation if you can't prove it. And believe it or not, there may be perfectly good reasons for wanting that land."

"Such as?"

"Willing sellers, to start. People are often reluctant to sell their property for public works projects, because they're often controversial, especially nowadays with people so quick to run to lawyers."

"I agree. Nothing can be good for everyone," I said. "There's always a downside for someone, or some group. But still…"

Amy didn't allow me to finish. "Good drainage is another reason for choosing one piece of land over another. How about the right size plot? Not too small or too large." She turned and caught my eye. "You know all this, but you've lost your perspective. Ever since that phone call a month ago you've been running around like a crazy person, handing out flyers, spilling your guts to the *LA Times*, cornering people on the street for Christ's sake. And look what it got you. Some fool in a Hummer tried to run you off the road."

"He was really after Connie." I shuddered at how close I'd come to dying.

Amy raised a well-penciled eyebrow. "Did the guy mistake

you for her, or the other way around? Or was it some sociopath who hates Subaru drivers? If so, maybe he had a point." I'll say this, she managed to keep a straight face.

"Very funny." I picked at a thread on the scarf I'd tossed over my T-shirt for the meeting. "I still think he was after Connie."

"Maybe, maybe not."

"Her death delays the deal, doesn't it? It sickens me to think that someone against the project location, someone on *my side*, would resort to murder, but that's the only thing that makes sense."

"Theoretically yes, but…"

"Wait." I interrupted, got a dirty look for my trouble, kept going anyway. "A couple of other things don't make sense. First, our cars look almost the same with the paint so dull and all, but the plates are different. Surely the killer would check before he pushed her over the cliff."

Do, re, mi, fa, so, la… More scale-playing. "Perhaps he got careless."

I unraveled another thread, and another. "Oh swell, a careless killer. Just what this town needs on top of having a sewer practically in our living rooms."

"Well, you do seem to have both on your hands." *Ti, do…* Amy drums while I unravel.

"You don't have to worry," I said. "In Tolosa where you live, the biggest problem is beer bottles the students toss on your lawns."

"Bella, that's unfair and you know it. I understand your position. Hell, I share it privately."

"You're against the deal?"

Amy nodded. "Privately, yes. The paper's neutral stance is something else. That's good business."

"I thought you'd support the sale because Connie's your friend. She did want to sell, right?"

"Yes, and I tried to discourage her. But she wanted to move on with her life and this was one way."

Move on with her life. What did that mean? "Stan indicated that Raymond used Connie to sway the crowd. But if she wanted to sell, then Raymond was right, much as I hate to admit it."

"Could be. But Bella, you know Raymond. He's not above exploiting Connie's memory if it serves his purpose."

"I guess. You know, I still can't get over the brutality of her murder. You told me the sheriff's report says Connie was parked when the guy approached her car. And the window was down?"

"Yes on both counts. The door flew off in the crash, but the window was still intact. It was rolled halfway down."

"I'm a devout coward but if I saw someone pointing a gun through my window, I'd at least try to start the car and get away. Why didn't she?"

"Dunno." Her eyes filled. "Maybe it was someone she knew. Or she might have been reading, or asleep. Connie hadn't been feeling all that well lately."

"Really? Then why was she out there that early in the morning?"

Amy shook her head. "I have no idea. All I know is that she liked the bluffs at that time of day, she was out there Monday and now she's dead."

"So with her dead, the threat's over for me."

"Aargh!" Amy looked like she wanted to shake me. "In a situation like this hate comes from all sides. You don't know who your enemies are."

"Enemies?" My heart beat a little faster.

"Sure. Take Raymond Mercado. The exchange you had with him gave me the creeps."

"Nah, he's a bully at heart. That business with the finger was so juvenile."

Amy cuffed the wheel. "Wake up and smell the sewage, Sister. You saw him and the water guy all cozy, cozy. Raymond stands to make a bundle if the deal goes through. With you out of the way there's one less obstacle to overcome." She took a deep breath, trying to calm herself. "I know I sound like a broken record, but I just hate the way he distorted Connie's wishes to manipulate the audience tonight. 'She would have wanted this.' Bull shit! Even though she wanted to sell, she would have hated being used like this."

I looked down and concentrated on another thread. Who was the real Connie Mercado? A sensitive, family-loving young woman, or a scheming husband stealer? Someone who wanted to preserve her family's heritage, or a person who wanted to sell their land and make a new start somewhere else? I might never know.

Amy reached over and removed my hand from the scarf. "You're going to have nothing but a pile of threads."

I took her hand and inspected her nails. "And you're going to have nothing but red stumps."

She smiled. "Touché. Last word. As your employer, but mostly as your friend, I'm telling you to cool it with the sewer."

I thought about my not-so-great options. "I have to keep my job, so I have no choice. And now you've got me scared."

"Good. That means you'll watch your back. I'm worried about you and also how our coverage of this goddamned sewer project will affect the paper's circulation."

"You're the managing editor, you get paid to worry," I said.

"There you go with the mouth again, Bella." Amy started the engine and tripped the door lock. "I'll stay to make sure your car starts."

The Subaru did start and Amy drove away into the night. I thought about what she'd said as I detoured to the market with one eye on the rearview mirror. Her words stayed with me as I hurried across the deserted lot to the well-lit store, as I looked over my shoulder before reaching into the freezer case for Ben and Jerry's, as I retraced my steps to the car.

A few minutes later I breathed a sigh of relief as I swung into our driveway. Mike's normal parking space sat empty. No big deal, he sometimes parked the pickup in the barn. The first floor lay shrouded in darkness. Only a night light winked through the billowing curtains of the East Wing. I know my husband and if he was there, both wings and the downstairs would be lit up like Dodger Stadium. I creaked open the back door.

"Mike?"

No answer. "Mike, I've got Cherry Garcia," I called in my most seductive voice.

Still no answer.

My heart tripped in my chest. Something didn't feel right.

"Mike? Sam? *Anybody?*"

I flipped the switch and gave brief thanks as light replaced darkness. But no dishes cluttered the sink, no Diet Pepsi cans lined the counter. And where was Sam? He rarely failed to wander out from his current nap spot to greet me.

Could Mike be ill? We hadn't talked all day. I checked our bedroom. Empty.

In the living room, the TV's huge black eye stared at me. "Mike? Sam?" As I stood there, the floor of Mike's East Wing, directly above my head, shifted. Not a creak exactly, but enough to announce a human presence.

There's a perfectly logical explanation for all this, I thought. I don't need to start writing grand opera. Still, as I ascended the staircase off the living room to Mike's nest, my breath came in shallow pants.

"Mike?"

No answer.

Finally, I reached the top. I grabbed the railing and swung around. Mike lay on his back in the recliner. His eyes were closed and he wore headphones, but the music had stopped.

9

I looked again and sighed with a mixture of relief and exasperation. Of course Mike couldn't hear anything—not with those damned headphones on. He was asleep, with Sam dead to the world at his feet. While I stood there, my husband shifted in his chair, causing the floor to creak once more. Sam the Watch Lab slept on.

I moved toward the chair, and immediately tripped over something. What the—? A cardboard box. I stopped and massaged my shin where it made contact with the sharp corner, aware now that other boxes in various stages of packing lay around the room. Housecleaning?

No, something more serious.

Mike opened his eyes and stared at me without recognition. Finally, he woke up enough for his brain to engage. "Hey, Bella. Wassup?"

I pointed to the boxes, noticing for the first time some snapshots of Ethan, his son, and Grace, his first wife, piled on the end table. Mike must have unearthed them as he packed. "Wha… what's all this?"

Mike removed the headphones and heaved himself out of the chair with a grunt and another creak of the floor. He ambled toward me.

"What are you doing with these boxes?" I swept an arm around the room.

He gave me a long, level gaze. "Moving out—"

"*But why?*" I howled, feeling hot, sudden tears on my cheeks.

He brushed them away with the sides of his thumbs, put sleep-warmed hands on my shoulders and gave me the gentlest of shakes. "Will you let me finish before you go off all half-cocked?" I nodded, feeling like an idiot. "I'm moving my stuff into that old office in the barn. That way Chris can bunk up here instead of sleeping on the living room couch."

Did I hear right? "Wait a minute. So you're okay with this?"

He nodded and I all but swooned with relief. "Sure. Had a chance to think about it and you're right. We could use a distraction. Get our minds off our petty problems. Besides, Little Mike's having back surgery next week."

His helper wasn't exactly small. Adding "Big" or "Little" to their names helped to keep the Mikes straight. Sort of.

"Back surgery?" I parroted. "Sounds serious."

"Yup, gonna be off a month. The kid can help me. Earn his keep."

I stared at Mike, pondering his change of mind. Our problems weren't petty and I didn't remember saying anything about needing a distraction. If Chris and Mike worked together, they'd get to know each other, maybe even become buddies. "You don't have to give up your study. Chris will be fine with the living room couch."

His eyebrows moved in a Groucho waggle. "You know how the couch backs up to our bedroom wall?"

I smiled. His train of thought was on its usual track.

Sure enough, Mike grinned. "We don't want to wake up the kid when I ravage your bones."

I closed the space between us, reached up and clasped my arms around his neck, leaning back so the lower half of our bodies touched. "I love you, Mike. And you can ravage my bones anytime."

Just like in the movies, we moved to the bedroom, shedding clothes as we went. Afterward, Mike retrieved the Cherry Garcia from the fridge. Sitting cross-legged on the bed, we took turns feeding it to each other from the carton. Finally, reluctantly, we had to remind ourselves that we weren't kids and tomorrow was a workday.

I tidied the bed while Mike laid out a clean uniform, something he did without fail every weekday night. Shaking out the pillow on his side, I noticed a tagged key on his night stand. "How come you brought one of the tankers home?" I asked.

He set his uniform down, moved across the room, palmed the key off the nightstand and dropped it in his shirt pocket. "Uh, had a problem with my pickup. Parked the tanker behind the barn. If the wind's right, shouldn't smell."

"Wait, wait a minute." I stayed his hand. "You're way ahead of me. What kind of problem? Serious?"

He held up his palms in a small sign of surrender. "If you must know, I had a fender bender—"

"A fender bender?" This couldn't be happening, not now, not after we'd made love. The ice cream curdled in my throat. "When and with who?"

He shook his head as though the subject was too insignificant for discussion. "Happened the other morning. No one else involved."

"What morning?"

"Monday, if you must know. Thought maybe you'd noticed it."

"Mike, there was a lot going on that day. I wish you'd said something."

"I didn't want to worry you and then I forgot. No matter. The pickup's already in the body shop."

I reached for my pillow and held it against my body. "What did you hit?"

"That guard rail behind the shop, the one you're always saying we should complain about to the county. My foot slipped off the brake as I was parking. It isn't that serious."

I hugged my pillow tighter. "You damaged county property and it isn't *serious*?"

"The guard rail's fine, but I creased the front bumper and knocked out a headlight."

"Did you call the insurance company? They usually want two estimates."

"No, I'm going to pay out of my own pocket. Our rates are already out of sight. It's not a big deal."

"Then what's the rush to fix it?"

Mike's eyes darted to the shuttered window. "Well, they found damage on the back of Connie's car—"

He let the sentence trail off and I stared at him. Mike knew what Amy had told me in confidence at the meeting, about the paint on Connie's bumper. Who told him?

Or did he know about the damage from first-hand experience? My heart plummeted to my toes. "Oh Jesus, Mary and Joseph, Mike, tell me you're not involved in her death."

He reached out, but I jumped back, not wanting him to touch me. "Of course, I'm not involved," he said. "But I didn't want some deputy to see my bumper and use it as an excuse start nosing around and asking stupid questions. You know how I feel about those dumb fucks."

Mike, the ex-big-city cop, had adopted a very elitist attitude toward the Tolosa County Sheriff's Office. Called the officers "Barney Fifes" and went out of his way to avoid social contact with them.

I shook the pillow, tossed it over to my side of the bed and stared at my husband. "That's stupid. If the sheriff's office put the body shops on notice, they might report it. Then you'll be in worse trouble."

"Not gonna happen," he said drawing out the words. "I took the truck to a Mexican guy in Santa Rosita. Works out of his house. Really cheap," he added as though trying to sell the idea.

"Did Little Mike see it happen?" He could verify the story if it came to that.

A head shake. "He had the other tanker out on a job."

"Santa Rosita is fifty miles south. Who followed you down?"

Mike crossed the room and slipped they key into his pants pocket. He painstakingly arranged both shirt and trousers over the back of the desk chair, all without meeting my eyes. "No one. Drove myself down. Took the county bus back."

"Really." That last part at least rang true. Unlike a lot of men, Mike loved to ride the bus, using the time to sleep or read.

"Do you realize how all this will look if the sheriff's office finds out?"

He raised his head and shook it slightly, a clear signal that he couldn't believe my stupidity. I know that gesture and it never fails to drive a stake through my heart. "They're not going to find out. This is Wednesday. I'll have the pickup back by Friday."

"Still think it was a dumb thing to do." How my husband, usually so orderly, so predictable, could do something so stupid, so maybe even *criminal*, was beyond me. Perhaps Connie changed him. He didn't kill her, I knew that, but if they'd merely (*merely*, listen to me) had an affair then he certainly had something to hide.

"Will you just quit stewing? It's been a long day, my ass is dragging and I've got to go in early." He sank down on the edge of the bed and began to fiddle with the alarm clock. As though responding to some inner signal, Sam appeared in the doorway. He ambled over, put his head on Mike's knee and gave him a look of pure adoration and something else. The look in Sam's soft honey-colored eyes signified absolute trust.

I watched them interact, Mike stroking the dog's muzzle and Sam nudging Mike's hand for more. Surely if Mike had something to hide, Sam would sense it.

It wasn't much to hang on to, but it was something.

10

It's so dark, how did I get here? And where's Bea? She was right behind me. Good, I can still see a little light at the entrance.

Turn around, Bella, walk toward the light, one foot in front of the other. You can do it.

What was that?
An explosion.
Oh God, it's pitch black now.
I'm choking.
Oh God, another blast.
Need to get back. It's so dark, which way?
"Bella, Bella…"
"Where are you, Bea?"
"This way. Follow my voice."
"I'm trying…" Another blast.
"Bea, Bea, where are you? Bea, help me. I won't tell, honest."

* * *

I bolted upright as another boom shook the house. An earthquake. I reached across the bed and found myself clutching an empty sheet. "Mike? *Mike?*"

Holy Mother of God, where had that man taken himself off to now?

Still another explosion rattled the windows. Not an earthquake, more like a sonic boom. Maybe thunder. Mike's pillow felt cool. He'd been up for a while. The bedside clock said 2:10.

I threw on my robe and padded barefoot to the kitchen. "Mike?" Maybe he went back up to the East Wing and fell asleep.

He wasn't there either. Frantic now, I ran downstairs, pulled on flip-flops by the front door and dashed down to the barn. Sam trotted out of the dog house where he slept on warm nights and stood as close to my leg as he could possibly get. I stroked his silky coat. "Where's Mike, Sam? You're supposed to know these things."

I looked toward the bay. No sign of a storm and no sign of Mike. Moonlight had turned the yard to bleached bone.

I walked down the dirt path past the old oaks that bordered the access road and scanned the horizon. As I watched, the sky to the east took on a grayish-rose pall. The air smelled like chemicals and rubber burning. Something bad had happened, and close by. I shivered. Where was Mike?

Aware of a sudden chill, I pulled my robe closer around me. As I stood in the driveway trying to decide what to do, headlights appeared on our access road. The tanker rolled into the driveway and Mike jumped down. "Where have you been?"

He pointed to the sky. "Looks like there's been an explosion or fire." He grabbed my elbow. "Come on, let's turn on the TV and see if we can find out what happened."

With Sam at our heels, we headed toward the house and Mike snapped on the TV in the living room. "Why don't you call the sheriff's substation?" I asked. "After all, you used to be a cop, I'm sure they'd tell you what happened, even if they're not ready to make a public announcement."

Mike looked at me and said—too quickly I thought—"No."

"That's silly." I reached for the phone. "Let me call."

He took the phone from my hand. "No, Bella."

11

Thursday morning:
I stared at Mike's *nalesniki,* pancakes with cottage cheese. He'd fixed them especially for me, but I couldn't get the fork past my nose. The first whiff of cheese, butter, sugar and cinnamon usually perked up my appetite. Today, it roiled my insides. I set the fork down and took a sip of tea.

"Something wrong with my pancakes?"

"No, Mike, they look wonderful. I'm just not hungry yet."

"Hmph."

On the early news we'd heard that Raymond Mercado's construction company had been burned. Arson was suspected. The office was destroyed, along with much of the equipment in the yard. A slight residue of burned rubber and chemical smells still lingered in the air, adding to my malaise. Dynamite stored in a shed on the property had caused the blasts. A terrible thing, but at least Raymond and his employees were okay. Raymond wasn't my favorite person, but I had no reason to want him dead.

Mike heaved a sigh. "Looks like this pounds another nail into our coffin as far as the state is concerned."

"Who would do such a thing?" Seemed to me that if one group of powerful people wanted the sewer on the Mercado land, another group of equally powerful people did not. What were ordinary citizens to do?

I took another sip of tea to clear my throat and gather my wits. "Mike, um, where'd you go last night?"

Mike looked up quickly, then half grinned. "What took you so long?" He brushed stubby fingers across his crew cut. "Couldn't sleep so I drove out to the bluffs to watch the moon on the ocean. I had things to think about."

"You went out there in the tanker?"

"Sure."

"Rotten timing, Mike."

* * *

"Hello, Bella, it's Janet. Ed's wife?" (As if I wouldn't know that voice anywhere.)

"Hey Janet. Heard from Mom lately?"

"Get a post card every week. Rome, Paris, London. You ever hear from her?"

"Um…sure. How are you anyway?"

"Don't ask. My knees are acting up so bad I can hardly take the steps. And my acid reflux and Ed's snoring keep me up all night. And then just when I get to sleep Chris comes in and bangs around the kitchen, eating everything I just lugged in from Kroger's. And the milk bill, why I—"

"When's Chris coming?"

"Monday. His flight gets into LA at four. He's expecting you to pick him up."

"Gee Janet, we're three hours north of LAX. I'm not sure my old Subaru will make it that far. Can you book him a flight on the shuttle to Tolosa airport?"

"Not really, the fare is so expensive. And I suppose we'll have to give him some spending money. And I need a root canal, and—"

"Uh, that's okay. I'll be there."

"Bella?"

"Yes?"

"You need to know, this kid has big-time issues."

"Really? What's his problem?"

"He smokes, and I think it's more than Marlboros. And the mouth on him. Why if I'd talked to my parents like he does, the old man woulda punched me into next week. And it takes an act of Congress to get him to church. Promise me you'll take him to Mass every Sunday."

"Don't worry. I have experience with troubled teens."

"You certainly do, Bella. How you could walk away from God's work like that I'll never understand."

"Janet, we've had this conversation. Chris and I will be fine."

"Hope so. Ed and I are at our wits' end. And I think my mother is coming down with the Alzheimer's. Her keys? Spends hours—"

"Janet, something's burning on the stove. Have a nice day."

"About time you did something for the family."

"You're welcome," I said to the silent phone.

I can do this. I can.

* * *

After Janet's call, I fed Sam, stacked the dishes and got ready for work. I was just turning the key in the deadbolt when I spied an unfamiliar car moving slowly up our access road. My heart thudded three times against my ribs. *Trouble, trouble, trouble.*

The car assumed the shape of a generic Crown Victoria. Law enforcement's vehicle of choice. A man unfolded himself from the front seat and began to walk toward me. Was he here about the fire at Mercado Construction? Oh dear. What if he asked me if Mike was home all night?

The man stopped by the Subaru, removed his sunglasses and ran his hand along both bumpers. I strode briskly out to meet him as though a visit from law enforcement was no big deal. "Hi. May I help you?"

"Mrs. Kowalski?" He pronounced our name as "Cow," rather than the Polish, "Kov."

"I'm Bella Kowalski," I said, correcting him.

The man nodded and held out his hand. "Good morning to ya. Ryan Scully. Detective, Los Lobos sheriff's substation." He sounded like he'd just stepped out of the Irish film *Waking Ned Devine*. The scene would have been charming under different circumstances.

I shook his hand and struggled to keep my tone conversational. "You're out early."

He studied me with wide-set eyes the color of Blue Ice. Forty pounds and twenty years ago he'd been an attractive man. "Tyin' up loose ends. Been handin' out flyers lately?"

Was he here to discuss that? Relief flooded through me, replaced by righteous anger. "Actually I haven't, but since when is that a problem?"

He looked at me and I noticed that one eye wandered a bit. "It's not, at least not to the Sheriff's Department. Sure and you've got some folks upset. Maybe upset enough to set fire to Mercado Construction. Got any ideas who might do that?"

Oh God, here it comes.

I fought the urge to wipe my palms on my slacks and shook my head, trying for a casual effect. "None at all."

"Figures. I'm on me way out to Raymond Mercado's right now, thought I'd stop for a wee chat first."

Crap. "O…kay. Would you like to come in?"

"That would be lovely now."

Detective Scully followed me through the front hall into the living room where he seated himself on the edge of a wing chair by the fireplace. He pulled a small, rumpled notebook and stubby pencil from his shirt pocket.

Like Mike, he licked the tip of the pencil. Must be a cop thing.

"Mind tellin' me what happened the other day?"

My mind turned to oatmeal. "What other day?"

He turned his head slightly so as to spotlight me with the wandering eye. The look unnerved me and he knew it. His words were delivered with studied patience, as though to an unruly toddler. "On Monday, the day Ms. Mercado died. Unless you'd be havin' something to tell me about last night."

"I don't." Why was he bouncing all over the place like this? Maybe to keep me off balance. My temples began to throb. "Uh, Monday. Sure." Probably wanted to check the story I'd told Deputy Marquez for inconsistencies.

Once again I told how I'd seen something unidentifiable on *Las Tablas*, how a closer inspection revealed a body, and how Connie's Subaru was wedged between the rocks and the bluffs.

"Any tire tracks over the edge?"

My ears were on fire; surely he could tell. "Um, let's see, it was dry, and the grass was tall. I remember it was mashed down, but I don't remember any tracks."

"Sure and there's no guard rail."

"That's true." What did that have to do with anything? Connie was shot. Silence while he caught up on his notes. I allowed myself to relax, but relief made me garrulous. "There's something else that may be important. I have a Subaru hatchback the same model and almost the same color as Connie's."

He nodded with his chin like he already knew. Of course he did. He'd checked both bumpers for paint transfers.

"That morning," I added, "on my way to the bluffs some guy in a gray Hummer tried to run me off the road."

He looked up from his notes. "Don't suppose ya'd be gettin' a license?"

"No, I was too shook up."

Detective Scully blew out a breath that would have done a horse proud. "The Hummer motorist might have reacted to those tree-huggin' bumper stickers plastered all over yer bumper."

I stood up. "Are we through?"

"In a bit, Mrs. Kowalski. Please sit yerself back down a wee moment."

Great. My rudeness had given him a perfect opening to grill me about Mike.

But once again he took a different tack and pointed to the grandfather clock ticking in the corner. "Might that be a family heirloom?"

"Yes, but not mine. Mike brought it from Chicago when he moved to Detroit, and then we hauled it out here."

"Yer husband have family back there?"

"Just second cousins. He was an only child. His parents and first wife and son are all gone."

Detective Scully gave me another wall-eyed stare. "Might want to ask yer husband sometime why he left the department."

"What do you mean, why he left? He retired."

"Just ask him." He rose and crammed the notebook and pencil into his pants pocket. They left a disconcerting bulge next to his fly. Almost hysterical, I fought the urge to giggle.

At the front door, he turned and asked in that offhand way that cops have, "Say, would ya know the color of yer husband's pickup, Mrs. Kowalski."

"Of course. It's gray."

Don't say more, Bella. Don't say more.

"Gray is it now? That's what I thought." He opened the door and let himself out.

Stunned, I stood at the open door and watched him drive off.

Back inside, I dialed Mike's cell number. "You've reached Mike Kowalski. Leave a message and I'll get back to you."

"Uh…never mind. I'll talk to you tonight." Those words almost never meant anything good. Was I ready to hear what he had to say? Or did I need more time? For what? To gather my thoughts or to hide my head in the sand?

Coward. I put down the receiver. Mike and I would have a long talk right after dinner, or at least before bedtime.

* * *

I went to work and had my usual hectic day. Thursday night came and went. After supper, Mike continued to lug his personal stuff from the East Wing to the small office in the barn. I took refuge on my sofa in the West Wing, where I fretted and procrastinated, knitting a blanket big enough for a woolly mammoth.

At least Detective Scully hadn't asked me if Mike was home when Mercado Construction burned. I honestly don't know how I'd have answered. Convent life presented moral dilemmas all the time, but nothing like marriage.

I did ask Mike casually if he'd had a visit from the sheriff's office, without naming names. He looked at me like I'd lost my mind. So why hadn't Scully followed up with Mike? Or maybe he had, and Mike just didn't want to say. I thought my husband and I shared everything, but apparently not. The thought made my stomach hurt.

Who was this man I married?

12

Friday noon:
"Obituary desk."

"Bella?"

Absorbed in entering our latest obituary into the computer, I jumped at the sound of the male voice in my earpiece. Detective Scully again? No, he would never call me Bella.

"It's Stan Mercado. Am I calling at a bad time?"

Weak with relief, I quickly closed the file. "No, not at all. How are you doing, Stan?"

The long sigh. "Okay. I wonder if we could get together and do Connie's obituary?"

"Sure. Come over any time."

"No, I…" his voice broke, "being in the office would remind me too much of last time, after my brother and sister-in-law died."

"Sure Stan, not a problem. Why don't we meet at Sinbad's for lunch? I'm dying for one of their Reuben sandwiches."

"Sounds good. Really appreciate this, Bella."

"Nonsense. It will do me good to get out for a while. Shall we say fifteen minutes? Bring Lana if you like. My treat."

A pause. "Thanks, but Lana probably has other plans."

Probably? "Okay, Stan. See you in a few. Are…are things okay with you two?"

Good one, Bella. Nothing like getting personal.

Stan didn't seem to take offense. "They could be better, but we're trying to work it out."

"I'm sure you will."

I drove to the restaurant thinking about Stan trying to work out kinks in a new marriage with a much-younger partner. Marriage at any stage was so difficult. Why hadn't someone warned me? Even after eight years, I couldn't seem to get the hang of this relationship business. On one hand, I couldn't stop thinking about Detective Scully's remarks concerning Mike's past. On the other, I was afraid to confront my husband and learn the truth.

I'd slept poorly last night. A second cup of morning tea brought an epiphany of sorts—I wasn't ready to know about Chicago. I gave myself permission to procrastinate. Now I was second-guessing even that decision and driving myself crazy in the process.

* * *

The weather was way too muggy for mid-June and I broke a sweat just driving two miles to Sinbad's. Our next car would have air conditioning for sure.

Vehicles of the lunchtime crowd filled the parking lot. After circling twice, I spied a place next to a Hummer. My heart gave a little lurch when I noticed it was gray. Silly. A parking spot is a parking spot. I pulled in next to it, killed the engine and hopped out.

I heard the yippy barking of a small dog inside. I couldn't see through the darkened windows, but the door felt hot to the touch. "Hey puppy, pipe down. I know you're roasting in there. Your person will be back soon."

I walked toward the entrance, out of his sight. No point in getting the little guy more upset than he already was.

"Bella," said a voice at my back.

I turned. "Hey Stan, good to see you."

We exchanged a quick hug and Stan frowned. "You seem tense. This too much of an imposition?"

"Oh no, not at all." I pointed to the Hummer three rows back. "It's so hot and the owner didn't leave a window open for the dog."

"Maybe we can help the pooch out." Stan walked back and tugged at the Hummer's door latch. He shook his head and moved back to my side. "Locked in. We tried. Wanna go somewhere where you won't spend your whole lunch being aggravated?"

"No, let's go inside. I'm starving."

We ordered Reubens, with Stan requesting the veggie version. Next came fountain drinks, napkins and straws. A table with a breeze opened up by the door and we grabbed it, displaying our plastic number for the server.

Once we were settled, Stan pulled a sheaf of papers from a brief case that looked like it had been through several Middle Eastern wars. He looked at me and pulled his shoulders forward in an apologetic shrug. "You're probably anxious to get back."

I took a sip of Diet Pepsi. "Will you quit? I have plenty of time. Let's eat first."

The server set our sandwiches before us and I eyed Stan's curiously. "What's the 'meat' in a veg Reuben?"

He pulled the sandwich apart releasing the pungent aroma of sauerkraut and melted Swiss. "Portabella mushrooms."

"Yum. I'll have to try that. We've been trying to eat healthier." I smiled. "Though I'm not sure Mike's committed to the idea. Your typical Polish diet is hardly low in fat."

"It's tough." Stan applied Dijon mustard to his sandwich as

though executing a fine painting. "I'm really opposed to eating critters, but damn, I can't give up my cheese habit." He took a huge bite, grinned and wiped a smear of mustard and melted cheese from his chin.

I swallowed my first bite. Heaven on rye.

"You're opposed to using animal products and yet you were raised around here. This is cattle country."

His grin turned lopsided. "One of those inconsistencies all humans have, I guess. I can't buy the whole idea that animals are only here to serve us. It's something I'm quite passionate about."

I put down my sandwich and studied him, the rounded shoulders, wispy gray hair, intelligent hazel eyes behind the owlish glasses. It would be easy to underestimate this gentle man. "What else are you passionate about, Stan Mercado?"

His eyes lit up. "My bride, Lana." He frowned, then shrugged. "I just wish she were passionate about me. But she's young, only twenty-eight. Says she needs time to, uh,…" He stopped and waved his hand. "You know." A lame smile.

Way too much information, Stan. "Of course." Change the subject, Bella. "What else do you like to do?"

"Teach, see light come on in kids' eyes." He shook his head. "Lana doesn't want children. I'm twenty-seven years older than her. It's too late for me to…" His sentence trailed off. "Well, it is what it is, and it will have to be enough, I guess."

"I know what you mean. I never had a chance to even consider motherhood while I was in the convent."

Stan smiled. "I should hope not."

I returned his smile and spread my hands. "And by the time I left, well, it was too late for me too."

Stan's look changed to one of such sadness that my spirit ached for him. In the ensuing silence, he munched through three more mouthfuls. A piece of portabella dropped from his sandwich. He picked it up and felt the texture, like a tailor examining fine cloth. "I'll tell you what else I'm into," he said. "Mushrooms."

"Mushrooms?"

"You bet. The texture, the color, the smell." He put the piece to his nose and sniffed it, then held it close to my face. "There are some amazing varieties in the stores now, but give me the wild ones every time."

I inhaled; the mushroom didn't smell like much of anything. "Give me the boring old Safeway ones every time."

A half smile. "You and Lana both. Hopefully the late rains have popped up a few more. I want to check out some of my old haunts in North County this afternoon."

"Good luck. The whole fungophile experience is just not something I'm curious about."

Stan shook his head and grinned to let me know there were no hard feelings. "Different strokes. They're not dangerous if you know what you're doing."

"'If' being the operative word." I took a bite of dill pickle. Like old friends we shared a laugh after the pickle squirted juice on Stan's glasses.

We were almost finished with our sandwiches when a tall woman with red hair strode past our table. I literally did a double-take. "Stan, wait here." I followed her at a discreet distance to the parking lot. Sure enough, she got into the Hummer.

I turned to Stan who'd come up behind me. "See that woman? She and her dog were at the CRUD meeting, and she's driving a Hummer."

Stan gave me a quizzical look. "So…?"

What could I say? A man in a gray Hummer tried to run me off the road. And a woman with a white dog had appeared in two places I'd been in the last five days. And, oh by the way, she drove a gray Hummer.

What did that mean in the whole scheme of things? This was such a small community I ran into people I knew all the time. "Never mind."

I pulled a yellow pad from my bag. "Shall we go back inside and get started?"

"Let's go to your office."

"Are you sure?"

"Absolutely." He grinned. "I can handle the newsroom."

Back at the office, after checking in with Amy, I sat down at the computer, opened Quark and turned to Stan in the side chair. "Let's start with the basics. When and where is the funeral?"

"Next Thursday, eleven o'clock at Saint Patrick's."

"Not the Mission?"

"No, Connie loved Saint Pat's. She'd..." his voice broke, "want it there."

I tapped away on my keyboard. "Private?"

He shook his head. "She wouldn't want that. Everyone loved Connie. What's not to love?"

What indeed? I turned toward him and squeezed his hand. Soft, with no rough edges, like the man himself. "I didn't know Connie that well, but I hear she had a lot of friends."

"She did. I'm surprised you two didn't get to know each other better. She and Mike seemed to get on so well. Why, they were always..."

I withdrew my hand. "Always what, Stan?"

His hazel eyes shifted, trying to cover the awkward moment. "It's just that, well, they liked to kid around."

"Really." The word, somewhere between a question and a statement, dropped like a stone. "And where did they do all this 'kidding around?'"

Stan made a tsking sound. "You know what I mean. They'd joke back and forth over coffee. Bella, trust me, it was no big deal. If you knew Connie, you'd know that."

"Well I didn't know her," I said coldly. Time to change the subject before I made an idiot of myself. "Is Rik coming to the funeral?"

Stan raised his eyes toward the stained ceiling tiles. "Last I heard."

"It's good for family members to be together at times like this." I considered telling him about Bea's murder, but it would hardly make him feel better. I turned back to my monitor. "We're getting off track here. What about the burial?"

"We—that is Raymond and I—have decided to have her buried in the church graveyard."

"Is that what she wanted?"

Stan heaved a shuddering breath. "Actually I have no idea what she wanted, but her heart was in that church. She was so full of life, I'm sure she never considered dying." His eyes were wet. "I just pray she didn't see the gun."

Not knowing what to say, I handed him a Kleenex.

He leaned across the desk to take it. "Connie was pregnant," he whispered.

13

I stared at Stan with my mouth open, not sure I'd heard right. "What did you say?"

"Pregnant." The word hung in the air like an unexploded bomb. I looked around to see if anyone else heard. Everyone in the newsroom was either on the phone or staring at a computer. Finally, I was able to breathe again.

"The baby was due in December," Stan said in hoarse whisper. "One of us was going to have a child. Another generation of Mercados. Manny and Margaret-Rose would have been so proud, especially after…" He began to cry openly.

"After what, Stan?"

He looked at me intently. "I'm telling you this on deep background."

"Obituary editors usually don't deal with deep background information," I said with a small smile.

Stan did an air-chop with his hand. "You know what I mean.

This is not for the obituary." I nodded and he continued, "Well, it was one of those family secrets they never talked about, the way people did years ago. When Manny and Margaret-Rose were first married I had a big fight with Manny and our father about my place in"—here he made quotation marks with his fingers—"'the family empire.' I knew none of the Mercado businesses were for me, but I had no idea what I wanted to do. So I spent a few years dirt-bagging around Europe before I entered UC Davis to study biology."

I nodded like I understood where this was going.

"Well, while I was away they had a set of twins, Connie and…" He hesitated and shook his head. "Sorry I can't remember the little tike's name. Maybe I've blocked it because of what came later."

Later? What did he mean by that? "Boy or girl?"

He hesitated. "You know I'm not sure of that either."

"How could you not know?" I almost shouted. I took a deep breath and lowered my voice. "Connie had a twin and you don't remember its name, or whether the kid was a boy or girl?"

He scratched his head, looking sheepish. "Lame, huh? I just don't recall. I was so into myself during college that not much else made it to the radar screen. And I was in Europe when the four of them moved to Mexico City for several years."

"Really? How did they manage that? And why do such a thing?"

"They managed it because our father, Manuel Senior, ran the construction business and Manny Junior, my brother, hired good managers for the other firms. He started some kind of importing venture down there. A few months later,…" he hesitated and his voice broke, "Connie's twin was kidnapped and murdered."

Dumbstruck, I stared at him. A child kidnapped. Murdered for no reason. Like my sister.

The Mercados seemed to have as much tragedy in their lives as the Kennedys. What good was all that money and power if everyone in your family died tragically? "I'll bet it was in all the Mexico City papers. What about up here?"

Stan shook his head. "Manny bribed the Mexican officials to keep it quiet to protect Connie. Long story short, the business failed and they came home and resumed their lives, at least as much as they could."

"So people didn't think it strange that they left with two children and returned with one?"

Stan took a moment to consider his answer. In the silence, I remembered that Amy told me Connie spent time in Mexico City as a toddler. She'd never said anything about a twin, much less that he or she was murdered. I wondered if she even knew.

He huffed a long breath. "As I said, I was pretty into my own thing at that time, but I think they told people the child died of natural causes. And people do have short attention spans." He gave me a half-smile. "I'm the living example of that."

"Whew. How fortunate that they *could* come back here. I'm sure they had horrible memories of Mexico City."

"Of course, but the story does have a silver lining, of sorts. The child's body wasn't discovered for over a year and while they waited for word, improbable as it sounds, Margaret-Rose gave birth to another set of twins."

I blinked. "Rik and Raymond."

He nodded.

"Wow."

"Wow is right," he acknowledged. "Like Connie, Margaret-Rose was very devout. They both saw the hand of God in everything, both good and bad. I think that even though Connie wasn't married, Margaret-Rose and Manny would have loved her being pregnant and believed it was meant to be." Once again his eyes filled.

Pregnant. That punch-in-the-gut word again.

"Do…do you know who the father was?"

Stan looked almost angry. "No, and I don't care."

Okay. "Was Connie depressed? Do you think—"

"That she committed suicide? Never!" Stan's palm thudded the desk. "She wanted this baby."

So that's what Amy meant by the "Especially not now," after

I asked if Connie killed herself. She *knew* Connie was pregnant. But maybe not that her twin was murdered. Like my own sister.

So why didn't I feel more kinship with this woman? Because I suspected that Connie, Ms. Good Catholic herself, had designs on my husband, that's why. "What were her plans? Didn't she want to move back to her family home to raise her child? It's such a gorgeous place."

"Actually, she wanted to sell it."

"Really? Why?" People never ceased to surprise me.

"Don't get me wrong. It was the family homestead and she loved it. After all, that's where she and her brothers grew up. However, she planned to establish permanent residency in Canada after the baby came."

"You're kidding. Why Canada?"

"Connie wanted out of here and Canada's a long way away." He rubbed at a scratch on the desk. "Too many bad memories. She and Raymond never got along. In fact they had one hell of a fight a few days before the, uh, before Connie died."

He couldn't seem to say the word 'murder' and I didn't blame him. "Do you know what about? Was it over the land sale?"

Stan shook his head. "Not sure. Maybe about the selling price, maybe he wanted her to have an abortion. With those two it might have been over the plot of some TV sitcom. They were like kids, always scrapping about something."

"Did you tell the sheriff?"

"Nope, and I don't intend to. What happens in the Mercado family stays in the family."

"As in 'what happens in Vegas stays in Vegas'?"

"Mmm," was his answer.

Protecting your family is fine and natural to a point, but not when it comes to murder. I looked at the resolute set of his jaw. I was right; it would be easy to underestimate this man. "How do you feel about the sale, Stan?"

He spread his hands on the desk and studied them. "How do I feel? If I had my druthers, I'd encourage Rik and Raymond to keep the land and turn it into an organic farm." He looked up at me, his eyes bright now and free of tears. "We could sell our products at the local farmers' markets, and to restaurants in town. It would be such a boon to this community."

"Sounds like a great plan. Have you talked to Raymond?"

"I've talked myself blue in the face. He wants to sell and that's that. So does Rik, apparently."

"What about your wife?"

His eyes betrayed the conflict he felt. "She's on their side. She's never had much and money is important to her. But Lana and Connie were really close."

I reached across the desk and touched his hand lightly. "I'm glad they were close, Stan. That's a good thing."

"Yeah." He sighed and grabbed his notes. "Let's get this over with. I need to be outdoors."

An hour after Stan left, I pushed away from the computer and read:

Obituary: Consuela Margaret-Rose Mercado
One of the Central Coast's bright lights shines no more.
After thirty-four years of lie on her own terms,

I changed the typo from "lie" to "life" and kept reading:

Consuela Margaret-Rose Mercado has joined her loving parents. Like Manuel and Margaret Rose, her life was snuffed out suddenly and tragically. Connie leaves behind grieving brothers Raymond of Los Lobos, and Rik of Las Vegas, paternal uncle, Stanley, and his wife Lana, both of Tolosa. Connie also leaves a legacy of unconditional love for her animals, who will be placed in good homes.

A Mass celebrating her life will take place at 11 A.M. next Thursday at Saint Patrick Catholic Church, with burial immediately following. The public is invited to both services and the reception afterwards at Consuela's Gently Used Treasures and Wedding Chapel.

Connie was born in Los Lobos, where she spent a happy tomboy childhood with her brothers on the family property. In high school she liked to hang out with friends Amy Goodheart and Brenda Livingston, dancing and going to the beach. After graduation, she traveled for several years. India, Tibet and Canada were favorite destinations. Back home, Connie opened a second-hand store and wedding chapel downtown. The tables in front of her store soon became a popular gathering place. Connie was licensed by the State of California to perform marriage ceremonies and many happy couples tied the knot in her chapel. She was a familiar sight whizzing off to garage sales around the county in her old station wagon. An animal lover, she volunteered at the local shelter and also gave many hours in the service of her church, where she was the coordinator of its Harbor the Homeless program.

The name Consuela means "consolation" and Connie was certainly a comfort to her late parents, Manuel and Margaret-Rose. She loved nothing better than to stop by for breakfast and an exchange of confidences. After their untimely deaths, hiking at Escarpa El Dorado became her passion. She also enjoyed antique jigsaw puzzles and it was difficult for customers to persuade her to part with even one from her large collection. A longtime journal keeper, Connie loved to spend the evening by the fireside with her animals, recording the day's events.

Connie loved children as well as animals. In lieu of flowers, the family suggests donations to children's organizations or the animal shelter.

As I read over the obituary, my heart shifted in my chest. Connie loved children and she was pregnant.

14

Monday of the following week:
Traveling south on the 101 freeway, I checked my watch just north of Santa Barbara. Barely noon and my nephew Chris's plane wasn't due until four.

I'd intended to use my driving time to think through all the things Mike and I needed to discuss. But I was lulled by sunshine that warmed my hands and the startling blue ocean as it hugged the shore. Further out to sea, a knot of storm clouds turned the water an abalone-shell gray.

Charming, but worrisome. Surely it wouldn't rain in June; that never happened. On the other hand, the muggy weekend felt more like Iowa than Coastal California. No doubt about it, the weather was definitely weird this year.

I'd always loved this stretch of the drive. Today, witnessing the raw power of the sea made me feel like I could handle anything. I resolved to put my problems aside for one more day. I'd have more perspective after I got home. My stomach rumbled in anticipation of a lunch stop in Camarillo. After that, it was over the Conejo Grade and into the northern tip of Los Angeles.

Traveling south, the worst part of the trip came at the end, dealing with LA's crazy traffic. I consoled myself with the thought that going home, the reverse was true—it was all downhill after Camarillo. By that time Chris and I would be having a heart-to-heart and the drive would pass effortlessly.

For the next hour, clouds moved in like storm troopers. As I approached the 405 interchange south of the San Fernando Valley, rain pelted the windshield and the metallic smell of ozone invaded my senses. My hands froze on the wheel. One by one I lifted each stiff finger and forced it to relax.

An interminable half-hour later I was searching desperately for the LAX turnoff. Right or left exit? Easy to miss when I was wedged between two semis, with rain sluicing off my windshield. Vehicles in the left lane whizzed by, spewing more water than the Subaru's wipers could handle.

Dang! Missed it! All of a sudden I had too many choices. Which spur would take me back to the turnoff? Choice 1? Choice 2? The decision was made for me as I was swept along in traffic moving south. Wedged between the two trucks like a mouse in a trap, I barreled over a high overpass with a roller coaster drop that left my stomach behind. I kept my eyes fixed straight ahead. One peek over the edge and I was a goner.

Once again I felt like the Hummer was pursuing me, but a check of the rearview mirror confirmed the same semi on my tail. My hands threatened to slip off the wheel; I carefully lifted first the left and then the right and wiped the sweat off on the sides of my pants. I felt lightheaded and my face was numb. "Don't pass out. Don't pass out," I muttered over and over. Just then I saw the sign: "Return to LAX."

Without even a signal I wheeled the old Subaru off the exit, rejoicing all the way to Lot C, which wasn't far. I grabbed a ticket and pulled into an empty space close to the entrance. I turned the ignition off, my knees knocking in time to the engine's chatter.

As my breathing slowed I noticed another sign: "Long Term Parking." Oh great. Definitely not where I needed to be. I checked my watch: only 2:54. Plenty of time to move to short-term parking. I had no idea where that was, but if I just followed my nose to the airport terminals, which I could see in the distance, how hard could it be?

First I'd have a short rest. I checked the gauges, noting with satisfaction the engine hadn't overheated. Rain pounded against the roof and windshield. I sipped from my water bottle and munched an apple, safe and drowsy in my warm cocoon.

Flights were so unreliable these days. Maybe Chris's would be delayed, maybe I had time for a nap.

Maybe you'd better move the car, Bella.

I turned the key in the ignition. *Click.* Tried again. *Click, click*—and then *click, click, click.* A hot flash grabbed me by the neck and threatened to explode my head. I waited for the chill that followed the sweat, tried the key again. Same result.

Okay, what's plan B?

Triple A of course. I reached in my wallet for the card and realized I didn't have one—I'd cut it up after we canceled our membership. A classic example, I now reflected, of penny wise and pound foolish. I reached for my cell, breathed a sigh of relief when Mike picked up.

"Where are you, Bella? Raining like hell up here."

"It's raining here too. I'm in Lot C."

"That's long-term parking."

"I know." The words were delivered through clenched teeth.

A brief silence. "You have time. Move to the short-term lot across from United. Just follow the signs to Terminal 7."

"Uh, that's what I called about. The Subaru won't start and the starter makes this funny clicking sound."

Mike swore softly into the phone. "Call Triple A I guess."

"I can't. Remember—"

"That's right." He swore again, not so softly this time.

"What should I do about finding a mechanic?"

"Nothing. Just leave the car and take the shuttle to the United terminal. Give me your row number and I'll try to get someone over there. Worst case, I'll borrow a drive-away and come down after rush hour and pick you and the car up."

"Mike," I wailed. "That could take hours. It will be after midnight when we get home."

He heaved an exasperated sigh into my ear. "Best I can do, Bella. You're not making my day either. Just go meet the plane and buy some magazines or something. And be sure to take your cell. I'll be in touch. Love you."

"Love you too," I said. What I really wanted to do was scream or cry or both.

* * *

After I reached the United terminal, I decided to go through Security and meet Chris as he came off the airplane rather than in the baggage claim area. If we were going to be stuck in the airport for hours, might as well be comfortable. We might even, I thought, hop a shuttle and treat ourselves to dinner at one of the nearby hotels.

By the time I reached Chris's arrival gate, first class passengers were beginning to deplane. I became aware of a general buzz as well as people with cameras and microphones. Media probably meant "Celebrity on Board." Unsure whether to hang back and avoid the crowd or press forward and join the fray, I opted for the fray. Less chance of missing Chris.

A thirty-something man of medium height strode through the jetway door with the air of someone used to attention. He paused and looked over his shoulder, then pressed forward as though late for a connecting flight. Dressed in black from turtleneck to fringed leather vest to leather pants, (which emphasized the emerging bulge of his midsection), the man adjusted the strap of the leather case slung over his shoulder, and arranged his face into a practiced smile, never missing a beat in forward momentum.

The media pressed forward. "How was the tour?"

"Mr. Mercado, how long will you be in LA?"

Mercado? Did I hear right?

"Is it true you're going to file for bankruptcy?" asked a reporter who stuffed a microphone into his face. My ears perked up at that word. That would certainly be a reason to want his sell his family's land.

Rik Mercado pushed the mike away, held up his hands in a "no questions" signal and said something to a teenage boy who'd finally caught up with him. Another man in black came through the jetway and joined the two in front of the counter.

But it was the boy, with his shoulder length, straight-cut yellow hair covered with a white painter's cap, who held my attention. He wore a backpack and carried an oversize skateboard.

His low-slung pants showed several inches of underwear and his shoes needed tying.

He looked familiar. Had I seen him on TV? At that moment, his blue eyes met mine. "Auntie Bella?"

"Chris?"

My nephew broke away from the men, hurried over and encircled me with thin, strong arms. I returned his hug, enduring the agony of skateboard wheels pressed into my spine. After a few seconds I held him away for closer inspection—same sweet kid apparently, but I wouldn't know him on the street. And why should I? There'd been big changes in eight years. "Your shoes are untied," I said, and stopped.

Nice one, Bella. Start out with something snide.

Chris looked down at his stubby black shoes. "They're, like, supposed to be that way." He shook his head as though I needed to get with it and pointed to the first man. "See that guy? It's Rik Mercado. He's heavy metal."

"Really?" I said like an authority.

"Yeah, he's, like, retro. The new Eddie Van Halen."

"Imagine that. So what are you doing with him?" As my nephew and I spoke, Rik stood talking with the other man. Both of them seemed unhappy about something. Rik shook his head and tapped the squared-off toe of his boot.

"I sat next to him on the plane. He's here for his sister's funeral," Chris said. "Bummer huh?"

"Sure is. How'd you get a seat in first class?" Stepmother Janet would never spring for one.

With the same infectious grin I remembered, Chris said, "Well, I was, like, looking for the head and like, accidentally got into first class, and was the flight lady ever piss…I mean angry. Anyway, I recognized Rik and he asked me to sit with him. The lady was like, still mad as hell, but what could she do?"

He waved a CD under my nose. "He gave me this. CDs are like, so over, but he signed this one. Rik's going to Los Lobos too, on the commuter. Wanna meet him?"

"No!"

Chris frowned. "No?"

"Well, maybe." His frown deepened and I backpedaled. "Uh, sure I'd love to."

As Chris and I approached, I heard Rik complain to the other man: "What do you mean the flight to Tolosa was canceled? What the fuck am I supposed to do, walk?"

At that point, the second man caught sight of us and put up his hands. "Stay back. Don't approach Mr. Mercado." Then he recognized Chris and dropped his hands. Rik reached out, pulled Chris forward and slung an arm around his shoulder. Flashes went off and a reporter asked Chris his name.

Chris had, if not fifteen minutes of fame, at least a couple as he clung to the skateboard. Using what seemed like several hundred "likes," he explained to reporters how he'd boarded the flight from New York in Cleveland and how Rik had invited him to share the empty first class seat next to him.

With the attention on Chris, Rik seemed to lose focus. He danced around, mugging for the few cameras not on Chris and talking behind his hand to the second man. His eyes met mine once. Apparently I wasn't worth a second glance.

While Rik fidgeted I had a chance to observe. If he and Raymond were twins, they couldn't be more different. Rik was dark-haired like Raymond and they both exuded that slightly sinister air. But that was it. Size-wise, Raymond had a good six inches on his brother. If they were birds, I decided, Raymond would be a raven and Rik a starling, always in motion, ready for a fight. Rik's eyes even had the beady, yellowish cast of those annoying birds who made Sam's life hell in nesting season.

When the media dispersed, Chris turned to the still-fidgeting Rik and said, "This is my Aunt Bella. She can drive you to Los Lobos. She works for a newspaper."

The word "newspaper" seemed to work a kind of magic on Rik's attention span. He looked at me with sudden interest and I reached out my hand. "Nice to meet you, Mr. Mercado. I'm sorry for your loss."

His face clouded over, but he said nothing, so I continued: "Under normal circumstances I'd be happy to drive you."

Yeah right, Bella. In my old Subaru.

"So what's the problem?" Rik's toe tapped.

"Well, I've had car problems and my husband is going to drive down tonight and pick us up. If you'd like to wait I'm sure we can find room for you."

Rik Mercado gave me a look that said, "Be serious, lady." The other man whispered something to him. "Right." He turned to us. "I'm a busy man. My manager here is going to stay in LA while I attend the funeral. Put some deals together for me, so I can make some money outta this trip."

Surely he didn't mean that like it sounded.

Rik waved off the manager. "He's gonna rent a limo and driver for me." He thought a few seconds. "Tell you what, why don't you ride with us? I can give you an exclusive for your paper."

"Oh, we couldn't. Chris needs to get his luggage downstairs and that will take time."

"We'd love to, man." Chris pointed to his backpack. "This is it."

"For two weeks? You're kidding," I said. "What about underwear?"

Chris tugged the waistband of his boxers. "Got 'em."

"Silly me."

"Well," Rik stared at us with undisguised impatience, "which is it?"

"Maybe," I said. "Let me double check my husband's plans." I stepped back and pulled out my cell. "Chris, don't go anywhere."

"Like I would, Auntie Bella."

A few minutes later it was settled. Mike hadn't been able to locate a mechanic. He would drive down tomorrow and pick up the Subaru. Chris and I would ride with Rik.

15

Thirty minutes later, the giant centipede glided to the curb in front of the United terminal. A stretch Hummer. My heart sank; I couldn't ride in that. The driver, who wore a black cap with a leather visor, alighted and stowed Rik's bags. He jogged around to the passenger door, opened it and bowed from the waist. "Madame?"

My throat tightened. This elongated monster looked unstable, as though it didn't have enough axles to support it. *"Madame?"* The driver gestured toward the open door. Rik tapped his foot and frowned. Chris nudged my elbow. The driver gave up on my dithering and turned to Rik. "Sir?"

Rik made brief eye contact with the guy, then hesitated. "Uh…okay." He slid into the limo.

Chris missed this exchange with the driver. His eyes were on me, his grin now shadowed with worry. Was I or wasn't I going to get in the damn car?

I couldn't refuse him this. I gulped down my anxiety like a dose of castor oil, accepted the driver's outstretched hand and stepped inside.

I paused, hunched over, as though entering a cave. The interior resembled a robber baron's railroad car. Padded black leather everywhere: ceiling, panels, bench seats that lined both sides of the passenger compartment. The inside smelled of saddle soap and what some wag called "conspicuous consumption." Rik parked himself in one of the matching black leather armchairs that faced the driver's section, separated by a wall of smoky glass. Soundproof, no doubt.

Lush burgundy carpet tickled my toes where they stuck out of my Birkenstocks. I started to take a seat on one of the side benches. "No." Rik pointed to the other chair. "Sit there. We can talk."

Chris parked himself on the end of the bench closest to the door, as near as he could get to his hero without landing in his lap. He stowed his skateboard under the seat, met my eyes and jerked two raised thumbs at me. I grinned and he pulled his Blackberry from his backpack.

"What are you doing?"

"Texting my friends," he said and began to work the keys with his thumbs. "They'll like, never fu…, never believe this."

I smiled. If you're a kid from Cleveland on your first visit to California it doesn't get much better than this.

The driver slid behind the wheel and started the engine. Rik frowned at the back of his head and punched a button on his phone. "Marty, me," he said. "Listen, did you vet the driver? Looks dicey." Silence then, "Okay, but I still don't like the looks of him. Get another one." Squawks resounded through the phone. "Okay, okay, I get it. If you're wrong, you're dead."

Rik swore, glaring at the now silent cell. Then he looked at me. "When you're as famous as I am, you can't be too careful."

Like I knew. "Of course."

Chris stared at him, open-mouthed, then once again applied thumbs to Blackberry.

Rik's black-clad chest rose in a sigh. "Stalkers and all kinda weird shit. I don't like the looks of this guy, but my manager says he used to work for Michael."

Jackson? Better not ask and appear the fool.

Rik reached into the padded console between us and extracted a bottle of champagne. He held up the frosted bottle. "Want some?"

"No thanks, I really couldn't." Rik grunted as though he considered me an insufferable prig. "Well, sure," I amended, "why not?"

He poured two glasses. What *would* the nuns at Holy Name think? Nothing good, I suspected. I raised my glass in a silent toast to those good women.

"Cheers," said Rik and we clinked glasses. I took a tentative

sip, then a larger swallow and felt the warm stomach and buzzing head that should have been a warning. I was nervous and
the champagne put an ever so slight barrier between me and the
jitters.

As the driver wheeled onto the 405 North, Rik relaxed into
plush leather. Sounding like Sylvester Stallone, he said, "Wanna
start the interview?"

"Sure." I rummaged in my bag, extracted a yellow tablet and
blue pen and wrote down the date and time for reference. I took
another sip of champagne. More buzzing in my head and stomach. Chris watched us with interest.

"So Rik, were you born in Los Lobos?" I asked.

"Born, bred and raised." Rik gave a barky laugh. "Got the
order wrong, I guess. That should be bred and born."

So he didn't admit to being born in Mexico City.

"No problem." I scribbled away, suddenly realizing my dumb
luck. Amy would not, *could not*, refuse this story. "I knew what you
meant."

Rik took a thoughtful sip then swished the wine around in his
mouth like Listerine. My stomach gave a lurch. I turned away so
I wouldn't have to watch him swallow. "Yup, our land's been in
the Mercado family several hundred years."

"Amazing in this day and age." I peered out the tinted side
window and wondered if the people in the next lane wondered if
there was someone famous inside.

"I know every inch of this road," Rik said, looking out the
other window. "Got started in LA right out of high school, playing in the clubs here. Used to drive up to see the folks at least once
a week." Another laugh. "It was a place to do my laundry and
get a home-cooked meal." He bit back the laugh when I didn't
crack a smile. Could he really be that much of a jerk? Even Chris
looked embarrassed and again fiddled with his Blackberry.

"How do you feel about the plan to sell the land?" I asked.

Rik put up his hand. "Hang loose a sec. I need to unwind
and this champagne's not getting it. I'm a white-knuckle flyer

and that landing was pretty bumpy." He studied the driver's bull neck. "To say nothing of this dufus driver." He turned to Chris. "Right, kid?"

"Right, Rik," Chris parroted.

Rik reached into his bag and pulled out a slim silver case. When he opened it, I realized that the skinny, loosely packed cigarettes inside weren't Marlboros. He took a joint and offered one to Chris. He didn't extend the offer to me. Chris put it behind his ear, carefully avoiding my eyes.

I'm too old for this.

"Chris, you give that back right now."

"Aw, Auntie Bella." Chris gave me the stinkeye, but handed over the joint. Rik sighed and made a big production of rolling his eyes, but returned both joints to the case without another word.

"Rik," I said, needing to fill dead air, "I'd like some information on your career. Do you have a press kit I can use for background?"

"I do, but Marty has the most recent ones. Tell you what, just check out my website, www.rikmercado.com. Internet's a great thing." Deprived of his dope, Rik gulped champagne. "Now where were we?"

To tell the truth I was having trouble with that myself. The champagne made my head feel like it was stuffed with cotton and my stomach was more than a little queasy. What I wouldn't have given for a cup of tea. I pushed the glass to one side and caught Rik's snide grin. Heaving a deep breath, I made an effort to sound sober. "Tell me about your brother and sister, what it was like to grow up in the Mercado family. How long since you've been back?"

"I lost count—seven, eight years."

"You didn't come for your parents' funeral." Not a question.

Rik's eyes widened. "What kinda crack is that? You some kinda nosy Barbara Walters bitch or something?"

The question totally surprised me and it took a moment to

respond. While I struggled to coordinate my mouth and brain, Rik helped himself to more bubbly and held the bottle up to see how much was left. In his own good time, he met my eyes. "Nah, tell you the truth, it did cause some kind of stink with brother Raymond. Connie was great about it, of course. What a little trooper she is—was."

He took a deep breath and shook his head. "Truth is I don't do death," he said in little more than a whisper. "Besides, how could it help them to come to their funeral?"

"I don't know, Rik, but it might have helped you." I paused. "Why now? Why Connie's?"

Rik chewed his lower lip as he set his glass in the holder. Then he rested his elbows on his knees and studied his open palms. "To tell the truth, I don't know. Maybe it's important to make up with my brother. Hell, ain't neither of us getting any younger. And Connie—she was special. Less than two years older than me and Raymond."

I reached across the console and touched his arm. "I understand. You don't have to talk about it now. We can finish the interview later." The inside of the limo began to spin and suddenly there were two Riks. I shook my head, and ran my fingers through my hair.

"Need a pit stop?" Rik asked.

I shook my head again. "No, I'm fine."

Rik looked at his hands (all four of them) as though his whole life were written there. "I was much closer to Connie than Raymond. This is on background of course, but my first girlfriend was one of Connie's friends. Amy was crazy about me, even though she was two years older. Used to hang around all the time. When she wasn't at the house, she and Connie were yakking on the phone. That little gal and I spent many an evening at the bluffs watching the submarine races, let me tell you."

He had to be talking about Amy, my boss.

"What are submarine races?" Chris asked.

Rik laughed. "Nothing you'd understand, kid."

"What was Amy's last name?" I tried to sound casual. Funny she never said anything to me.

"Uh, let's see, they say you never forget your first girl, but I'll be damned if I can remember her last name. Married some guy named Goodman, I heard."

"You're talking about Amy Goodheart. She and Connie are—were—still close friends. She's the managing editor of the *Central Coast Chronicle* where I work, so you needn't worry about the details of your romance showing up in her paper."

"No shit?" Rik poured himself the last of the champagne.

"Yup, she's also the owner, publisher and general all-around handy woman."

"Ain't it a small world." Rik raised his glass in a small toast.

"It is if you live in Los Lobos," I said.

16

Rik's cell chirped, and he settled back into what looked like a long conversation. I rested the back of my head against the seat. If I just closed my scratchy eyes for a second...

The next thing I knew, the limo swayed sharply to the right. My eyes jerked open. Were we rolling over? It swayed again, this time to the left and I saw the sign that read: Los Lobos Road. We'd made the wide arc off 101.

I took a deep breath, trying to get my bearings. I was in big trouble. Why, oh why, did I drink that champagne? I leaned forward and laid my head sideways on my knees to keep from being sick. From this rather ridiculous position I surveyed the scene.

Rik and Chris had both dropped off, Chris slumped sideways, sleeping the sleep of the young. Rik's head was thrown back and his mouth had dropped open. If his fans could see him now.

I wrinkled my nose. A familiar ropy aroma filled the limo. I'd smelled plenty of pot on the streets of Detroit. For the next ten minutes I concentrated on not being sick.

Finally, Rik sneezed, sputtered and snorted his way to consciousness. He peered out the window. "Where are we?"

I sat up straight and ran stiff, aching fingers through my bed-head hair. "Almost to Los Lobos."

"Crap," he said, "I don't have time to go to friggin' Los Lobos tonight." He had a furtive, even frightened, air about him that seemed strange to say the least.

At the sound of Rik's voice Chris's eyes popped open. "Wassup?" he asked in a goofy voice.

"Hey, Chris," I said, "back among the living?"

"Huh?" My irony seemed to be lost on him.

Rik spoke into the mike attached to the console. "Driver, turn around. Drop me at the Tolosa Hilton. I don't wanna go to Los Lobos."

"Sir, we're entering Los Lobos now. Shall I turn around?"

"Crap." Rik dropped the mike.

17

Five minutes later the limo swung into our driveway. I craned my neck, expecting to see Mike's truck. Not there. Maybe he'd decided to pick up the car tonight after all. Maybe I was an idiot for not checking my cell. I'd snapped it off during the interview with Rik. Score another one for the champagne.

Wide awake and wide-eyed, Chris powered down the window and stuck his head outside. It was well after eight and the yard lanterns gave the house and windmill a *Better Homes and Gardens* appearance. In the lemony glow, the bitch-to-clean diamond window panes sparkled and the heavy oak door took on a hand-rubbed sheen. Even the shrubs looked greener.

"Wow! Do you like, live here?" Chris asked, turning to me with a grin.

"Sure do." I gathered my things and suppressed a yawn. A long day and the champagne hadn't helped. Bed would.

Sam ambled around the side of the house. Hearing my voice, he paced back and forth beside the vehicle.

"Be out in a second, Sam," I called.

Chris leaned out the window. "That your dog?"

"Yup."

"This house is way cool," Rik observed, rubbing champagne- and pot-puffed eyes. I blinked several times; my own eyes felt as though I'd spent a month in the Gobi Desert.

"I remember coming here when I was a kid. Used to be a working windmill, true statement?"

"That's right," I said. "Though the mill hasn't operated since the end of World War Two."

Rik nodded, apparently no longer interested in the mill or what I had to say about it. He fidgeted, first with his short pony tail, then the fringed leather vest, finally pulling his attaché case into his lap, opening and closing the zipper.

I gritted my teeth. The man was *so* annoying.

"Do the blades still like, turn, Auntie Bella?" Chris asked.

I gazed at the paddles standing in stark relief against the moonlight. As always the sight of them calmed me. "They're called paddles, Chris, and they're tied down now so they can't turn."

Chris's face fell, making him look more like seven than seventeen. These sudden shifts from teen to grade-schooler and back again in less time than it took to say "awesome" were disconcerting. Possibly I'd get used to them.

"That doesn't mean those paddles aren't trying to turn. They make the whole house creak when it's windy."

"Awesome," said Chris. "Like a real haunted house."

Rik dropped back into the conversation. "From what I remember about the Central Coast, it's windy all the time."

I laughed. "You're right about that." I turned to Chris. "We even have a resident ghost. Her name's Emily Divina and I'll tell you about her later."

"Awesome." Chris grabbed his skateboard and backpack, opened the rear door of the limo and swung long, skinny legs out. His untied shoes crunched on the gravel as he headed for the front steps, which glistened black from the rain. Sam loped after him.

"Chris," I called, "come back here."

He backtracked, a puzzled expression on his face. Sam stayed close to his side. "*Whaaat?*" Chris said, stroking Sam's head.

"Don't you have something to say to Rik?" I hinted like a proper parent.

"Oh sure." Chris climbed back into the limo. Sam followed, bringing with him a slight doggy odor. I expected his usual slobbery welcome. Instead, tail between legs, raised hair on back, he eyeballed Rik.

Strange. Sam usually liked everyone.

"What's with the dog?" Rik asked. His legs were crossed and he swung the toe of his boot in a menacing way. At least Sam thought so. He growled deep in his throat.

"Sam, stop it," I snapped.

My nephew stood there as though he'd forgotten the lines to the script. "Well, Chris?" I prompted.

"Uh, sure." He swiped his right hand on the side of his pants and thrust it at the still-seated Rik. "Thanks for everything, man." He dropped his eyes and his toe worried the carpet. "Maybe we can like, hang together while you're here."

Two frown lines appeared between Rik's eyes. "I don't know, buddy—" Seeing Chris's face drop, he hesitated, then snapped his fingers. "Hey, I've got a great idea. Why don't you come back to the hotel with me tonight? I'll rent a car tomorrow and bring you back."

Chris turned to me, his look a mixture of hope and something that said he knew this wasn't quite kosher.

When pigs fly, Rik.

I gathered my things and stood up. "Sorry, that's not possible. Chris needs to stay here."

"Wait a minute. Don't get your underwear in a bunch, Auntie. I'll get the kid his own room. It's just that—" He stopped suddenly and looked straight ahead.

All of a sudden it hit me; Rik didn't want to be alone with the driver. I gave myself a mental shake. Too bad. No way was I putting my nephew in jeopardy, no matter what Rik's problem. He was a grownup. Sort of. He'd have to figure it out for himself.

"Sorry."

Chris actually looked relieved, but Rik decided to backpedal. "Uh, tell you what. Why don't you and your Aunt Bella come to the funeral on Thursday? I'm leaving on Friday and me and my brother have to find some shit of Connie's first." He stopped like a man who's said too much. "I mean, er, we have business in the next couppla days." He smiled at Chris. "Hey pal, we can hang together at the service and the wake afterward."

There's still something strange, I thought, something that doesn't belong. Why would he want to spend time with a teenager he's just met rather than the brother he hasn't seen in years? Then again, that might be the whole idea.

Chris turned to me, pleading in his eyes. "Can we, Auntie Bella? Please?"

I shook my head. "Chris, I hate to act like the bad guy here, but funerals are private. I don't think—"

"Bull," Rik said. "The whole town will be there. Everyone loved Connie."

Hmm. Stan said the same thing, that everyone loved Connie. Including perhaps my husband?

Out damned thought.

"Please, Auntie Bella?"

I jerked my mind back to the teenager in front of me. "We'll see," I said, the time-honored hedge of all parents.

"See ya Thursday." Rik gave us a dismissive wave, then pulled out his cell. "Hey Marty, on my way to the hotel. Yeah. ETA fifteen minutes. Stay on the line with me, man." The door closed with a rumble and the Hummer snaked its way down the driveway.

I'd kept quiet about the smell of pot inside the limo, but now I got right into Chris's face, hands on hips like an outraged schoolmarm. "Young man, I want it absolutely understood that you are not to use any controlled substance, with Rik or anyone else, while you are our guest. Is that clear?"

"Sure, Auntie Bella," Chris set his backpack on the hall bench and gave me a wide, blue-eyed stare. "What's the beef?"

"The 'beef' is that I smelled pot in the limo. And please remove your hat in the house."

Chris fingered the painter's cap like he'd forgotten it was on his head, shrugged and dropped it on the backpack.

He looked at me and my chest contracted. The Dutch-boy haircut stopped just short of the collar of his Che Guevara T-shirt. He had Bea's cowlick, which stood up on the back of his head like a clump of straw. I smoothed my own cowlick, now gray like the rest of my hair. Bea's would have been gray too, if she'd lived.

"*Whaaat?*" Chris pulled a face.

"Uh, what do you have to say for yourself about the pot?"

"You know what it *smells* like?" Chris's jaw went slack.

"I certainly do. Smelled plenty of it when I was a nun."

"You did? Did they, like, smoke in the nun house?"

I couldn't help smiling. "Hardly, but there was plenty of it on the streets of Detroit."

"Jeez!" Chris shook his head. "I, like, didn't realize nuns were so…" He stopped as though searching for a word "…so with it."

I grabbed Chris by the shoulders and spun him around. "I'm

'with it' because I've had to be, when I was a nun and now. Promise me you won't use any more pot while you're here."

Chris made a small sign of the cross over his heart. "Word."

I tried not to laugh at the street talk coupled with the small-boy gesture. At least he didn't deny that he'd smoked pot with Rik. That told me he was basically an honest person.

"Want me to sign a contract?"

"A what?"

"A contract that we write together and both sign. Janet's always threatening to do that, but she never follows through. All she knows how to do is yell and complain."

Privately I agreed with him, but I wasn't going to be drawn into a discussion of Janet's faults. "The contract sounds like a good idea. We can write it in the morning. Now let's get you settled in your room. I think you'll like it."

That was an understatement. Chris loved Mike's East Wing, especially after Sam loped up the stairs and settled on the end of the daybed with a long "goodnight all" sigh. The Lab had eclectic sleeping habits, with many napping spots inside and out, but he never invaded Mike's space. I shrugged. It's easier to ask forgiveness than permission.

Where was that man anyway? I looked at my watch hands now slipping past 8:30. There'd been no messages on my cell.

Chris unzipped his pack and dumped his few things onto the daybed: dingy socks, ditto three wadded up T-shirts. Also a single pair of board shorts, some chewing gum and a can of Red Bull.

I grabbed a T-shirt and started to drape it over a hanger, then stopped. Why bother? The shirt was grayish-yellow with holes in the front. I fingered the holes, probably the result of too much bleach. "So how come you didn't bring more clothes?"

A grin chased itself around Chris's mouth. "Janet said you'd take me shopping."

I'll bet she did. "Glad to, but who pays?"

The grin found its home. "She says you do."

"Hmph. Figures. What did your dad have to say?"

Chris bunched up his shoulders and turned away, suddenly busy with a thread on the daybed cover. "He never sez anything. He's so whipped."

"Chris, watch it. I'll gladly buy you some clothes. We can get some for school while we're at it."

"Awesome."

I reached for the T-shirt and hanger again. "We'll hit Penneys tomorrow morning when they open."

Chris's eyes narrowed. "You've got to be shi—, kidding."

"The mouth, Chris, the mouth."

He backed away, palms up. "Okay, okay. I get it. But you were like, kidding about Penneys, right?"

"Dead serious. This is the sticks. We don't have Urban Outfitters and stores like that here."

Chris looked around as if he'd been dropped into Indian country. "You *do* have a computer?"

"Sure."

"Maybe we can order online."

"That's okay by me. Now put this stuff away and you can help me start supper."

In less than ten seconds his things were wadded into the top drawer of the filing cabinet Mike had emptied. He stuffed the gum in his pocket, popped open the Red Bull and took an enthusiastic swig.

"You'd better not drink that or you won't sleep tonight," I said.

He wiped his mouth on the back of his hand and stared, first at me and then at the can. "You know about this stuff?"

"You bet. Drink it all the time."

"Auntie Bella!"

"Just kidding. Come on down and earn your keep. I have a feeling you're going to be expensive."

Fifteen minutes later the mingled aromas of eggs scrambled with sharp cheddar, and butter-browned Yukon Gold potatoes, onions and fresh rosemary filled the kitchen. I was just cramming thick sliced Tolosa Sourdough into the toaster when I heard the unmistakable sound of tires on gravel. Thank goodness.

As Mike stomped through the back door, I said, "Hey you, it's about time. Did you go to LA?"

He shook his head. "I wish. No, worked late. Got behind with the pumping because of the rain. Jesus H. Christ, what a downpour." His eyes found Chris's and he stuck out his hand. "This must be the famous Christopher Jensen. Last time we met, you were still in diapers I believe."

Nice opening, Mike. Chris was nine.

"Hi, Uncle Mike." Chris gripped Mike's hand in a manly way, but shot me a glance that said, "Is this guy for real?"

He'd finished the Red Bull, so I asked, "Chris, would you like a cup of chamomile tea with dinner? It'll help you sleep."

Chris looked at me like I'd offered him an illegal substance. "Milk's fine."

"In the fridge. Glasses in the first cupboard."

I carried two loaded plates to the table. "Mike, there's plenty of food," I called over my shoulder. "Help yourself."

"I'm so hungry I could eat a grizzly," Mike said, earning another "for real?" look from Chris. Mike retreated to the small bathroom off the kitchen where he always showered and changed into his house attire: white T-shirt, baggy pajama bottoms and geezer slippers.

After the three of us were seated elbow-to-elbow around the small table, Mike reached out and clamped his hand on Chris's forearm. "Glad you're here, buddy. I can use help with the pumping this summer."

Buddy? When did that happen?

Chris scooped up a forkful of eggs. "What're we pumping, Uncle Mike?"

Mike and I exchanged looks. "Sewage, my son. Sewage."

"Oh gross!" The fork clattered onto the plate.

18

Chris faded early despite the Red Bull. He'd overcome his repugnance at the idea of pumping sewage long enough to polish off a soup bowl of rocky road ice cream. Truthfully, he'd pretty well yawned his way through it. And no wonder. The clock on the wall edged toward eleven, two A.M. Cleveland time. Even by teen standards, it had been a long day.

Mike had called him "buddy" and later, "son." I took that as a good sign.

I was beyond tired, sliding toward numb. After Chris said his goodnights, Mike and I lingered over a pot of peach tea. My fingers found his across the small table. We sat silent and dreamy for a few minutes, inhaling the fruity, fermented perfume of the tea. "Going to be different with a teenager in the house."

Mike nodded. "Hmm. Seems like a good kid."

My turn to nod. More conjugal silence.

Finally, "Bella?"

Something about the way he said that made me flinch. "What?"

Please don't wreck the mood. Please don't.

"You've been distant for almost a week now. Something I did? If so, please say." He took a tentative sip and gave me a lopsided grin. "I'm not good at handling the silent treatment."

Here it was. This was the opening I'd been waiting for. So why did I want to run into the bedroom and fling blankets over my head? "Well," I gulped, "for starters, Detective Scully from the sheriff's office came by last Thursday morning after the fire at Mercado Construction."

Mike dropped his head to take another sip, but not before I'd seen the flash of irritation in those steely eyes. And something new. Fear.

"Bella, that was what, five days ago? Why didn't you tell me sooner?"

"I don't know, I didn't want to worry you I guess." I pulled a loose thread on the side of the place mat. "I was hoping it would all go away."

Mike put down the mug. "I don't understand you sometimes."

Make that all the time, I wanted to shout. That would start a fight and I needed answers, not arguments. The thread I pulled had loosened another one and I pulled it too.

"So—did he ask where I, where *we*—were that night?" I noted his careful insertion of the word "we."

"No, thank goodness." I pulled another thread and worried the three into a knot with my index finger. "I'm glad I didn't have to tell him that you were gone."

"Do you honestly think—" He grabbed my arm.

I pulled back. "I don't know what to think. And you're hurting me."

"Sorry." His hand retreated to his Chicago PD mug and he took a sip of tea, watching me over the rim. "Well?"

"No, Mike, I don't think you had anything to do with the fire, mostly because it's so silly. But that's not all. Detective Scully inferred that you left the Chicago force under a cloud."

The mug froze halfway to his lips.

"Is it true?"

Mike's "Bastard!" and the slam of the cup told me all I needed to know.

I struggled for control. "I…I think you owe it to me to tell me what happened."

Mike placed his palms flat on the table. "You're right, of course. There's not much to tell, really. A suspect died of asphyxiation after we pepper-sprayed him. The family said we'd overused the damn stuff, and we didn't call for backup fast enough. Hell, I called as soon as I could, but we didn't know the guy had asthma. He wore one of those bracelets, but we didn't see it. You know how it is when a suspect is out of control and high on crack besides."

"No, I don't. Tell me."

"A cluster fuck." He rubbed the back of his neck. One part of me wanted to rub the tense spot, the rest just sat there watching my life disappear. Mike grimaced. "Christ, the guy was all over the place. Kicking, screaming, your typical crackhead. Like wrestling an octopus."

"So what happened?" Even gripping the teacup with both hands couldn't keep my teeth from clattering against it.

"Well, it was an election year and there had been, as there always are, allegations of police brutality, and the incumbents wanted a couple of trophy cops to hold up as bad examples for their constituency. My partner Gus and I turned out to be the patsies."

"What happened to your partner?" I didn't really care, but I asked the question to gain think time.

"Got busted back to beat cop. He was younger than me. Heard he left and went to law school." He grimaced. "Figures. I lost touch with him after I came to Detroit."

"And what about you?"

"The powers-that-be suggested it would be a good time for me to retire and I did." His voice had a bitter edge and his eyes were like razor blades. "I left Chicago never wanting to see the damned place again."

The hurt was so palpable I could taste it. Boiling anger and sadness started deep in my gut and rolled up the back of my throat like bile. I tried to swallow it down and couldn't. My eyes felt hot. "What…what about me? Why didn't you tell me from the get-go?"

Mike reached for my hand. I yanked it away and started on another loose thread. "Bella, you're going to wreck that place mat."

"I know, but I can't stop." Tears spilled down my cheeks and I swiped at them with both hands.

Mike's arm inched across the table, palm up. He wiggled his fingers.

"Oh hell." I folded my hand into his.

He put the tips of my fingers to his lips and kissed them one at a time. Two tears leaked from his closed eyes. He opened them and stared at me, looking like the Mike with whom I'd fallen in love.

"You ask why I didn't tell you? Fear and common sense."

"How so?"

"You were the best thing, hell the only good thing, that happened to me since…since before Grace died and Ethan disappeared into that murky lake. I just couldn't risk losing you. All these years I was afraid that somehow you'd find out accidentally, and now it's happened."

I looked at Mike, knew he was hurting. I wanted with all my heart to offer him some reassurance that it was okay, that I understood. But my own hurt was too new, too raw. "How do you suppose the sheriff found out?" I mumbled.

Mike sighed and rubbed the back of his neck again. "The cop good ol' boy network is alive and well, so I suppose he made a couple of phone calls."

"But why check up on you?"

"I have no idea."

"Do you have any enemies in Chicago who might make trouble?"

He snorted. "Someone who's been a cop for thirty years has plenty of enemies, but I don't know of any specifically. Someone from the sheriff's office might have found something on the Internet. God knows it was all over the papers at the time. Guess we could Google my name and Chicago and see what comes up."

"Not now," I said. "I really don't care how he found out. But why did he need to tell *me* you left under a cloud. And why now?"

Mike stared out the kitchen window at the garden, now shadowed in moonlight. "I think he suspects that I—or we—have something to do with Connie's murder. Possibly this is his way of driving a wedge between us."

Hmm. A wedge, that was it. Divide and conquer. Why hadn't I seen it before? "But that's stupid. Killing Connie, especially in such a brutal way, to delay the sewer is so ridiculous it's laughable. So is thinking you had something to do with the fire."

"I know that, and you know that, but does he?"

"Point taken." I paused. Suddenly I was back on the bluffs, ready to step over the edge, not able to stop myself. "Mike?"

"Hmm?"

"Was there something between you and Connie?"

"*What?*" He huffed the word as though I'd said the most stupid thing imaginable. "Don't you know me better than that?"

I stared at him, not able to believe that he could ask such a question. Wasn't it *obvious* that I didn't know him better than that? I felt the flush on my cheeks as I went in for the kill. "After what you've just told me, I'm not sure I ever knew you at all." I gulped a deep breath. "Stan said he used to see the two of you together."

A long silence while Mike brushed his fingers over his crew cut, once, twice, three times. Again he rubbed the back of his neck. "Christ, Connie always seemed so vulnerable that I guess she aroused my protective instincts." He gave a "he-he" laugh. "You know how us guys are."

"No, I don't." My fingers inched toward the place mat, but I pulled them back. "Why don't you tell me."

"Bella, come off it. When a woman's in trouble, most guys feel like they need to help. There's nothing sexual about it. It's probably just a throwback to Victorian times or something. Christ, I don't know. You're sure helping me dig a deep hole here."

"No Mike, you're digging that hole all by yourself. How did you help Connie?"

"Well, I guess I let her use me as a sounding board for her problems."

"Such as?"

"She and Raymond didn't see eye to eye on anything. Sometimes I gave her advice after they had a beef. You know, the man's point of view. And—"

"And what?"

"She asked me for advice about permanent residency status in Canada. You know she planned to move there after the land was sold?"

"Stan said that." I concentrated hard, trying to absorb what he'd told me. My husband as confidant of another woman. Like Chicago, another part of his life hidden from me.

"And God, it seemed like I was always tweaking that damn Subaru for her. At least you take care of yours."

"Thanks," I said, the word sharp and bitter and hurt.

Mike got up and began to clear the tea things. "Look, I've had it. Ready to turn in?"

"And if I'm not?"

"Then I guess you'll stay up and read or something," he said to the window as he put the cups in the sink.

I rested my head on the place mat. "Look, Mike, I—"

"Not tonight, Bella. It's been a long day." I heard the scuff, scuff of house slippers on the kitchen floor, smelled the distinctive smell of him, Irish Spring and something like apples. He stopped before me and leaned over "Kiss?"

"Sure." I raised my head and brushed his lips knowing that I still wasn't ready to ask the one question that would make everything all right. Or not. The only thing that really mattered.

Was he the father of Connie's baby?

19

Tuesday morning:

I slept the sleep of the truly exhausted and awoke, if not refreshed, at least able to face the day. Lying there, not yet ready to open my eyes, I became aware that something was different. My arm found its way to Mike's side of the bed. Empty.

I shot up and focused on the block-shaped numbers of the bedside clock. 7:30. Mike always left for work by seven. I must have slept through the alarm. Sometime in the night I had become aware of his body against mine and felt his need. My body responded and our lovemaking was both grappling and urgent. We must have sounded like a couple of fifty-year-old elephants in heat. What would Chris think? He must have heard. The East Wing was directly overhead.

I threw on my robe and headed for the kitchen. I expected to find Chris at the table wolfing Cheerios. I was greeted by three empty chairs. He wasn't due to start work until tomorrow, but maybe he went off with Mike anyway.

Maybe he didn't. I did a mental forehead smack. The kid was seventeen. Dynamite was probably the only way to get him out of bed. I'd let Mike deal with that tomorrow.

A yellow Post-it winked at me from one corner of the kitchen window. In his neat script Mike asked me to please get Chris a couple pairs of heavy jeans and some work boots.

Okay, you could lead the clothes horse to water, I thought, but could you make him—?

Lousy metaphor, Bella.

While I filled the teakettle, I surveyed my kitchen garden. Baby vegetable sprouts, their leaves still wet from yesterday's rain, soaked up the morning sun. Their world was as it should be. Ours, unfortunately, was not.

Mike and I were both scared to death, and for good reason. Considered possible murder suspects, the loss of our business if the sewer deal went through, losing our home due to costs and fines if it didn't, our marriage slipping away on a sea of anger and mistrust. Why weren't things like they were a month ago, before this sewer mess started, before Connie died?

"Auntie Bella?"

Pulling my robe together I whirled around. "Chris. You scared me."

"Sorry."

"That's okay, you didn't mean to. What would you like for breakfast? Do you drink coffee?"

"Do you have Red Bull?"

When he saw the expression on my face, his palms shot up. "Just kidding." A killer smile. "I cook awesome pancakes if you have cornmeal. Want some?"

"I do and you bet." I set the filled kettle on the stove. "Bacon with those?"

"Auntie Bella, I'm vegetarian, remember?"

"That's right." At supper last night, while Mike scowled, Chris announced that besides veggies and fruits, he also ate eggs and dairy products, and once in a while fish, fresh caught of course. Oh, and organic chicken. Sometimes. No pork. Except for barbecued ribs on major holidays. Whatever.

"Great. You fix the pancakes while I grab a quick shower." I pointed him toward the pots and pans, instructed him to keep the kettle on low boil and beat a quick retreat.

As we devoured thick, golden pancakes with lightly browned edges covered in warm currant jam, he asked about Connie. Because there wasn't any reason not to, I told her about her murder and my own experience that day.

"Wow." He swallowed a mouthful of pancake and washed it down with orange juice. "Were you like, scared?"

"Terrified." I pushed my plate away. Just talking about it gave me stomach flutters.

"Do they like, know who killed her?"

"Nope, but she was pregnant." The information just kind of tumbled out. I eyed the block of knives on the counter, wanting to cut out my tongue.

"So? There's a couple pregnant girls in school."

"In Catholic school?" I asked.

"I go to public. Janet says we can't afford tuition for Catholic." He rolled his eyes.

My "why am I not surprised?" brought forth a conspiratorial grin that I didn't discourage.

"Yeah, we had a bunch of preggers last year. Big bellies all over the place."

"Really," I said, the word not a comment, but not a question either. Judgemental as hell. "What do people say?"

His stare made me feel like a Stone Age specimen. "No one like, says anything. Why would they?"

I shrugged. Different generation. Who was I to judge? "The only reason it's important is that pregnancy might be a motive for her murder."

Chris pushed a forkful of pancake into a mound of jam. "You mean like, if the guy was married and didn't want the wife to find out. Or if the wife smoked her."

"Exactly." My heart fluttered. If Mike and Connie had an affair, and if Detective Scully knew, he might suspect me of killing her. Actually that gave me a double motive; the first—to delay the sewer—was ridiculous, the second not so much so.

I thought of Mike and how we were last night. All we had could slip away. I heard Chris's voice but he might have been speaking in tongues for all I understood. A numbness flowed over my body like ice water.

"Auntie Bella, are you okay?" Chris rose from his chair.

I gripped the table. "Uh, I'm fine." Tried out a smile. "Guess the pancakes were a little too sweet first thing in the morning."

"You think so? Want some water or something?" He gave me a funny look. "You're not pregnant, are you?"

I shook my head to clear it, suppressed a grin. "No, most definitely not. Ahem. Now, what were you saying?"

"That Rik doesn't seem too broke up about his sister being offed."

I took a bracing sip of tea, swallowed hard. "Difficult to tell. People show their emotions in different ways. I don't think he'd come home for the funeral if he didn't care."

"I s'pose." He polished off the last of the pancakes, rose and picked up the plates. "You said you had a computer?"

"Sure. What for?"

He gave me a "well duh?" look. "So we can write the contract."

"Chris," I toyed with my favorite place mat, "we don't really need a contract, do we?"

Another killer smile and a head shake. "Uh, uh."

"Good." A smile of my own.

"But could we like, order clothes online? Then check my e-mail? If that's okay."

"That's fine, Chris."

An hour later we were still looking for things Chris deemed suitable and I could afford. Most of the stuff he liked I wouldn't wear to wash my car, and the prices were, well, insane. For the first time, I felt some small sympathy for Janet, "small" being the operative word.

"Stop!" I pushed back from the computer. "This is hopeless and I have to be to work by one. Let's just go to Sears and get your work clothes. Maybe you'll see something you like in—"

I stopped. How would we get to Tolosa? The Subaru was in LA. Bet Mike forgot that when he left me the note. I picked up the desk phone.

"Who're you calling?" Chris asked.

"Mike. He needs to take us to town so I can rent a car." Funny, we'd talked about that last night, but then both put it out of our minds. Which said something about the state of our minds. While I waited for Mike to pick up, I prayed that he wasn't on his way to LA and he would come home soon.

* * *

He wasn't, and he did. By eleven a spiffy red Neon sat in Sears parking lot and Chris and I stood on one foot and then the other in their checkout line. Chris handed the jeans and boots to the clerk as though they were hazardous waste. He leaned toward me. "Still don't see why I need these."

I fished out my credit card. "Trust me, tomorrow this time you will."

"Bella?"

I turned. "Stan? What are you doing here?" The man did turn up at the most unexpected times.

With a grimace, he held up a somber tie. "For the funeral tomorrow. Lana would have a cow if she knew I bought a cheapie, but I'll never wear it again." Small pause. "At least I hope not."

I grinned. "Our secret." The clerk waggled outstretched fingers at me and I handed her my card. While she processed it, I introduced Stan to Chris.

"Stan," I said, "you work at the college. Do you know where the kids buy their clothes?"

Chris and I moved aside and Stan handed the tie and a twenty to the clerk. "Actually, a lot of them bought second-hand stuff at Connie's shop."

"You're kidding," I said. "They drove all that way?"

"It's only twelve miles." He grabbed the bag, pocketed the change, and nodded thanks to the clerk. "Connie had a real eye for what kids like. She took a lot of stuff on consignment." He paused to hold the door for us. "Say, I'm headed that way. After I talked to Raymond and Rik this morning we decided to clear out the stock while Rik's here."

I nodded. Rik must have gotten to the hotel okay last night.

Stan paused as though he'd just had a light bulb thought. "Say, why don't you come and have a look at what's there?"

"Can we, Auntie Bella?" For the first time in an hour Chris looked as though life didn't totally suck. His term, not mine.

Stan smiled at Chris. "I'll make you such a deal, son."

"Isn't the shop off-limits right now?" I asked.

"Nope, the sheriff's office did a cursory look-see, but that was it."

"Please, Auntie Bella?"

"Okay, sure, why not?"

"Awesome."

20

By noon Chris had several armfuls of clothes that he actually liked and they hadn't cost a dime. While he stuffed the plastic bags in the Neon, I chatted with Stan in the parking lot. Being in a murdered woman's shop had felt strange and now I turned my face to the sun, happy to be outside.

A generic Ford sedan passed the shop, then suddenly made a U-turn and shot into the parking lot. The driver pulled up next to us and stopped with a spray of small rocks that burned my shins. Rik jumped out. He was in our faces almost before I figured out who it was. "Stan, what the hell you doing?" He pointed at me and Chris, who stood frozen, white plastic bag in hand, mouth open. "Did you let them inside?"

Stan put up his hand. "Rik, get a grip. I let the kid pick out some clothes. There's so much stuff in there he's doing us a favor."

Rik wasn't about to be mollified. "I thought we agreed that nothing went out the door until we'd gone through everything. Raymond will have a shit fit."

Chris stepped forward, head down, and thrust the plastic bag in Rik's direction. "Here. I'll get the rest out of the car."

"Forget it." Rik swiped his hand at the bag, hopped back into the sedan and slammed the door. The Ford wheeled out of the lot and I noticed the Mercado Motors license holder. The family owned the dealership. Why hadn't he helped himself to a flashier model?

Understandable if he wanted to remain incognito, but my gut told me it was something more sinister. A reporter at the airport had asked him about bankruptcy, apparently common knowledge in the entertainment world. Was he being targeted by someone he owed money to? A deranged fan?

I motioned for Chris to stow the bag in the Neon and leaned toward Stan. "What was that all about?"

Stan shrugged. "Beats me. My nephew, the space case. He hasn't changed at all." He turned the key in the lock and poked it under a flower pot by the back door.

"Aren't you afraid someone will find that and clean you out?"

Stan grinned. "As I said, all the crap in there, they'd be doing us a favor."

* * *

I stood in the doorway of the West Wing and hiked my purse onto one shoulder. "Chris, there's salad stuff in the fridge for lunch. I'll be back by six."

Chris sat at my desk, staring into the computer screen as though it held the secret of all life. Littered with gum wrappers, wadded Kleenex and his omnipresent Blackberry, my desk looked like it had been invaded by aliens.

"Awesome. Want me to start dinner?" he asked, his eyes still on the screen.

"Sure. I think we'll barbecue hamburgers." The "h" word got his attention and he looked up to protest. "Don't worry. You can defrost enough veggie burgers for all of us." Mike would have a cow, I thought, and smiled at the accidental pun. "You can also fix a tray of lettuce, tomatoes, onions, pickles, the whole McDonalds thing."

"Awesome," he repeated and again tapped keys. "I'm writing an e-mail to Janet and Dad. Should I tell them where we got the threads?"

"Better not." I grinned. "That might earn you a trip home quicker than you want to go."

Whoosh! The sheaf of papers on my desk took flight. Chris had opened the slider without drawing aside the curtains. Propelled by afternoon breeze, the billowing sheers blew into the room like uninvited guests.

Tap, tap, tap. Intent on his task, Chris didn't seem to notice.

Choking back my irritation, I snatched up the papers and moved to shut the slider. "Leave it," he said. Small pause. "Please. I need air."

"Okay," I said, snapping open the sheers. "But put something heavy on the loose papers. And in the future, open the curtains before the door. When you shut the door, you have to lift it slightly or it won't slide. Here, like this." I demonstrated for him.

He watched with almost no interest, then plunked a mug filled with pens onto the papers. "Okay, I get it. Sorry." I studied him. Can I do this? I wondered. Share my living space with someone so young, whose sensibilities are so different? He probably wasn't any more unconscious than Bea and I were at that age, but still… What was I going to do with him all day? He needed a friend his own age, but where to find such a creature?

Without warning, Chris spun the chair around and pointed at Emily Divina's portrait on the opposite wall. "Sorry about the curtains, but I couldn't like, breathe. That lady creeps me out. Her eyes keep following me."

I studied Emily's familiar countenance, the dark hair parted in the middle and swept back over her ears, a scrimshaw brooch at the neck of her pleated shirtwaist, the thin, straight-arrow mouth. All of this was overshadowed by her dark eyes, which reflected sadness and a latent passion destined to end in tragedy. Like Connie's graduation picture. I shivered.

"Emily's our resident ghost, the one I told you about last night," I said.

Chris gazed at Emily, wary but excited, too. "Does she like, knock on walls and moan and stuff? I heard some crazy sounds last night."

Mike and me. The windows were open, after all. My lips twitched trying to suppress a smile. "Must have been your imagination. Emily doesn't make noises, at least none that I've heard. But you're right, her eyes follow people. I'm used to it, but I can see why you were creep—I mean, unsettled."

He peered at the portrait. "How come she's so sad?"

"Emily killed herself by jumping from the widow's walk." I pointed past the billowing curtains to the balcony outside.

"Widow's walk?" A faint vertical line appeared between almost-white eyebrows.

"The balcony around the windmill. Mike calls it a catwalk because it was used to repair the paddles, but I like widow's walk better. That's where women watched for sails on the horizon, the first sign that their men were coming home from the sea. And since many of them didn't—"

"I get it. Is that why she offed herself, because her husband didn't come back?"

"Not exactly. She jumped after her lover drowned in a shipwreck. In a snit, her husband, the miller, turned her portrait to the wall."

Chris shook his head. "Why didn't he just throw it out or something?"

"I have no idea. The first thing I did after we moved in was turn it around so Emily could face the world."

"Awesome." He bobbed back and forth, testing Emily's powers. I sighed. Emily wasn't the only one being tested.

"Have anything planned for the afternoon?" I asked.

"The beach." He turned back to the computer and unwrapped another stick of gum. The bulge in his jaw indicated several already. "Do you like, have a Boogie Board?"

"Sorry no, but Mike's old long board is in the barn." Cripes, why did I tell him that? "Look, I don't want you going in the ocean by yourself. You need to find a buddy."

"I'll never meet anyone hanging around here all day, will I?" He rolled the gum stick into a wad, stuffed it in his mouth and chewed hard. "I'll be careful," he said, the words garbled. A small gesture on his T-shirt. "Cross my heart, hope to die."

My own heart turned over. "No, I forbid it. This area is famous for riptides." It hit me then, what a grave responsibility we'd assumed. If anything happened to my nephew, Bea's son, on our watch...

"And don't say that ever again."

"Say what?" He gave me an oh-so-innocent, blue-eyed stare.

"Hope to die."

21

Thursday morning:

The day of the funeral, Our Lady of Capricious Weather again unleashed their fury on the Central Coast. Chris and I stood with other mourners around the closed coffin, preparing for the trek up the hill to Saint Patrick's Cemetery. Looking around, I felt like I'd been dropped into one of those Agatha Christie novels where everyone stands around with long faces and dripping umbrellas.

It seemed strange to attend the funeral of a woman I hardly knew, especially since she might have a history with my husband. But Rik had invited Chris, and I have to admit, I had a morbid curiosity bordering on obsession about today's event.

My nephew and I shared an umbrella handed to me by the funeral director as we left the church. I guess they needed to be prepared for anything: Kleenex for tears, smelling salts for fainters, umbrellas for the vagaries of weather. The last were rarely needed at his time of year. June weather was almost invariably cool and cloudy, with no rain.

Except for this year.

An hour ago we'd entered the packed church with sunshine warming our backs and shoulders. The storm blew in off the ocean as Father Rodriguez began the Mass of Christian Burial. Outside, wind raged, and when the bishop of Tolosa County began his eulogy, thunder rumbled through the old brick church. He frowned, and looked up as though daring God to interrupt his carefully chosen words. I guess God was unimpressed because he sent another clap of thunder. And that wasn't all; the lights dimmed briefly during Holy Communion. Very biblical, or very Agatha Christie, depending upon your point of view.

The weather's temper tantrum did nothing to lessen my own sense of foreboding. Mike had called from a job site to say he'd be late, but would join us at Mass. So here we were, Mass over, burial service about to begin, and still no Mike. Maybe he couldn't face this. That made me feel even worse.

We stood beside a group of pygmy oaks at the end of the church yard. I sneaked one more peek over my shoulder, still hopeful that Mike would appear.

No such luck, but a shiver shot through my body when I spied the red-haired woman from the CRUD meeting and the restaurant parking lot. She and Lana, Stan's wife, carried on an intense conversation by one of the two snarling lions that flanked the church steps.

Now that was interesting.

Just as interesting and certainly more ominous, Detective Scully stood with his back to the church door, surveying the crowd. Three men in dark suits, sunglasses and law enforcement haircuts fanned out around him. Scully would surely notice Mike's absence. Were the dark suits detectives I didn't recognize, or where they Feds? Had they been called in because of the fire? I made a mental note to ask Mike if the FBI was called in for major fires where arson was suspected.

I felt the wave of restless energy that ripples through a group before it begins to move. Even though the church was packed, only about twenty mourners had elected to make the trek up the hill. The rest had probably gone straight to the wake. Possibly Mike did too.

Clang! Clang! Clang!

The metallic sound of the church bell plunged a knife into the heart of the morning silence. A flock of mourning doves exploded from the belfry. Their wings made a sinister whoosh as they swooped over our heads. Instinctively I ducked. I hate birds, thanks to Alfred Hitchcock.

The doves veered right and flew toward town. Father Rodriguez held up a large wooden cross and began the long climb. I wondered why the bishop wasn't conducting the burial ceremony. Pressing business, most likely. I'd seen him sneak a peek at his cell during the recessional. Pallbearers hefted the casket and fell in behind Father.

Chris tugged at my sleeve. "Can I wait in the car?" Dressed in an old sports coat of Mike's that I had to practically bungee him into, he looked as miserable as any teenager in similar circumstances.

"No, you may not wait in the car," I said, trying out parental-style manipulation. "I need you." I felt numb, unable to conjure up any emotion except a deep desire to put this day behind me.

"Where's Uncle Mike?" he stage-whispered as we dug our shoes into the damp sand of the path. Thank goodness I'd rejected Amy's insistence that I needed heels.

"I have no idea." I tried to ignore the burning in my calves as we left the oaks behind and snaked up the narrow path that wound through undulating beach grasses. Their stalks, dripping with rain, soaked the bottom of my skirt. The soggy denim made a slap, slap, slap sound against my legs. I shivered.

"This place stinks!" Chris held two fingers to his nose to block out the putrid odor of wet vegetation.

"Shh."

Finally, we reached the crest of the hill. Chris breathed hard beside me, and I remembered what Janet said about him smoking on the sly. I moved closer to see if I could smell it on him, then pulled back.

Now was not the time.

I gazed around. The cemetery looked very old, very rustic, the few grave sites poorly tended. No flowers, no plastic windmills, no teddy bears. Simple headstones, many weather-beaten and chipped, surrounded by short grasses bleached to old ivory. A few sheep stood in a nearby windbreak of dark green eucalyptus trees. Perhaps the sheep were in charge of graveside maintenance. The thought made me smile. Almost.

Connie's body and that of her fetus would spend eternity next to her parents on this windswept hill. From this lonely piece of land, their earthly remains would get to know the sea in all her colors and moods. I looked out over the ocean. The rain had transformed it into sea of quicksilver.

Tears stung my eyes. I felt glad for them and did not try to brush them away. At least I could feel *something*.

We gathered around Connie's coffin at the burial site. The rain had slowed to an irritating drip. I moved the umbrella to shield Chris at my elbow. "How long will this take?"

"Shh," I said, "it's starting."

"May the Angels lead you into Paradise; may the martyrs receive you at your coming." Father Rodriguez spoke in barely a whisper. He sprinkled holy water on the coffin and showered some into the open grave. I couldn't bear to look into the hole; Chris, on the other hand, couldn't seem to stop.

Sweet Jesus, this was a mistake. He was thinking of his mother. Why did I subject him to this? Why hadn't I sent him straight to the wake? Why didn't I go myself? We'd have to leave before they lowered the body. I couldn't watch that either.

"I am the Resurrection and the Life." The priest shook incense over the casket and then in our general direction. The smoky aroma, made more acrid by the damp air, transported me back in time and distance to the convent. There, attendance at daily Mass was compulsory. No excuses, no sniveling, no matter how big a storm from Canada or how severe the monthly cramps.

Once I left that sheltered environment and moved to a two-bedroom, inner-city apartment with three other nuns, I'd seldom attended Mass, except on Sunday. There seemed to be little relationship between what happened on the altar and the violence on the streets, especially after Bea's death. If Mother Teresa could have doubts, so could I.

"Our Father, who art in heaven,..."

The beginning of the Lord's Prayer startled me back to the present. The priest gave us a wan smile and motioned for people to join in.

I'd never met Father and had never been to Mass at Saint

Patrick's. In fact, today marked the first time I'd been to church in months. Mike and I, when we chose to go at all, drove to the mission church in Tolosa. The larger congregation seemed more impersonal, and for us, that was a good thing. We could lose ourselves among them. What was left of my Catholicism craved anonymity. I didn't want nosy parishioners keeping track of how many times I sat in the pew while others received communion.

"From the gate of hell," the priest began. His olive skin had a pale cast that made me wonder about his health.

"Deliver her soul, Oh Lord." The mourners mouthed the responses from hymnals we'd been given. Some barely opened their mouths, some just stood there. Besides Stan, Raymond and Rik, I recognized only CRUD member Charles Cantor, Brenda Livingston, spokesperson for the wastewater project and Connie's lifelong friend, and Amy, of course.

"May she rest in peace."

"Amen."

I studied these people, trying to see into their hearts. Did one of them hate Connie enough to kill her?

"Oh Lord, hear my prayer."

"And let my cry come unto you."

Under their shared umbrella, Brenda and Amy clung to each other, struggling to answer the prayers without collapsing. Surely neither of them was a murderer.

"The Lord be with you."

"And with your spirit."

Charles Cantor stood next to Brenda and Amy, his smooth round face pale under a black fedora. Rain collected on the brim and periodically he swiped at it. The damp air fogged his glasses, making it impossible to see his eyes. Brenda was here as a friend; Charles must be attending as CRUD's official representative.

"Eternal rest grant unto her, O Lord!"

"And let perpetual light shine upon her."

Stan and Raymond stood closest to the coffin, each keeping a safe distance from the other. How sad that uncle and nephew couldn't find it in their hearts to be close, since they'd suffered so much tragedy. Misfortune doesn't always unite people.

Mother and I certainly drew apart after Bea died. She blamed me, and in a way, I felt responsible. Bea was gunned down on the sidewalk in front of my apartment, the accidental victim of a gang shooting. After I saw how little the Detroit PD did to find the killer or killers, I'd taken matters into my own hands. I questioned street people and walked house-to-house interviewing neighbors. Wrote endless letters to the *Detroit Free Press*. If anyone saw or knew anything, they weren't talking. Finally I had to acknowledge that I'd bumped up against a dead end, to mix a metaphor.

"May she rest in peace."

"Amen."

Snapped back to the present by the drone of prayers, I realized that Stan's wife Lana had opted out of the burial service. Maybe she wasn't up to faking grief she didn't feel.

Oh come on, Bella, cut the woman some slack. Stan had made a point of saying Lana and Connie were close. Most likely she'd just gone ahead to help set up food for the wake. On the other hand, she didn't look like the catering type.

Stan, wearing his Sears necktie, stood with his shoulders hunched, seeming to shrink into his ill-fitting suit. In my wildest dreams I couldn't imagine this gentle soul as a killer. But people were rarely what they seemed.

Raymond seemed more than capable of such an act. He stood worrying a piece of turf with the toe of one ostrich skin boot. He looked up and his heavy-lidded eyes telegraphed a mixture of anger and impatience. He and Connie didn't get along, but that didn't mean he murdered her. They both wanted to sell the ranch and now the sale would be delayed. There was something unsettling about Raymond—an undercurrent of suppressed violence I couldn't define.

Rik stood well apart from Raymond and Stan. He didn't belong; he knew it and so apparently did they. But like Stan, he loved Connie and had no obvious reason to want her dead.

I felt another tug on my sleeve. "They almost done?"

"May the souls of all the faithful departed, through the mercy of God, rest in peace."

"Amen."

"Soon," I whispered. Something drew my eye to the windbreak of eucalyptus just to the north. The sheep were gone, but Mike stood there watching, hands clasped behind his back. My heart began a wild dance. What on earth was he doing? Why couldn't he just walk over and be with me, with us? Was he afraid I would pick up on something—a tightening of the lines that bracketed his mouth perhaps, or the throbbing temple vein that even his inscrutable cop face couldn't hide?

I simply did not know what to think about Mike. The very core of my being wanted to believe this man I'd loved and trusted for eight years couldn't be a killer. But he'd kept a serious secret from me, one I deserved to be told, for all the time I'd known him. And more recently, he'd begun a relationship with Connie that was at least cordial, and perhaps intimate. If he wasn't the father of Connie's baby, he knew who was.

Some things you just understand instinctively. I knew that in the quiet and deep part of my soul.

22

Chris moved from my side to stand near Rik, who was so deep into himself he didn't seem to notice. What a selfish man. Why would Chris want anything to do with him after the fuss Rik made over those old rags from Connie's shop?

My eyes searched the eucalyptus again. Mike had company. Just behind him stood the red-headed woman from Sinbad's parking lot. Why was she here, and even more important, why was she standing close to Mike? That strange woman seemed unduly interested in, not only the Mercado affairs, but ours as well.

I shivered, alone and hidden under the black cocoon of my umbrella. To save myself, to say nothing of our marriage, I might have to find Connie's killer myself.

That made no sense of course; all I knew about law enforcement I'd seen on *CSI*. Mike never talked much about his job in Chicago and now I knew why.

Maybe, just maybe, if I found the killer it would redeem me in some small way for not answering the door sooner when Bea knocked frantically, all those years ago. She was always a drama queen, but why didn't I sense real danger? Mother was in the bathroom and didn't hear her. Why did I have to finish that damned phone conversation? While I chatted with Mother Superior about soup kitchen supplies, my sister was gunned down on my doorstep.

The priest raised his hands: "*Go in peace.*"

The service was over. Chris and I loped down the hill, leaving the other mourners far behind. The wake would be held in the wedding chapel behind Connie's shop. It was only three blocks away and the rain had subsided. We decided to leave the Subaru, safely retrieved from LA, in the church parking lot and walk.

Standing in the entrance, I felt like I'd stumbled into a wedding or birthday bash. People milled around in the garden adjacent to the chapel. A bar had been set up. Margaritas in hand, they smiled and chatted and listened to strolling *mariachis*.

"Wow!" Chris froze beside me. "Are all California funerals like this?"

"Chris, you're not in Kansas anymore."

He gave me a puzzled look. Not surprising. *The Wizard of Oz* and Dorothy and Toto were part of the dark ages for him.

Inside, the chapel walls were decorated with colorful silk banners. *Piñatas* dangled from either side of the raised area that served as a speaker's platform and altar. I scanned the crowd lined up at the buffet table. Mike wasn't there yet, surprise, surprise. I tried my cell and got his "away" message.

"Can we like, eat now?"

The combined aromas of corn, chile, onions and cheese made me realize I was starving. "Let's."

At one end of the long table covered with a green cloth, we grabbed silverware and scarlet napkins. As we moved down the line, smiling women in peasant blouses and rainbow skirts heaped our plates with fragrant tamales and Chili Verde, beans creamy with milk and butter, and cumin-spiced pink rice. One girl, younger than the rest, slipped Chris an extra tamale. "Be sure to try the *tres leches*," she said with a shy smile, pointing to small pieces of buttery cake on paper plates. "I helped my *abuela* make it."

"Grandmother." I whispered in reply to Chris's puzzled expression.

"Oh." He put meal and silver down, picked up a piece and gave it the sniff test.

The girl giggled. "It won't bite you. It's made from three kinds of milk, that's why we call it *tres leches*."

Chris took a tentative bite, rolled it around in his mouth, then a larger one. His face lit up and he turned to the server. "Awesome."

"See you later." I waved and moved away to give him and the girl some space.

Balancing a large plate of food, plus silver, napkin and drink, and left to my own devices, I looked for a place to sit down. A stunning platinum blonde sat alone at a table by the door. Lana, Stan's wife.

"May I join you?"

She shrugged, raised her glass to eye level and swirled the red wine into a vortex. I sat down and forced an awkward little smile. While she gazed into her glass, I stared at her. Couldn't help it. The dark eyes were so at odds with her improbably-blonde hair. Stan had mentioned that she was only twenty-eight, but the hard lines around her mouth looked more like mid-thirties. Who was I to judge? Maybe she had a tough life.

An awkward (to me anyway) silence ensued. She continued to swirl while I fiddled with napkin and silver. Finally I could stand it no longer. "We met at the CRUD meeting, Mrs. Mercado. I'm Bella Kowalski." Not one eye flicker of response.

She pointed her glass more-or-less in my direction. "Charmed."

That was apparently it for conversation. My mind searched frantically for something to fill the vacuum of dead air between us. "I'm the obituary editor at the *Central Coast Chronicle*? I worked with Stan on Connie's death notice?" Why was I making everything a question? "I want to say how sorry I am for your loss."

"I'm not." The flat appearance of her dark eyes affirmed the truth of that statement. Strange. Stan had said Lana and Connie were close.

She sipped her wine. Stunned by her response, I toyed with my food, praying for someone, anyone, to join us. We must have been giving off strange vibes because no one did. Just as I was about to move, it hit me: I could turn this into an opportunity. "Mrs. Mercado, that woman you were speaking to at the church?"

Lana looked up with a glimmer of something I couldn't pinpoint. Hostility, anger, fear? All three? I pressed on. "I've met her somewhere, but I can't remember her name. Can you help me out?"

A shrug of shoulders barely covered in basic black. "No, she just asked how to get here."

I looked around. "She doesn't seem to be present."

"No, she doesn't." Lana returned to her wine.

I pushed my food around some more, mumbled excuses (not that they were needed) and went looking for Chris and his new friend. I wandered outside and examined the plants in the walled garden between the shop and the wedding chapel. The plants, both green and flowering varieties, were abundant and beautifully kept. Someone, probably Connie, had spent a lot of time on them. I wondered who'd do it now.

An interesting specimen grew from a basket of moss attached to a large ficus. I reached up to touch the antler-like fronds and heard behind me, "Interesting, is it not?"

I whirled around. The man standing at my shoulder still looked wan, but at least he wore a small smile. I put out my hand. "Father Rodriguez, I don't believe we've met. I'm Bella Kowalski."

His hand felt warm in mine and his smile widened. "I know of you. The activist."

I put my hand on my chest. "Not really, it's just that I—"

"You don't need to explain. People need to hear the truth about what is happening in their town."

I started to comment, then decided now was not the time. "Uh…it's great that you could conduct the burial service. Was the bishop called away?" I asked, thinking of the older man sneaking a peek at the cell phone under his chasuble during the recessional after Mass.

He smiled. "Ah yes, a busy man." A hush while I studied the fern, trying to think of a suitable reply. "Beautiful, is it not?" he asked.

"I'm not sure I'd call it beautiful, but it's certainly exotic. Do you know what it's called?"

"Staghorn fern. They grow on the island of Kauai."

"Really. Have you lived in Hawaii?"

He nodded. "Yes, for many years. But I was born in the Philippines."

Aha, that explained his formal speech. "And how do you like the Central Coast?"

He shrugged. "It is beautiful, but certainly not home." He indicated the fern. "On Kauai they grow much larger than this poor fellow. It's a bit cold here for him, but our Connie, she… she," his voice broke, "just kept trying."

"You knew her well then?" I blinked, realizing it was a nosy question.

He nodded solemnly. "She…she was our angel. She did so much for our parish, so much help, so much," he hesitated, "…

money. I cannot imagine how we can go on without her." His shoulders began to shake and his eyes filled with tears. "I cannot imagine how *I* will go on without her."

Surprised, sorry, and to tell the truth, a little embarrassed at his grief, I reached over and patted one heaving shoulder. The nun in me had been taught that priests were off limits and it felt strange to touch one in that intimate way.

We stood together for a few seconds, then Father stepped back. His red-rimmed eyes darted back and forth like someone who realizes he's said too much. "Please excuse me." He bolted out the side gate into the parking lot.

23

The wooden gate banged shut behind Father Rodriguez. In the last fifteen minutes, I'd received two opposite impressions of Connie. Lana hadn't even pretended to be sorry that her sister-in-law was gone. Perhaps that wasn't surprising; Stan would most likely inherit everything if something happened to Rik and Raymond. With three members of the family dead within two years maybe that wasn't such a stretch. I thought again of the Kennedys.

Father Rodriguez's outburst had totally surprised me. Was he involved with Connie? Priests became intimate with female parishioners all the time. Abuse scandals aside, if that occurred, it probably was a consensual affair. To rid my mind of such thoughts, I returned to admiring the staghorn fern.

"Bella?"

I whirled around. It took me a moment to recognize Charles Cantor, minus the hat. "Hi, Charles." Behind thick lenses, his eyes looked like blue dinner plates.

He hesitated. "Uh, I was wondering if I could call you. I have something important to talk to you about."

He looked so troubled my heart went out to him. "Of course, you can call me anytime. We're in the book. Better yet, let's talk now."

His eyes darted around. "No, not here. It may not be safe. I'll call you." With that, he disappeared up the steps and into the shop.

Wow. With Lana, Father, and now Charles, I was zero for three here. I turned back to the garden area and spied the Mercado boys and Stan. Three men in dark suits and sunglasses stood behind them against the brick wall of the wedding chapel, the same guys who were at the church. Rik's body guards, I guessed, not FBI or sheriff's detectives. No sign of Ryan Scully.

Whatever. I'd had enough of the Mercados and their issues for the moment, maybe forever. Time to head for home. Now where was Chris? A peek inside the chapel confirmed his new friend back at her station. He was nowhere in sight.

Swallowing my annoyance, I decided to check the shop which was open today so the catering company could use its small kitchen. While I stood there, a smiling worker passed through the open back door and made her way among the crowd to the chapel carrying a fragrant, foil-wrapped pan of food.

The spicy aroma followed me as I climbed three rather rickety steps to the store. Inside, there was so much clutter that the neatness freak in me begged for large garbage bags. How did Connie find anything in this mess?

The other day Chris and I had stayed in front by the window, near the racks of used clothing. The view from the back was quite different. Scattered around was enough bric-a-brac to satisfy the most ardent Antiques Road Show junkie: several sea chests, an old armoire or two, and those were just the beginning. Thank goodness I didn't have to inventory all this junk.

After almost bumping into a full suit of armor just inside the door, I ran my hand over his breast plate. "Hey, big guy. Seen my nephew?" I looked around to see if anyone had heard me talking to a hunk of metal.

Apparently no one had. Not the caterers clattering around

in the kitchen, not the few people near the entrance. Back here it was so dark—why didn't someone turn on the lights, for Pete's sake? I squinted, searching for Chris. Where had that kid taken himself off to? Honestly, he was as bad as Mike. I seemed to spend half my life waiting or searching for the male members of my family.

After much groping I found the light switch beside a floor-to-ceiling bookcase that dominated one side wall. The fluorescent bulbs sputtered and hissed and finally spewed forth watery blue light. Not great, but better. A couple across the room smiled their thanks.

My eyes moved upward, taking in the packed shelves. So Connie was a lover, or at least a collector, of books. Besides the usual mysteries and romance novels, the shelves held a collection of children's literature, everything from Doctor Seuss to Harry Potter.

A spiritual advisor once told me you can know someone's heart by the books they read. I reached for a book and studied the front cover. I'd picked "The Holy Twins," a children's book about Saints Benedict and Scholastica. I'd first become acquainted with them in Saint Gregory's "Dialogues," required reading for novitiates. Benedict founded the Benedictines, still a thriving religious order, in the sixth century. His fraternal twin Scholastica, who spent most of her life in a convent, is the patron saint of nuns. "Sister Scholastica" jokes aside, I'd always felt a certain kinship with her.

I studied the book's cover, a clever and colorful fusion of primitive and religious artwork. The book was an interesting choice for Connie, or maybe not. She was certainly devout, or so everyone said. I took a step back, stared up at the volumes and it hit me. These books were for sale, for cripes sake. They didn't necessarily reflect her personal taste in literature.

I spied a weighty encyclopedia of saints next to "Dialogues" on the top shelf and was just reaching for the roll-around ladder when I sensed someone behind me.

I turned to see Kathy Tanner, head librarian at our local

branch. We usually chatted during my weekly visit. Kathy often referred to herself as "Los Lobos' token black woman." An almost true statement; few African Americans lived here. But she was much more than a token anything: book lover, reading advocate, Chamber of Commerce Woman of the Year. She held a paper plate of cake in one hand and a plastic fork in the other. "Lot of books, eh?"

"Sure are," I agreed. "I wonder what will happen to them now."

"The Mercado boys donated them to the library. Too bad they can't be in our sale on Saturday. The family wants to go through them first." She pointed the fork at the top shelf. "The ones up there are from Connie's mother's collection. They were both really into saints."

I showed her the Benedict and Scholastica book. "I can tell."

Kathy set the fork on the plate, leaned close and cupped her hand over her mouth. "I think donating the books was the uncle's idea." Her head moved slowly from side to side. "Left to their own devices, the brothers would probably drop them in the nearest dumpster."

"Really?" Somehow that didn't surprise me.

Kathy picked up the fork and stabbed the cake. "They're a pair all right. Now Connie, she was a sweetie and she did so much for the library. She'd agreed to work the sale this Saturday, as she always did. But now, of course…" She didn't have to finish the sentence.

All of a sudden I found myself facing the business end of the plastic fork. "Hon, would you like to work in her place? We're so short-handed that even one extra person would make a difference."

Busted. "Oh, I couldn't possibly. Saturday is my busiest day, and my nephew's here from Ohio and…" *Yada, yada, listen to yourself, Bella.* "I'd love to."

"Great. Can you come at seven to help finish sorting?"

Seven—on a Saturday morning? "Sure thing."

She walked away eating cake.

What had I done?

About that time Chris ambled through the front door. He stopped when he saw me, reversed direction and then apparently thought better of it. "Wassup, Auntie Bella?"

The smell in his hair and clothes preceded him. "Were you smoking, Chris?" I asked as he came closer.

"Just cigarettes." He crammed his hands in his pockets, fanning out the pleated pants to make them wider at the hips, and studied the floor.

"And who bought them for you?"

"Uh, like, I brought them with me?" He seemed to be asking the toes of his shoes.

"Who bought them for you?"

"Uh, Rik?"

"That's what I thought. Come with me."

A few reluctant steps behind, he followed me into the garden where Rik sat talking with Raymond and Stan. The guys in black suits hovered, as guys in black tend to do. I invaded Rik's personal space and found myself facing a wall of serge.

Rik rose and signaled for the bodyguards to back off. "What can I do for you, Bella?"

I was shocked, and somewhat flattered that he remembered my name, but undeterred in my mission. "Did you buy cigarettes for my nephew?"

He looked at Chris standing behind me and his eyelid dropped ever so slightly into a wink.

How dare he?

"The kid's seventeen. What's the big deal?"

"It's against the law for starters," I said. "Don't do it again." Behind Rik, the suits glowered, Stan frowned and Raymond's expression was unreadable.

I turned on my heel to face Chris, surely the most embarrassed kid on the planet. "Come on, it's time to get out of here."

* * *

The talk we had in the car went better than I expected. I offered to buy Chris nicotine gum, patches, send him to a counselor, a doctor, whatever he needed. He in turn assured me that he only smoked when bored or stressed, which with teenagers, seemed to be pretty much all the time.

We finally agreed, *dear God help me*, that he would hand over his cigarettes and I would dole them out two a day. If he couldn't make it on those, and no cheating allowed, we'd take it to the next level, whatever that was. What would stepmother Janet say to that? Not that I cared. If there was ever a time to be practical, this was it.

As we drove along Los Lobos Road, I sniffed. The car smelled like mildew from all the rain. Better have Mike check the window gaskets for leaks before another storm hit.

Chris sat silent beside me, perhaps contemplating life on two cigs a day. I told myself I was doing him a favor; by most accounts the things were truly lethal. Nevertheless, did I really have the right to inflict my personal beliefs on him? Maybe I did as long as he was in my care.

I glanced at him, taking in the tawny hair that brushed the sport coat collar, his bright blue eyes, the straight posture despite being clearly in a funk. The future was his for the taking and smoking could short circuit that.

Snap, snap. Snap, snap. Chris had picked up my phone and was flipping it open and closed, open and closed. "Look, if you're going to fool around with that, do me a favor and check my messages."

Silence while he worked his thumbs. "There's like, one from Uncle Mike."

"Would you like, play it please?" I asked, swinging into the left lane to pass a tractor. He turned up the volume and I heard Mike's metallic cell-phone voice say that Little Mike's back was worse and he'd been admitted to the hospital. Then he, Big Mike, had an emergency call that ended in time for him to come to the cemetery, then he got called out again. He was sorry, he hoped things went well and thanks for attending in his place.

Okay. A perfectly reasonable scenario. I decided to give him the benefit of the doubt.

24

Thursday evening:

Long after Chris and Mike were asleep, I sat in the West Wing, a cup of cocoa on the desk beside me. My eyes were drawn to the darkened window. As so often happens after a rain, the fog rolled in. I watched it play hide-and-seek with the moon above the tree line.

Through the half-open window I heard a foghorn far out to sea. I shivered and tugged the window shut. Usually I found the sound comforting, but tonight it seemed to warn of danger ahead.

I felt eyes boring into my back and swiveled in my chair. "Emily, did you hear a foghorn the night your lover drowned?" She watched me from her picture on the wall, her expression inscrutable as always.

Enough already. In the last twelve hours I'd had conversations with a suit of armor and a woman who died more than a hundred years ago. What did that say about my state of mind?

I snapped open a copy of Tuesday's *Central Coast Chronicle* and turned to the obituaries. With Chris coming, plus getting ready for the funeral, I'd been too busy to check it. I always studied my work after it was in print, looking for phrases that worked, or didn't, or God forbid, a typo that escaped the editor's eye.

I studied the text, written in the sentimental, schmaltzy style families prefer. A clue to her death could be buried there. Connie was one of those people that everyone loved. Except the person who killed her.

Lana came to mind. She'd been such a snot at the funeral. But just because she wasn't grieving for her niece by marriage didn't mean she'd murdered her. She had nothing obvious to gain. The most likely suspect was someone who had the most to lose from the land sale, or the father of her unborn baby. Could be one and the same person.

Mike? No, I would not allow my mind to go there.

Charles Cantor? On the surface at least, he was all for the sale. I wondered what he wanted to talk about. Perhaps I should call him. A quick glance at the clock. After eleven; the call would have to wait until tomorrow.

I took a sip of cocoa and grabbed a pencil. A long time later I had smudged black circles in the obituary text, a disjointed list in the margins, and no idea of what to do next. Of course I'd circled the names Raymond and Rik. Did one of them kill her to stop the sale? Or for some other reason? To paraphrase a controversial political figure, I didn't know what I didn't know about their family life.

How about some other disgruntled person opposed to the sale? That was the most obvious motive, but was it that simple? What about Connie's lifestyle? She might be devout, but even devout people have illicit sex. I often wondered if saints had sex. I'll bet they did.

Connie was pregnant so she was having sex with someone. Mike? Again the finger of suspicion pointed to him. The thought was like a knife in my heart.

"Why don't you ask him, Bella?"

"Shut up, Emily. Because I'm a coward, that's why."

I looked again at my circles. Connie was active in her church. What about Father Rodriguez? This afternoon he'd said he had no idea how he'd get along without her. His words sounded so personal, but he probably meant as a friend and colleague.

She worked in the homeless program. Had one of her clients shoved her over the cliff? Not likely, very few homeless had access to any vehicle, much less a Hummer. "Murder by Hummer."

Hmm. Not a bad title for a mystery. I yawned and stretched. I'd been at this too long.

Another sip of cocoa, now gone cold in the cup. I was still missing something, but what? Antique jigsaw puzzles? Not likely.

Wait a minute. My pencil point stabbed the word "journals." Like many of us, Connie was a keeper of journals. Maybe, just maybe, the minutiae of her life might provide the answer to her death. Also, whether she was having an affair with my husband.

One thing for sure. I needed to peek at those journals.

25

Friday:

"Good morning, *Central Coast Chronicle*, obituary desk. May I help you?"

"Bella? It's Charles."

"Charles, I'm glad you called. What's on your mind?"

"Uh, well, I saw something…"

"Saw something? Where? When?"

"Out at the bluffs. The day Connie was killed."

"Charles, if you were a witness, you'd better go to the sheriff. Ask for Detective Ryan Scully. Don't wait. Your life could be in danger."

"…So afraid." *Click.*

"Charles? Charles? Don't hang up!"

* * *

"Hello."

"Hi, Stan, it's Bella. Glad I caught you at home."

"It's summer vacation, Bella. I'm home every day. Drives Lana nuts. Interferes with her watching the shopping channel."

"Hmm. Stan, I need a favor."

"I'll help if I can. What do you need?"

"Uh…remember you said Connie kept journals?"

"She…did." I detected hesitation in his voice.

"Do you think you could get them for me? I'll return them almost immediately."

Silence, then "I'm sure you have a good reason, but no can do, Bella. One, I don't know where they are, and two, my nephews got really upset the other day when I let you and Chris in the shop. There's no way I could get them now. Sorry."

"Okay, Stan. Thanks anyway."

"Bella, a word to the wise. The lock on Connie's house is pretty flimsy. As for the shop, you know where we keep the key."

* * *

That evening after Chris and Mike turned in, I dressed in dark clothes and retrieved a small flashlight from the kitchen junk drawer. My head pounded as I stood in the hallway, stuffing the flashlight and a credit card into the front pocket of my black sweatshirt. I pulled an old Raiders watch cap down over my hair. Driver's license? Better take it. Getting stopped without a license might lead to awkward questions.

I couldn't believe I was doing this. After advising Charles Cantor to go the sheriff, I was taking matters into my own hands. Unless I missed my guess, those journals would never make it to the sheriff's office if they contained anything incriminating about the family. I'd just have a little look-see. If Detective Scully needed to take a look, I'd drop them off anonymously at the substation. If not, I'd return them to Connie's house.

How could I do that? I'd worry about that later.

"Where you going, Auntie Bella?"

I whirled around, sure my heart would leap out of my chest. Chris stood there in boxers and an extra large Grateful Dead T-shirt from Connie's thrift shop. "Why aren't you in bed?"

"Because I'm standing here asking you where you're going."

What could I say that he would possibly believe? "Uh, I'm—"

Chris studied my choice of apparel. The temperature was probably in the high sixties and already I was beginning to sweat. "Are you gonna like, break in somewhere?"

I tugged at my cap. "Of course not. I'm just like, going for a walk."

He raised a skeptical eyebrow. "This time of night?"

I stuffed a stray piece of hair under my knitted cap. "Sure, why not?"

"Because that's bull crap." His eyes lit up. "Take me with you. I can be your lookout."

"Absolutely not. You're in my care and I can't put you in danger. Now get back to bed and forget you saw me."

"No way, Auntie Bella."

"I said go to bed."

He didn't budge. "If you won't take me, I'll like, tell Uncle Mike."

I know when I'm licked. "Get your clothes on, Chris."

"Can I grab a smoke first?"

"No."

* * *

Connie had lived in a small house a block from her store. As we drove east along Los Lobos Road, I told a wide-eyed Chris I thought the answer to Connie's death might be in her journals, and how I planned to search for them.

"O-*kay*!" He tugged the hood of his black sweatshirt over his forehead and drummed restless fingertips on the dash. That kind of enthusiasm made me wonder about latent criminal tendencies.

After we crossed the intersection at Ninth Avenue, one of three traffic lights in town, I heard a faint snore. Chris had dropped off. So young, so innocent. Well, young anyway, I thought with a smile.

We passed Connie's store and it was all I could do to keep from screeching to a halt in the middle of the street. A white car stood half-hidden under some trees just beyond the parking lot. Looked like Rik's rental Ford, but I couldn't be sure. He'd said he would leave today; possibly his plans had changed. I slowed down, snapped off my headlights, turned around and made another pass.

Looked like a duck, must be a duck.

I drove east for half a mile while I sorted out my thoughts. Should I call the sheriff's office? Rik *was* Connie's brother, he had every right to be there. But why at midnight? On the other hand I certainly didn't want to call attention to myself, now did I?

I turned around once more and pulled into the parking lot of the strip mall that contained two of my favorite haunts, Lockhart's Bakery and Volumes of Pleasure, a quirky independent bookstore. Mike and the other contractors lined up early to buy the bakery's famous Danish pastries, then carried them across the street to eat at the tables in front of Connie's shop. She supplied the coffee, I guess. And maybe other things to Mike.

Stop it, Bella.

There were two other cars in front of Lockhart's and a light on in the back of the shop. Bakers started early. The aroma of sugar and cinnamon made my stomach rumble. Alas, food would have to wait until I had my mitts on the journals.

Seeking anonymity, I parked between two cars and squinted through my dirty windshield at Connie's shop. Hello, what was this? A thin band of moving light, perhaps from a flashlight.

"Hey, Auntie Bella, what are we like, doing here?"

I jumped and slapped a hand to my chest. "Chris, you scared me."

He rubbed sleep from his eyes. "Sorry."

"That's okay, I was watching the shop and forgot you were here." I pointed across the street. "See that white Ford over there behind the trees?"

"Yeah? So what?"

"I think it's Rik's."

"No…sh, I mean, no kidding. I thought he was leaving today. He didn't even call and say goodbye."

"Well, maybe his plans changed."

"Yeah. Is he like, looking for the journals, too?"

"Conceivably. If so, he probably tried her house first."

"If he finds them, we're screwed," Chris said.

"Mind your mouth, Chris, but basically that's right."

"Come on," Chris said, "let's check it out."

We crept across the deserted boulevard, looking both ways. Nothing in sight. What did I expect this time of night? As we paused on the sidewalk in front of the shop, a flash of lightning over the ocean and the smell of ozone warned of another electrical storm. Sudden terror clawed like a cat at my chest.

"Any windows side or back?" Chris whispered, eyeing the two that flanked the front door. No light showed through the blinds. Perhaps what I'd seen before was just a reflection.

"No windows on the side, but there's one in back. I'm not sure we could see anything from there, though."

"Then we're screwed," said Chris, and this time I ignored his word choice.

In silence we pondered our next move. Then Chris came up with, "Why don't I stay here and keep watch while you like, peek through one of those front windows?"

"I knew I brought you along for a reason."

He pulled out his ever-present Blackberry. "Got your cell?" I nodded and he said, "Good. We can stay connected."

"Great. If any cars come along, sing out, and we'll duck down behind those outdoor tables."

"Got it. You warn me if Rik starts to come out."

"For sure," I said.

While he remained on the sidewalk, I edged up to one window whose blinds were ajar. "Chris, can you hear my heart beating through the cell?"

"Chill, Auntie Bella, your heart's fine. Go for it."

"Okay, I'm facing the window. Is the street clear?"

"Yup."

I pressed my nose against the glass and forced my eyes to adjust to the darkness. I was starting to wonder if this was a waste of time when a bluish light jolted my senses. Rik stood in the display area with a camp lantern. He turned it toward the window where I stood. I ducked back against the wall. Finally, the light moved away from the window. I screwed up my courage and peeked in. He set the lantern on a desk by the back wall and begin pawing through stacks of papers.

"What's happening?" Chris's voice squawked through the ether. At the sound, Rik stopped and turned toward the window. I ducked again, maybe not fast enough. Had he seen me?

"Chris," I whispered into the phone, "I think he heard you. Don't say anything unless it's an emergency."

"Yo!" Chris said, way too loud. I winced.

I spent a long minute waiting for the front door to bang open. When it didn't, I approached the window once more. Rik was now searching the file cabinet next to the desk. This seemed to take forever.

Apparently satisfied, he moved to the floor-to-ceiling bookcase against the east wall and spent ten minutes digging through the books on the two lower shelves. Finally, he stepped back, hands on hips. Even with glass and distance between us I heard his "Son of a bitch!" He stomped toward the front door.

"Chris, hide! He's coming out!"

26

With no time to get behind the tables, I shot to the east wall and took cover behind a fat pine. I'd be toast if Rik found me.

"Hide, Chris!" I repeated into the phone.

"Can't. No time." I peeked through the branches and saw him head east along Los Lobos Road as though out for a midnight jog.

The front door slammed. Rik came around the corner and stood in front of the tree, swinging the lantern. I smelled his sweat. He stared briefly at Chris's hooded figure, gave an almost imperceptible shrug and walked to his car. A minute later the Ford turned out of the driveway and headed east toward Tolosa and the 101 Freeway.

Weak with relief, I squeezed out from behind the pine, waited until the car melted into darkness, and spoke into the cell. "Come on back, he's gone."

Chris halted under a streetlight by the gas station. "Did he see me?" I watched him say the words into the Blackberry as I heard them in my ear. What a strange sensation. He circled around and started my way.

"Yeah, but I don't think he recognized you," I said to his approaching figure.

A few seconds later my nephew stood beside me, slightly out of breath. I'd put him in real danger. What if Rik had recognized him? This wasn't a game we were playing. I headed for the street. "Come on, that's it. We're going home."

"No way." Chris grabbed my arm. "We're like, just getting hot. Did he find the journals?"

"No, but let's think about this. We don't know if that's what he was searching for. Whatever it was, he got tired of looking, and soon. He doesn't have much concentration. I think he's AD/HD."

"Could be. Lots of kids at my school like that." Chris peered through the dark window of the shop. "Where'd he look?"

"The desk, file cabinet and two lower shelves of the bookcase."

"Not the upper ones?"

"No, I think he got bored. As I said, no attention span."

"You have a credit card, right? For slipping the lock?"

I patted the front pocket of my sweatshirt. "Sure do."

He nodded. "Gangster."

"Gangster?"

Chris grinned. "Means the same as 'cool.'"

"Oh," I said, "I thought 'cool' was cool."

He heaved a deep sigh. "Auntie Bella, that is so not cool." A quick peek through the window. "Let's finish searching the bookcase first. With two of us, it'll go quick."

Ah, the confidence of youth. I studied my nephew, looked at the shop door and realized two things: No way could I expose him to that risk, and I didn't need a credit card to get in. Stan had reminded me on the phone the key was under the flower pot.

"Chris," I said. "This is an order. Take yourself across the street and wait in the car. Stay low, stay on the cell and tell me if Rik comes back or you see anything suspicious. If anyone challenges you, tell them…"

Oh dear Lord. Tell them what?

"Do you have a driver's license?" If so, he could just drive home.

He brightened. "A learner's permit."

Worse than I thought. "Look, if anyone challenges you, call Uncle Mike. He'll know what to do."

"No way, Auntie Bella. I'm staying with you."

My mind searched frantically. "Chris?"

"Yeah?"

I handed him my keys. "Go back to the car and have a ciggie."

"Okay." He trotted off.

Feeling like my feet were planted in molasses, I forced myself to turn and inch my way along the side wall of the shop. I retrieved the key and let myself in the back door. I snapped on my trusty flashlight, shielded it with my hand and took a moment to get my bearings. The heat build-up inside this old structure was unbearable. No wonder Rik was sweating.

"Chris, I'm inside. You in the car?"

"Yeah."

"Good. Can you see my flashlight?"

"Nope."

"Stay low."

"Okay."

I looked up at the wall of books. What would it take to search them all? My spirits sank. The wall clock said close to 1:30. The real work lay ahead.

Rik had left books scattered on the floor, apparently getting careless as he tired of the search. I started to pick them up. Bad idea. He might notice when he came back. If he was serious about finding those journals, he *would* come back.

Where to start? I flicked my light over another, smaller bookcase. Hmm. Piled with jigsaw puzzles. Stan had made a point of saying Connie collected old ones. Maybe she hid the journals with them. I looked back at the other bookcase and decided I couldn't tackle those shelves yet. And I might get lucky with the puzzles.

"Yo!"

My heart gave a jolt. "Chris *what*?"

Silence for three heartbeats, then, "Um, nothin', I guess. Cat jumped on the hood."

"Okay. Stay cool. I mean 'stay gangster'."

"Auntie Bella, will you quit?"

After my heart returned to normal, I moved back to the puzzle shelf. To calm myself, I opened each box. Some were filled with wooden pieces, some with the more familiar cardboard ones. Some were very old and no doubt valuable. A few had no pictures on the box cover. What a challenge to put one of those puppies together. When I reached the bottom of the puzzle shelf twenty minutes later it was obvious that I'd also hit a dead end.

"Yo!"

I snapped the flashlight off. "What is it, Chris, another cat?"

"No, sheriff's car."

Oh dear Lord.

"Put out your cigarette and stay low."

"Don't have one, and I am."

Now I heard the car outside the shop. I moved to the window

and gazed through the blinds. Chris was right. Two deputies—
the last people I needed. Headlights sliced through the night. Car
doors slammed one after another as the deputies stepped from
their vehicle.

I moved away from the window and flattened myself like an
aging Gumby against the front door. Not the smartest thing to do
if they had a key, I realized. Too late. I was committed.

My heart felt like a brick in my chest. One deputy played a
flashlight through the cracks of the blinds while the other jim-
mied the door. It shook like an earthquake against my spine. I
steadied my feet and pressed my back hard against the door. The
rattling seemed to go on forever.

Finally, I heard "Okay, lock's solid," and footsteps retreated.

But my worries weren't over. What if the deputies recognized
the Subaru, with Chris in it, across the street? With my lousy luck
one of them would be Deputy Marquez who interviewed me at
the murder scene. What if he called Detective Scully? Could this
get any worse? Defenseless, I awaited my fate, too scared to even
mouth a Hail Mary.

I must have banked the heavenly equivalent of an emergency
stockpile. A moment later car doors slammed and gravel crunched
under moving tires. The car pulled out onto Los Lobos Road.

"They're gone," Chris said, stating the obvious.

"I know." Finally, I allowed myself to breath a sigh of relief.
The adrenaline rush from this near encounter gave me renewed
energy. I moved to the bookcase, stared up at the hundreds of
volumes…and my rush fizzled. Maybe there were no journals.
Maybe Connie destroyed them before departing this world. But
she didn't know she was going to die.

I was missing something. What was it? Rik had begun on
the bottom shelves, the easy choice. I needed to think and work
smarter. If I wanted to keep something private, I'd hide it in plain
sight, but I'd also pick someplace difficult to reach. Where? The
top shelf, of course.

I positioned the library ladder and began to climb. Three

steps off the ground, I began to sweat. Four, and my knees shook. I needed Chris to steady the ladder. I stopped, huffed a deep breath, remembered the deputies—and Rik—and kept going.

Finally, I reached the top shelf. Balancing myself with one hand on the ladder, I leaned back and studied the titles. As Kathy Tanner said at the wake, all these volumes were about saints. Saint Gregory's "Dialogues" was as good a starting point as any. I reached for it, then noticed the encyclopedia of saints I'd seen earlier.

Hmm. Something odd about that one. From this vantage point, the encyclopedia looked too fat for its spine. I pulled it off the shelf and several notebooks tumbled to the ground. *Could it be?* I held up the empty spine as though Chris could see it. "I think I found the journals."

"Awesome. Want me to come over?"

"No!"

I scrambled down the ladder and gathered up the notebooks, five in all. I opened one and played the flashlight over a page covered with crab-like writing.

Bingo.

I decided not to press my luck. Quickly, I stuffed a fat book inside the encyclopedia so it would appear normal to the casual observer and returned it to the shelf. When everything was as I'd found it, I snapped off my light, replaced the key and scurried across the street with my booty.

Closer to the Subaru, I could just make out the tip of Chris's black hood. He unlocked the driver's-side door. I got in and plopped the notebooks on the console. We hi-fived. "Couldn't have done it without you," I said, patting the books.

"No sweat," he answered with studied nonchalance.

Easy for him to say. I started the car and took a deep breath. The car and Chris didn't smell like smoke.

"Did you have your cigarette?"

"No," Chris said. "Too scared."

* * *

At home, before Chris trudged up to bed, I extracted a promise that he'd roll out in time for the library sale. I checked our bedroom and found Mike on his back, arms thrown out, snoring like a Trojan. If he woke up and missed me, he'd probably think I was sleeping in the West Wing.

The kitchen clock said 3:10 A.M. Might as well stay up; I'd have to get up in three hours anyway to be at the library by seven.

I made a killer cup of Earl Grey, loaded it with honey and carried it and the journals up to the West Wing. With a shiver of anticipation and a pinch of dread, I stared at the five notebooks. All had identical black and white marbled covers. They made a tidy pile on my desk, an invitation to pry into the secrets of Connie's heart.

I glanced at the portrait on the wall. "What do you think, Emily?"

No response. Probably too late even for ghosts.

I picked up the first journal. At least I thought it was the first because it looked the most beat-up. Briefly, I considered leafing through all of them to see if Connie mentioned Mike anywhere. I sipped tea and contemplated this, then shook my head. No, I would start with the first. No reason except that exhaustion brings out my obsessive-compulsive tendencies.

I opened the journal and tried to read the first few pages. Agony. Few of the entries had dates and the writing was almost impossible to decipher. Connie had started this one when she was in seventh grade, with the usual junior high concerns of homework, girlfriends, crushes on boys.

I don't know how long I sat there, reading the minutiae of pre-teen life. I picked up the next notebook and found more of the same. Still, I felt compelled to press on.

I now considered Rik the most likely murder suspect. Why else would he go through her shop in the middle of the night? And he said he was leaving today—no, yesterday—and then he didn't. Once he went back to his rich-and-famous lifestyle, that would be it.

If I went to Detective Scully and told him we'd seen Rik in the store, he'd probably say, "What of it?" Even if more evidence surfaced later and Rik was arrested, he had money to hire high-powered lawyers.

Or did he? Weary as I was, I remembered the reporter at the airport asking him about bankruptcy. God, was that only last Monday?

Despite the tea, the honey and the importance of my task, my head nodded over the pages. Afraid I'd break my neck, I gave up and lay down on the sofa, pulling the old afghan around my shoulders. Before I dozed off, I looked up at the portrait on the wall.

"Emily, I'll get back to those journals right after the library sale."

My pronouncement must have caused the gods to smile and shake their heads.

27

Saturday morning:

Mike and I faced each other across the breakfast table. I gazed groggily into yet another cup of tea, then pushed it away, for once having no taste for it. "What's on your schedule today?"

Mike checked his watch as though already late for an appointment. "I need to clean up some paperwork at the shop. Should take until late afternoon. You?"

"The library book sale, remember?"

"That's right." His eyes narrowed into that look I dreaded. *"Whaat?"*

"Did you sleep well?"

"Not very." I concentrated on buttering an English muffin. When I offered him half, he shook his head.

"Look," he said, leaning across the table, "you don't have to break your neck on the sofa. You can sleep in the bed. I won't bother you until," he hesitated, "until this thing is settled between us."

Finally, at last, an acknowledgement that there *was* something to settle. On three hours sleep I wasn't ready to go there. "It's not that. I slept in the West Wing because I stayed up late doing stuff. Didn't want to disturb you."

"I slept just fine." The edge in his voice made me wonder if he did. If not, why not just ask me where I was until 3 a.m.?

His place mat looked bare without its usual mug. "Let me make you some coffee," I said, anxious to make nice.

"No thanks." He rubbed a spot just below his breastbone and I studied his face. He did look a bit gray about the gills.

"Are you all right?" I pushed the chair back and started around the table. "Do you have a fever?"

Mike put up both hands to fend me off.

"I'll make you some breakfast. How about oatmeal?"

"Bella, for chrissake will you just lay off? I don't want breakfast. I'll grab something later."

"You look pale. Want me to call the doctor?"

He shook his head. "Wouldn't do any good. I dunno. I just feel like something awful's going to happen."

That was a first. "Did you have a bad dream?"

He shook his head. "Not that I remember." He fingered the spot below his breastbone again. "And I have a touch of indigestion. Not much. I'll be okay." Cop eyes dared me to disagree. He glanced at his watch. "Better get Chris up."

As if on cue I heard the click of dog toenails on the tile floor. Sam wandered into the kitchen, followed by a yawning Chris. He was dressed in clean and fashionably ragged Levi's, blonde hair swallowed by the black hood of last night's sweatshirt. "Ready, Auntie Bella?"

"In a minute." I turned to Mike. "If you feel worse, call me right away, okay? But call the doctor first."

"Yes, Mother." Mike gave me a weak grin.

* * *

"Well, that does it for murder." I'd finished sorting the umpteenth box of Anne Perry and P. D. James mysteries. I'd been too busy in the last three hours to think about Connie's journals or Mike's health. Since I hadn't heard, I assumed he was better, or at least no worse.

I straightened up, massaged the crimp in my back and glanced over at Kathy Tanner. She had a black marker in one hand and a fistful of labels in the other. "Want me to start on the cookbooks next?"

"I'll do those." Kathy consulted her watch. "Fifteen minutes 'til the sale starts. Why don't you take your break now, Hon?" Two worry squiggles formed between her dark eyes. "Forgive me for saying so, Bella, but you look like hell today."

"That's okay. I had a really rough night. Be back in ten minutes." I left her to interpret my remark as she saw fit and ambled across the parking lot toward the concession stand where Chris and a girl with dark braids worked side-by-side.

The girl looked familiar, but I couldn't place her. I stood at the counter as Chris, without acknowledging me, turned to retrieve something from boxes piled behind the stand.

"Good morning."

The girl's head bobbed, but she didn't meet my eyes.

Hmm. Shy, sleepy, or just plain grumpy? "I'll have a coffee, black, and let's see, are those *churros*?" Once again a polite nod only. "Yes, I'll have one of those."

Chris moved to the girl's side, carrying two stacks of cardboard cups. "Oh hi, Auntie Bella," he said as though he'd forgotten we inhabited the same planet, much less driven here in the same car. He set the cups down next to the large electric percolator on the counter and turned away.

"Would you like to introduce me to your co-worker?"

Good one, Bella. Why push yourself on them?

Chris looked around as though I'd spoken to someone else. "Oh, right." He fiddled with the already-tidy piles of cups.

"Miranda, this is my aunt, Mrs. Kowalski. Auntie Bella, this is Miranda."

She met my eyes and then I remembered. She served at the wake yesterday, looking much younger now with her hair braided. I reached out my hand. "*Hola, Miranda. Como esta?*"

Miranda's eyes registered surprise. Oh dear, did my attempt at Spanish sound patronizing? Apparently not. Her face lit up with a twenty-four-carat smile. "How do you do, Mrs. Kowalski? I am very well, thank you."

Impressive. This child even pronounced my last name correctly. "I remember you from the funeral yesterday. The food was delicious. Did your family prepare it?"

"But of course," she said, spreading fingers with short-clipped nails on the counter. "We do weddings, funerals and parties of all kinds. It is our family's business. My mother and aunts cook and serve the food and my uncles play *mariachi* music." She reached for a piece of wax paper, selected a rich brown *churro* and handed it to me, first shaking off the excess sugar. "*Mi abuela* made these."

"*Gracias.*" The churro's heavenly cinnamon-and-sugar scent reminded my stomach that it had been three hours since that boring English muffin. I took a bite and rolled the crispy pastry around in my mouth. "Wow. Please tell your *abuela* these are superb."

"I'll be happy to." Miranda beamed, showing none of her earlier shyness.

Chris passed me a steaming cup of coffee. "Auntie Bella, would it be okay if Miranda and I go to the beach after we're done here?" His eyes scanned the azure sky. "Today's the first really nice day we've had, and Miranda's going to like, give me a surfing lesson."

I hesitated. "You'll have to rent a decent board. And how are you going to get there?" I gave him what I hoped was a meaningful stare. "As you *know* from *last evening*, I will be *very busy* this afternoon."

"No problem," Miranda said. "I have both an extra surf-board and my own car."

"And you also have a driver's license?"

She smiled to show she understood my question was prompt-ed by concern for Chris, not rudeness. "For two years now. I graduated high school last week."

I returned her smile, letting her know I appreciated her cut-ting me some slack. "Well, in that case, how can I say no?"

I also wondered, but did not ask, why an eighteen-year-old girl would be interested in a boy a year younger. I studied my nephew, trying to see him as Miranda might. The almost white hair, crinkly blue eyes, the very image of a California surfer. Let's face it, he was a hunk.

Chris accepted my money for the coffee and *churro*. "And can I like, go to Miranda's house for dinner afterward? Her grand-mother's making more tamales."

Miranda shot him a look of disapproval.

"*What?*" Chris turned to her. "You invited me, didn't you?"

"Of course. But I just don't see why you have to keep saying 'like' all the time."

"Okay," Chris said, looking aggravated and chagrined, "let me get this straight. You don't like me smelling like cigarettes and you don't like me saying 'like' all the time. Are you like, sure you like me at all?"

The repeated "likes" may or may not have been acciden-tal; Miranda chose to take it that way. Another killer smile. "Of course I *like* you. It is just that my family has taught me to have high standards."

Good for you, Miranda. This girl knew how to handle her-self. I turned to Chris. "Of course you can stay for dinner. Just watch out for riptides and be home by nine."

Chris rolled his baby-blues. "Yes, Janet."

"Don't be snide." I wondered what Stepmother Janet would have said about Chris's plans. Not that I intended to call her and find out. Come to think of it, she hadn't phoned to see if the kid was okay, and neither had my brother-in-law. Chris claimed he was keeping in touch by e-mail. But wouldn't you think a concerned parent would want to speak to me, at least once? Their attitude made me wonder if the concerned parents act was just that—an act. Bea must be worn out from twisting in her grave.

Miranda said, "I'll send some tamales home with Chris."

My mouth actually watered at the prospect. "Yum, thank you."

I turned around with my coffee and churro and noticed Kathy Tanner talking to a sheriff's deputy in his car across the street by the tennis courts. I wondered what they were discussing. Kathy's son was Tolosa County's sole African-American deputy.

The son/deputy drove off and Kathy crossed the street to the library parking lot. Her complexion had assumed a grayish cast. Did the deputies spot my car last night after all? If so, why talk to Kathy?

Oh God, was Mike okay? Suddenly I couldn't feel my own face. Kathy approached and laid a honey-colored hand on my arm. I steeled myself for the worst. She leaned forward and whispered, "Keep this under your hat, Hon, but Martin just told me they found a body sprawled across Connie's grave."

This couldn't be happening. Instinctively, I crossed myself. "Who?"

"Charles Cantor from CRUD. Someone shot him in the head." She shuddered. "And he was nekked."

28

Saturday afternoon:

I got home a little after four. The Beast, newly repaired, sat in its normal parking spot by the front walk. Good. I could hardly wait to discuss the murder with Mike. Did he have a premonition about this new killing this morning? Knowing my husband's secular nature, that seemed unlikely. But at this point, nothing was too ridiculous to consider.

We'd touched base by cell shortly after the sale started and he'd said that yes he felt better, and yes he'd heard about the murder on the radio. Then customers clamored for attention and I had to cut the call short.

One thing for sure. I needed to tell him about Charles Cantor's earlier call. I wondered if Charles was the mysterious Deep Throat who leaked news of the land sale in the first place. Maybe not. He acted as the sale's most enthusiastic supporter, and Paisley Potter had all but accused him of accepting a bribe to make it happen.

Yeah, Bella, it may be a cliché, but things are not always what they seem.

Kathy Turner had declared the sale a success despite the anxious knots of folks standing around whispering among themselves. Bad news does indeed travel fast. We'd even had a local news anchor thrusting a microphone into people's faces. Remembering my experience with the *LA Times*, I said "no thanks," in words not exactly that polite.

By noon we'd sold out of mysteries. Is there something about murder that whets the appetite for more? The cookbooks disappeared next. Murder and mysteries, funerals and food. Go figure.

I parked next to Mike's truck and Sam came loping around the corner of the house, lips folded back in a dog smile. Despite being eager to get inside, I spent a minute or two sideways in the driver's seat, giving him extra love pats. "Good boy, Sam. We're going to have a hike again very soon." He almost melted with pleasure at the word "hike" and tried to climb in the car. "Hey wait a minute, I'm exhausted. Does Monday fit with your schedule?" Apparently it did. He trotted off toward the side yard.

When I opened the front door, a blast from the TV almost

popped my eardrums. Mike lay stretched out on the couch in the living room. On the tube, macho cowpokes struggled to mount and ride cranky bulls. I frowned. Something wrong; he never watched *Championship Rodeo*. Well no wonder, he was asleep. I tiptoed over, grabbed the remote and clicked the Off button.

He sat up. "Hey, I was watching that." His hand reached for the remote.

"You weren't either," I held it over my head and glanced down at him. He looked like a halibut three days without ice. Worse than this morning, and he'd looked pretty bad then. Currents of alarm chased each other up and down my spine. "I'm calling Doctor Davis. This is ridiculous."

He tried to stand up, then sank back, sweat beading his forehead. "No, I forbid it."

I went from zero to sixty in less than a second. "Forbid? Who are you to talk to me that way?" My tirade was cut short by the doorbell.

Company.

Mike gasped like there wasn't enough air in the room, or the entire house, to fill his lungs.

I walked to the door and peeked through the side window. Detective Scully stood on the porch. Just what we needed. How come Sam hadn't sounded the alarm? Probably off chasing a rabbit. My legs turned to rubber, but I pasted a smile on my face and grabbed the knob. "Detective Scully, what brings you here?"

"Sure and would yer husband be at home, Mrs. Kowalski?"

"Yes, but he's not well. This is not a good time—" I tried to close the door.

Scully placed the flat of his hand on the oak panel and pushed his way in as though I hadn't said a word. "Won't be takin' but a minute."

Mike stood by the fireplace, both hands on the mantel, as if to hold himself up. He glanced sideways at our visitor. "Detective Scully, what brings you here on a Saturday?"

Scully ignored the question. "That pickup's lookin' a lot better these days, Kowalski."

Oh-oh.

"If I didn't know better I'd say that front bumper was brand new." He nodded slowly. "By all the saints, brand spankin' new."

"Last I checked it wasn't illegal in this county to get a new bumper," Mike countered.

Scully turned to me. "Mrs. Kowalski, would ya be excusin' us now? Yer husband and I have a bit o' private business."

I tried to catch Mike's eye. *Should I go or stay?*

"Anything you say to me can be said in her presence." Mike got my message. He clung to the mantel like a shipwrecked man to a lifeboat.

"Achoo!" Scully reached into his pocket, pulled out a handkerchief and let loose a great honking sneeze. His nose did look kind of red.

"Are you okay?" I asked.

Scully sniffed. "Just a wee bit of a cold. I'll be fine."

"You need to stay in bed and drink plenty of liquids," I said, hoping this would make him go away.

Scully opened his mouth to reply, but before he could utter a sound the door banged open and Chris appeared in the archway. He took in the three of us and jerked his head, first at the detective, and then at me as if to say, "What's he doing here?"

"Something wrong with yer neck, lad?" Scully asked.

Chris went scarlet. "No sir."

"I thought you were going surfing," I said.

"Uh, came to get some board shorts. Miranda's like, in the car."

Thank goodness. At least she won't have to hear this.

Chris pushed through the room and bolted up the stairs to the East Wing as if he couldn't get away fast enough.

At this point, in his own inimitable fashion, Scully changed tack. "Suppose ya folks heard about the latest murder."

Mike stood there like a statue while I said, "We couldn't help but hear. Why would anyone shoot Charles Cantor and leave him on top of Connie's grave? And what was he doing there anyway?"

Scully studied his fingernails. He looked up and his eyes narrowed. "Wouldn't really comment about an ongoin' investigation except there's stuff all over those things ya folks do with yer computers." He made whatever it was sound like an unnatural act.

I took a shot in the dark. "Blogs? Blogging?"

He snapped his fingers. "That's it. Sure and they ought to shut the things down, whole Internet too."

I debated answering this and decided it wasn't worth the trouble.

"What…what time was he killed?" Mike asked and looked at me. Just a glance, but it was enough. He knew I'd been out last night, perhaps Chris as well. But that was ridiculous. Why would I kill Charles? Perhaps Mike feared one or both of us had witnessed the murder and were now ourselves in danger.

"Sometime between midnight and four." Scully paused and looked toward the hall that led to our bedroom. "I suppose ya were here asleep at that hour."

"*Absolutely*," I said, "absolutely." I looked up the staircase and saw Chris staring down at us, his eyes round as two blue moons. Auntie Bella lied to law enforcement. Some role model I turned out to be.

If Scully saw Chris he gave no indication. Instead he turned to Mike. "How about yerself, Kowalski? Sound sleeper like yer wife?"

"…Need to sit down." Mike released his hold on the mantel, moved toward the sofa and stumbled. I grabbed his arm. Ignoring my own heart, which felt like it might hammer its way out of my chest, I said, "Get in the car, Mike. I'm taking you to emergency now. You could be having a heart attack."

"I'll be callin' EMT for you, Mrs. Kowalski." Scully reached for his phone. "Yer husband looks like he could use 'em."

For once in his life Mike didn't argue.

29

Saturday evening:

It was after ten when I drove home from the hospital. Fog swirled around the Subaru. I hugged the white line, hands gripping the wheel. To take my mind off conditions outside, I concentrated on two things for which I could be grateful: Mike had passed the initial tests, and they were keeping him for observation. I would have been scared to death to bring him home.

One glimpse of my pale and sweaty husband and the admitting clerk had grabbed a wheelchair. An EKG and other tests didn't indicate a heart attack, but Mike's new cardiologist, Doctor Simpson, explained that didn't rule one out. So-called silent attacks don't show on an EKG. The doctor explained that a feeling of impending doom is one symptom of a coronary. Also, his blood pressure was off the charts. They'd grounded a grousing Mike until Monday for more tests and to bring his pressure down.

I'd ridden with Mike in the ambulance. Chris and Miranda followed, Miranda in her car, and Chris (with his learner's permit, God help me) driving the Subaru. As soon as Mike was out of danger, I'd sent them on their way for supper at her house and to take in a movie in Tolosa. I hoped Miranda would drive carefully. She was a sensible girl, I told myself. Of course, she'd be careful.

A plate on the kitchen counter welcomed me. Tamales under a foil blanket. Their succulent aroma filled the room, beckoning like a siren's song. Later. Right now, with the house quiet, I'd work on the journals.

I set my purse on the counter and a little warning bell dinged in my head. Something relating to the hospital. What was it? I thought a moment. My credit card, that was it.

Even though we have insurance, the admitting clerk insisted

on an imprint of my card. I'd searched my purse and realized with a pang that I left it in the front pocket of the sweatshirt I wore last night, now buried deep in the wash pile. Hastily, I wrote a "take credit card" note and set it on top of my purse.

A few minutes later, with a cup of fresh mint tea beside me on my West Wing desk, I opened the first journal to where I'd stopped early this morning. Once again I grimaced at the crab-like script. Feeling like Sisyphus condemned to endlessly rolling a stone uphill, I sipped tea and planned my attack.

Perhaps it would be smarter to concentrate on entries for the last two years. I'd start before her parents' death and end with the last entry.

"Of course it would, Bella. But you might find out about Mike. Are you ready for that?"

I stared up at Emily's portrait. The words seemed to have been spoken by her, even though I knew they came from inside me.

"Stop!" I said.

"You want to know, don't you?"

"Emily, you're starting to sound like Bea. Quit nagging already."

I turned my back on Emily and studied Connie's obituary tacked to the bulletin board above my computer. Stan had told me that Connie shared confidences with her parents. Maybe she'd written about those. Maybe not, but it seemed like a good place to start.

I hesitated, then sighed and cracked the last journal. The first few pages detailed more cat rescues than I ever thought possible. Several sojourns to Santa Barbara for estate sales. It was going to be a long night.

I turned more pages. Subaru trouble, good Samaritan Mike to the rescue. Could be trouble ahead. My pulse drummed in my ears.

Mummy's arthritis, Daddy's acid reflux. Fascinating.

Interesting that a thirty-four-year old woman called her parents Mummy and Daddy. Perhaps Connie wasn't as emotionally mature as she might have been. I was no psychologist, but I knew that if something traumatic happened during her formative years, like her family's experience in Mexico City, it could affect her emotional development. I read on. About half-way through the year, a month or so before the elder Mercados died in the plane crash, I hit pay dirt:

> After private detective's report, Mummy and Daddy said they plan to cut R. from the family trust. I'm glad. He liked to hurt animals when we were little, maybe he still does. Drowned Fluffy in the tub and made me watch, said he'd kill Snowball if I told. Can't tell Mummy and Daddy after all this time and break their hearts.

Wow! No wonder Connie hid her journals, no wonder Rik wanted to get his mitts on them. I stared at the words again, the pain in them rising from the page.

Wait a minute. "R." could also mean Raymond. Possibly Rik wanted to get the goods on his brother, a situation as old as Cain and Abel.

I glanced first at Emily—who gave me an enigmatic Mona Lisa smile—and then at my watch. Almost twelve. I'd been at this for two hours. I should call someone, but who? Certainly not the Mercado brothers. Detective Scully? And tell him what? That I broke into Connie's shop last night and found these incriminating journals.

Just like in the movies, the doorbell rang. Chris must have forgotten his key. I ran downstairs and opened the door without thinking.

Very big mistake.

"Rik, what a big surprise. What can I do for you?"

Sam appeared out of nowhere and stood close to my leg.

Rik snarled, "Do for me? You can start by letting me in out of this goddamned fog."

I began to push the door closed. "If you're looking for Chris, come back in the morning." Rik didn't have exclusive rights to rudeness.

Like Detective Scully this afternoon, Rik pushed back, almost knocking me off my feet. He strode across the threshold. "Came to see you. I have something of yours." Ignoring Sam's low growl, he reached into his pocket and pulled out a small, shiny, blue and white rectangle.

My credit card.

30

I put a hand to my chest. "My goodness, Rik," I said, sounding like Scarlett in *Gone With the Wind*. "Wherever did you find that?"

Rik snorted. "Next to the flower pot at Connie's shop. We found it this afternoon."

"We?"

"Me and my brother, and Lana. When we came to clean out the store."

Lana didn't appear to be the cleaning type, but that was beside the point. "I can't imagine how it got there."

The yellow flecks in Rik's eyes sparked. "Don't shit me, Auntie Bella. We know you have Connie's journals."

We? I took the moral high ground even as my heart played Ping-Pong in my chest. "I don't know what you're talking about."

"Of course you do." A nervous ha-ha. "With me being so famous and all, we can't have things getting out about the family."

Again the first person plural. Did Raymond, and perhaps Lana, know there was something incriminating in the journals? Or just Rik? What about Stan? He'd all but told me where to look for them, and I wasn't sure why. And if Rik and/or family members put two and two together with the credit card and the journals, I might have other callers tonight.

Well, first things first. I reached around him, grabbed the knob and yanked the door open, forcing Rik to move his *tush* in a big hurry. "Get out of my house."

"Huh?"

"Get!"

Sam tucked his tail between his legs and threatened to give teeth to my words. Rik put up his hands. "Nice doggie." He turned to me. "Okay, Bella, have it your way, but we'll see what the sheriff says." With that he pocketed my credit card and walked off into the fog.

I didn't believe for one minute he'd go to the sheriff's office, but I needed to talk to someone and Sam didn't have any answers. I glanced at my watch and sighed. Midnight. Calls would have to wait 'til morning.

31

Sunday morning:

"Bella, what's going on? It's not even seven yet." Amy's voice sounded so sleepy over the phone I felt a twinge a guilt.

"I haven't slept all night and I need to talk. Mike's in the hospital—"

"The hospital? What's wrong?"

"They thought he had a heart attack but the EKG didn't show anything. They're keeping him until Monday."

"That's good. Sleep in, call me at ten."

"There's another problem. Rik."

"What about him?"

"I don't want to say over the phone. Can we meet, say at the hospital cafeteria?"

"Sure thing, Bella."

* * *

An hour later, Amy and I faced each other over a small table in the noisy and crowded cafeteria. People in green scrubs came and went. The place smelled like a stew of disinfectant, burnt coffee and bacon grease. I popped a straw into a carton of orange juice while Amy took a tentative sip from her faux latte. Bracelets jangled as she wrestled plastic wrap from her bear claw.

I gave her an update on Mike. According to the nurse on duty, he'd had a restful night and was still sleeping.

"Great." Amy leaned forward. "So what's this about Rik? And why bring me into it?"

"Well, Rik told me that you two were an item in high school."

Amy spat her bear claw across the table, nailing the Golden Lab on my T-shirt. She reached across the table and scrubbed at my chest with a napkin. "When did he tell you that?"

"On the ride from LAX in the limo."

"I don't know what he was smoking, but I wouldn't let that creepy little twerp within a hundred feet of me. For one thing, he's two years younger, a big difference in high school, you may remember. And what does this have to do with now?"

I swallowed hard and told her about Connie's journals. How Chris and I spied Rik through the shop window. Also how I let myself in with the key and found the journals after he left without them.

"And that's not all," I said. "My credit card dropped out of my pocket when I put the key back. Rik has it."

"Ouch." Amy winced. "Bad, bad. That places you at the scene."

"I know," I wailed. "What should I do?"

"Nothing for now. Let's concentrate on the journals. Have you read 'em?"

"Started to. Didn't get far before Rik showed up waving my credit card."

Her eyes widened. "What did they say?"

"That sometime during junior high, someone Connie called R. killed her cat and threatened to do the same with another one if she told."

Amy hit the table with her fist. "I knew it!"

"Keep it down," I cautioned, looking around. "Did she tell you?"

"No, but sometime around eighth grade Connie…" Elbows on table, she hesitated, coppery nails glittering as she raked both hands through her hair. "She changed."

"Changed how?"

She tilted her head, thinking. "Little ways. Nothing I could put my finger on, but she was quieter and she looked sad all the time. She pulled down the sides of her cheeks so that her eyes drooped at the corners. "Like this." I nodded and she went on, "She was never very good in school, and her grades got even worse after that. There was a time when I wondered if she would graduate high school." She paused to reflect. "That goddamned Rik. I always knew there was something different about him."

"But…but, the diary only says R. Could be Raymond."

Amy's eyes constricted behind her glasses. "Oh it's Rik all right. Raymond's a jerk, always has been a jerk, but he's basically all mouth. Rik used to tear the wings off butterflies and swing kitties around by their tails. We used to say the neighborhood cats had a contract out on him." She laughed grimly. "I wish."

"Another thing," I said. "Connie's parents hired a private detective to investigate R."

"No shit." She gulped latte and stared at me. "When?"

"About a month before they died."

Another gulp. "Now that's surprising. Margaret Rose never wanted to hear anything bad about her kids. Even as adults, after most parents realize their offspring have faults, she insisted they were perfect."

"Hardly that."

"You better believe it." Amy's eyes widened and she whispered, "Do you suppose the plane crash wasn't an accident?"

Our eyes held across the table. "My God, Amy, I never considered it. What should I do?"

"Take those journals to the sheriff's office today. Today, hear me?"

"I can't, Amy."

"You have to. You could be an accessory if you hide them."

"I probably am anyway. I stole them, remember? And Rik has my credit card to place me at the scene."

"Screw Rik. If you come forward now, it will go easier on you."

"Still can't. Chris was with me." I put my face in my hands. Could this get any worse?

A few seconds later I felt a pressure on my forearm and looked up. "Tell you what," Amy said. "I'll come by this evening and pick them up, take them to the sheriff in the morning."

"And say what?"

"That Connie left them with me in case something happened to her. That I'd forgotten where I put them. My word against Rik's, if it comes to that, and it won't. My guess is that Mister Rik is going to find he has pressing business on the continent of Australia. And soon."

I reached across the table and touched her hand. "Owe you big time."

Amy smiled. "All part of the service."

"What should I do about the credit card?"

"Take the initiative. Report it stolen. Again, your word against Rik's."

"He claims Lana and Raymond were there when he found it."

She swiped the air with her hand. "Worry about that later. Your card has been missing for several days and you don't know how it turned up at Connie's shop. That's the story and all you have to do is stick to it."

"Um, okay." I finished off my juice and set the carton on the table. "Amy, I can't let you lie for me. Then you'd be the accessory."

She grimaced, obviously having second thoughts herself. "You're right. But it was a helluva good idea. Cancel the card anyway. And take those journals to the sheriff. Right now, you better get upstairs and see Mike."

Mike. "Amy?"

"Yes, what now?"

"I know Connie was pregnant."

Amy lowered her head and spoke to the empty cup. "Figured you did."

"Is Mike the father?" I thought I already knew the answer but I needed her to confirm it.

She fingered a spot on the table. "Can't say."

"Can't, or won't?"

She looked up and there was both pain and anger in her eyes. "I'm telling you Connie swore me to secrecy. Some things transcend death and secrets are like that."

Hmm. I knew a secret about Bea, that I'd never told anyone, that I'd carry to my grave. I understood.

Amy rose and began to gather our trash. "You need to talk this over with Mike."

32

Sunday afternoon and evening:
Turned out I couldn't talk anything over with Mike. After I got back upstairs he was having more chest pain, so much he didn't even notice the bear claw stain on my T-shirt. They did another EKG which still didn't show anything conclusive. Doctor Simpson scheduled a coronary angiogram for Monday morning. This

test would show any blockages in the arteries. As an added precaution, he also ordered an MRI.

After stepping into the waiting area to call and cancel my credit card, I spent the rest of the day with Mike. We watched a golf tournament and PBS reruns. Actually I did most of the watching. They'd given him something and he acted dopey, slept a lot. One more day and we'd know something for sure. At least I hoped so.

I watched him sleep, feeling even more betrayed than last week, when I found out about the incident in Chicago that forced his early retirement. And based on my conversation with Amy, I was pretty sure Mike fathered Connie's baby.

What was next for us? I had no idea. On the surface, having an affair with Connie made no sense, but then neither did keeping secret what happened in Chicago. My husband seemed to be a man who relished his secrets.

Around five I finally left the hospital, worn out from thinking too much. The nurse said I could spend the night, but after Rik's visit the previous evening, I didn't want to leave Chris alone. And truth to tell, I needed to be away from Mike for a while.

As I drove west from Tolosa on Los Lobos Road, dark clouds gathered on the horizon. At least I would be home safe and dry when the next storm hit.

Chris had left a note on the kitchen counter. Out with Miranda, back at nine. So much for not leaving him alone. At least he left a note, which was more than a lot of kids would do.

He and Miranda were getting pretty thick, and quickly. I made a mental note to have a birds-and-bees talk with Chris. Was I really up for that? No, but I doubted whether his father, or God forbid, Janet had. Someone needed to do it. It wouldn't be the first time I'd warned at-risk kids to use protection if they were going to be sexually active. That would have gotten me booted out of the Holy Name order if they'd known. Despite official church policy, I didn't consider it a matter for confession either. Guess I really was a "cafeteria" Catholic after all, someone who picked and chose dogma to suit herself.

Enough. With Chris gone, I could devote at least four more hours to the journals. First thing tomorrow I'd take them to the sheriff's office. After all, this *was* Sunday.

I felt a little shiver of anticipation along my spine. Mike considered it weird, but I loved being safe and dry at home while a storm raged outside. Tonight was no exception.

I fixed myself a salad and sprinkled it generously with gorgonzola in place of dressing, relishing its funky smell. I considered a glass of Merlot, settled for Earl Grey. The journals would require all my wits.

With salad and tea at the ready, I went to work. I'd put a Post-it where I left off, about a month before the elder Mercados died, after they'd received the private detective's report about the mysterious R. I wondered what the report actually said. The parents might not have told Connie the details. Amy had mentioned that Margaret-Rose was in denial about her kids.

Surprisingly, Connie had written nothing about her parent's death and funeral, which must have been a horrible shock. Perhaps both events were just too painful. I felt a pang of sympathy for her. Despite being born into wealth, she'd led a sad life.

The next entry had been written six months later and told of receiving an e-mail from a woman named Corinna. No clue as to their relationship or where the woman lived. Hoping to find another entry, I leafed through the rest of the notebooks. On one page I found a drawing I'd missed the first time through, stuck between two pages.

Interesting. I held the pencil sketch up to the light. It looked like a map, but in typical Connie fashion, offered no clue to location of same. Three labels indicated "south wall," "north wall," and "table," with an arrow pointing under a crudely drawn table. Something hidden under the floor or taped to the underside of the table? No way to tell. I studied the drawing for several minutes, but nothing else revealed itself. This might be another reason why Rik was so hot for the journals.

I put a Post-it on the page and found two more entries mentioning the mysterious Corinna. Again a frustrating lack of detail, but the women had made plans to meet. Connie didn't say where, but the date almost jumped off the page at me.

Dear God, it was the day she died. I looked again, not believing what I was seeing. Had the woman set her up? Amy was right. I really needed to hand these journals over to the sheriff.

In another revealing entry just two days before she died, she said she'd caught Raymond searching her house for the journals. They'd argued, with Connie insisting they were private property. Hmm. Stan told me they'd quarreled. The entry pretty much proved Raymond knew there was something in them that cast the family in a bad light.

I became aware of a creaking sound, wind straining against the tethered paddles of the windmill. If Mike were here, he'd be outside checking them. I'd just have to hope the restraints held. A worried glance out the sliding doors confirmed the storm clouds moving closer. I shivered and gathered my sweater, and my wits, around me.

My uneaten salad began to reek of gorgonzola ripening in real time. Too involved to move the bowl, I kept my place in the journal with one hand, reached across the desk and inched a pad of yellow-lined paper toward me with the other. I flipped to a fresh sheet and scribbled:

1. Which Mercados knew there was something incriminating in the journals?
2. Who was R? Rik, Raymond, someone else?
3. Did he—or she—kill Connie?
4. Did R. work alone or did Corinna, the mysterious e-mailer, set Connie up?
5. Was the plane crash an accident?
6. If not, did R. arrange it?
7. What about the map? Did it point to something valuable?
8. Did the map have anything to do with Connie's death?
9. What did the private detective's report say?
10. Where is the report now?

I pressed on and soon had a tidy list of questions. Making the list provided no real answers, but it was temporarily satisfying and helped to lay out the pieces to the puzzle. Rain sheeted against the glass as I sat there wondering what to do next. The creaking of the windmill paddles grated on my nerves until I wanted to scream. Something else I couldn't control. Perhaps I should call someone to check them. But who? I sure didn't want Chris out there tying them down in the wind and rain. Despite my best efforts, at every turn I seemed to be putting him in danger.

More rain on the glass. The storm was getting serious and the Subaru's hatchback leaked. Better move it to the barn. I knotted a scarf around my head like a *babka*, Polish grandmother, and ran downstairs and outside. As the wind and I played tug-of-war with the Subaru door, a truck bounced into the driveway. I squinted against the rain.

Oh crap. Raymond. Here we go again.

Where was Sam? Raymond parked his industrial-strength Jimmie behind the Subaru and slithered out of the cab. "So Bella, where do y'all think you're goin'?"

Silently I considered my answer. If I told him I was on my way to the hospital he might decide to follow, or worse, insist on taking me. If I told him the truth, he'd know I was in for the night. No way could I let that happen.

Raymond and I stared at each other through the now-driving rain. "You gonna ask me in?"

"No. Come back in the morning."

He shook himself like a spaniel. Water sluiced off his dark hair. "You know why I'm here. The journals. We can't let those leave the family."

"That's not my problem." We stood close together, a little oasis of tension in the midst of the storm. I stared at Raymond and he stared at me. So, both Rik and Raymond knew about the incriminating material in the journals.

Not knowing what else to do, I lied through my chattering teeth. "I told your brother and I'm telling you. I don't have them."

Raymond narrowed his crow eyes. "Hope that's true, *Bella.*"

"And why would that be, *Raymond*?"

He cocked an index finger under my nose. "If it's not, I might have to kill you."

The finger was so close to my face I had to cross my eyes to see it. The more I stared, the bigger it got, thick and meaty like a hairy Kielbasa. Honestly, I couldn't help it. I leaned over, opened my mouth and chomped down.

Raymond blinked, then jerked away, hunched over and held the afflicted hand between drawn-together legs. "Ow, ow, ow," he bleated, like a sick calf. He opened his legs, brought the finger to eye level and inspected it. "You bitch, you probably gave me AIDS."

I grabbed his finger and examined it. Hairy, limp and damp from the rain, like the man himself. "Raymond, I didn't even break the skin. Get outta here, you big cry baby."

His eyes went darkly opaque. "You're a sick woman, and you'll get yours. I promise you." With that, he climbed back into the truck and fishtailed out of the driveway.

I leaned against the Subaru, oblivious to the rain and the water Raymond's truck had sprayed on me. He'd called me sick, but what about him? And his ridiculous brother. Raymond and Rik. Amy called them the Evil Twins; they were that all right. Did they work as a team, or as separate scum bags? Was I truly in danger with the journals in my possession?

Was Pope John Paul Polish?

I should leave, go somewhere, but where? If the storm kept up, it was only a matter of time until Los Lobos Road flooded and Sam and I would be cut off. But if the road was out, they couldn't get to us, either.

Oh dear God, what about Chris? Better call and warn him to stay at Miranda's. I drove the Subaru into the barn and threw a tarp over it in case the barn roof leaked, too. As I was about to slide the heavy door shut, I noticed Sam curled up on a blanket in the corner. "Hey, boy. Want to come inside?" He wagged his tail, but showed no signs of moving. I pointed to an open window. "If you want out later, jump through that, okay?"

He rattled the links of his collar, the standard "yes" response.

Back in the kitchen, dripping wet and shivering, I reached for the phone.

"Hello, Miranda?"

Silence, then a cautious, "Yes?"

"It's Bella Kowalski. Is Chris there?"

"Right here, Mrs. Kowalski."

"Hi, Auntie Bella."

"Chris unless you start for home right now, you better stay the night. I'm afraid the road will wash out."

"I'll—"

The phone went dead. I stared at it, feeling helpless. No, I could call back on my cell. Then I remembered. I'd left it on the console of the Subaru.

33

I decided against braving the storm once more. Chris was a sensible kid. He'd stay at Miranda's. I hoped her parents were home.

Stop it, Bella.

I dried, changed clothes and applied myself to the journals, trying to ignore the chaos of wind and rain. The paddles creaked ominously. They could come loose and wreak havoc on the house if the weather got much worse. I stared at the rain blowing horizontally off the ocean, then at the green numbers on the desk clock. Barely seven, and almost dark. Strange in June, so close to the summer solstice.

Discovering that I'd skipped a few pages in Connie's last journal, I skimmed over them. What was this? Mike's name was all over these pages. How could I have missed that? Maybe I'd skipped them because I didn't want to face the truth.

My hands shook so I could hardly hold the book. As I read on, I wanted to throw it across the room. Honestly, the woman was the queen of obfuscation. Mike says no, says no again, (Good for you Mike!), Mike says maybe, back to no, Mike says yes, and then—here the Fog Queen became shockingly clear—he'd made an appointment with Doctor Olvera. Quickly I grabbed the Tolosa County Yellow Pages. Only one Doctor Olvera listed. His specialty: In Vitro fertilization and artificial insemination.

Oh dear God. Mike had provided the sperm for Connie's baby. Here before me was the black and white evidence, the smoking gun.

Sick to my stomach, I put my head down on my arms, letting the journal slide to the floor.

Some time later the lights flickered, all the clock numbers turned to eights and the room plunged into darkness. Power out. Damn. What else could happen?

Candles. I rummaged in the desk. No, the kitchen. Outside—pandemonium, wind howling, paddles straining against restraints, rain beating a tattoo on glass.

Halfway down the winding staircase, I heard something that turned me to stone; the unmistakable sound of shattering glass. It came from the back of the house. The kitchen? I thought about the glass door. Mike had always said that door was unsafe. I cursed myself for leaving Sam in the barn. With the sound of wind and rain, he probably didn't hear a thing

I crept down the remaining steps and across the breezeway to the door that opened into the dining room. Standing in the shadows, I wondered if I could make a dash through the dining room to the hall and out the front door without being seen. I'd run to the barn, get in the Subaru and be out of here before the intruder realized I was gone. With all the noise outside, he'd never hear me.

Except, the car keys were in the kitchen.

The breath tightened in my chest. My senses were so acute that each sound from the kitchen, a cupboard or drawer banging, stuff being smashed against tile, felt like a physical blow.

As the intruder moved into the dining room, I stifled the urge to cry out. From the shadows of the breezeway I glimpsed a dark, wide-brimmed fedora. Charles Cantor wore a hat like that at Connie's funeral. But he was dead.

The man rummaged through the drawers of the sideboard, scattering linen and silverware with abandon. If he looked my way I'd be road kill. Time for Plan B, whatever that was.

He seemed focused on the search and I took advantage of his concentration to sneak back across the breezeway. I tiptoed up the stairs, entered the West Wing and eased the door closed, wishing for a lock. Only a matter of time until he found me. And the journals, if that's what he was after.

Hide them.

Where? Desk? First place he'd check. Closet? Too obvious.

In the corner by the sliding doors, my knitting overflowed its wicker basket. I grabbed the journals from the desk and shoved them under skeins of yarn, a jumble of knitting needles and pattern books. I tossed an afghan-in-progress over all. Not perfect, but it would have to do.

Now to hide me. Again, not the closet, I'd be trapped like a rat. I scanned the room. How about the widow's walk? Fighting gusts of wind, I struggled out the door and clutched the railing to keep from being blown over. Keeping my back to the wall, I inched to the front of the windmill. Hmm. Driveway empty. Intruder must have parked on the road. I shivered and not just from rain beating into my face.

A flash of something shiny drew my eye to the patch of trees by the access road. The wind parted the wet leaves, revealing something, I wasn't sure what. I strained to see in the gathering dark. A car? No way to tell.

Maybe I could jump to safety from here. Leaning against the wind, I peered over the railing and wished I hadn't. Twenty feet down, at least. Crawl down and hang off the struts?

Sure thing, Bella. When your arms give out, you'll be hamburger.

I studied the dark outline of the windmill paddles. I could climb up one of them onto the roof. Even the idea made me shake. One paddle dipped almost to the railing by the sliding doors. Quickly, before I lost my nerve, I eased my way back. I hoisted myself onto the railing; it swayed alarmingly. Entire section loose. Still, I'd have to chance it. Just as I'd gained a toehold on the bottom slat, I sensed movement behind me. I turned, stumbled and fell to the deck.

The Fedora stood just inside. But it was the gun that caught my eye.

34

Terrified, but curious too, I scrutinized the face under the fedora. Not Charles Cantor, and certainly not Rik or Raymond. Blond wisps escaped beneath the brim. I focused on the cold, dark eyes.

"Lana?"

She gave me a twisted smile and waved the gun. Not wanting to die on my backside, I scrambled awkwardly to my feet, trying with difficulty to keep my hands in the air. She used the gun to motion me inside. I sneaked a glance left and right. Could I run around to the front and…

And do what, Bella? It's pretty hard to outrun a bullet.

I stepped through the door like the good little girl I become when the chips are down. "We can talk," I said, trying to keep fear and desperation out of my voice. Just words perhaps, but another corpse might prove awkward. Then again, maybe not.

"Shut the door."

"Can't," I lied. "Slider's stuck."

She frowned and waved the gun. "Unstick it."

I turned and tugged at the door. Nothing happened. You have to lift the door to slide it and I wasn't about to close off my only escape route. "See? It won't budge. You try."

"Forget it." Was it my imagination or did the gun shake a bit? Luckily, the wind had died down enough so it wasn't making a shambles of the room.

"Give me the journals," Lana said with quiet menace.

This conversation would be monotonous if it weren't so scary. As with Rik and Raymond, and even though my kneecaps knocked against each other, I feigned innocence. "What journals?"

She aimed the gun at my belly button. "The ones you stole from Connie's shop. We found your credit card."

"*We?*"

"Rik and Raymond."

The usual suspects. "Was Stan there also?"

One well-penciled eyebrow lifted. "Stan's out of the family loop."

The way she said this made it sound more sinister than merely being ostracized. "Where is he now?" I asked as casually as I could.

"He's sick." She snickered. "The fool got a bad mushroom."

"Lana, that's serious. He could die. You need to get him to the hospital."

She smiled in a chilling way. "I think we'll let nature take its course."

"But you can't. He…he's your husband."

"Of course I can." She yanked off the fedora and tossed it on the chair beneath Emily Divina's portrait. "He's one of them."

"Them?"

"Mercados, famous, powerful, ruthless, and all dumb as sticks."

I sensed my survival depended upon saying just the right things. Anything could set her off and I'd be dead. "Connie wasn't like that," I said, then wondered if even that was a mistake.

She shook her head slowly from side to side. "No, she was just dumb."

"So, did you kill her?"

Her smile said it all.

I was dead meat. Feeling sick, I tipped my chin toward the fedora. "Charles Cantor?"

"What do you care?"

"I do care. He and Connie were human beings. I'm trying to understand why they died."

A flicker of menace showed in her eyes. "What's to understand? You're going to die too."

I'd known this from the moment I saw the gun. Actually, that's not quite true. One part of me knew I was going die, the other part felt like the cavalry would ride up any minute and save me. That was the part that kept me from being scared. (Well, too scared.) Also, I'd be damned if I was going to die like Bea and not know why.

What was that? Someone behind Lana. Oh-no. Chris stood frozen in the doorway. How much did he hear?

With every cell in my body screaming to make eye contact with my nephew, I concentrated on Lana. "What's to understand? For starters, why you would kill your husband's niece."

She smiled like I wasn't quite bright. "She was more than that."

"What do you mean?"

She drew the words out for maximum effect. "She…was…my…sister."

I stared at her, too stunned to say anything, aware only of the rain.

She bowed slightly. "Corrina Mercado, at your service."

I studied her: the Mercado eyes, dark and troubled, the black roots of her platinum hair, the tall, strong body. Same almost everything. Connie's long-lost twin. "But you're dead."

She waved the gun. "Do I look dead?"

"No, but…but how could that be?"

She sucked in her breath. "It's a long story, and I'm not going to waste all night telling you, but in Mexico things like this happen all the time."

Corinna, the e-mailer and Lana, the sister-in-law: one and the same person. All of a sudden it hit me. "If you're Corrina, then Stan's your uncle!"

She smirked. "Marrying Stan was my passport into the family."

"Oh gross." Apparently this was more than Chris could handle. He stood frozen, the sopping Grateful Dead T-shirt pasted to his torso.

Lana spun around and before I could tackle her, wrapped her left arm around his throat and pulled him toward her. The other hand held the gun to his temple. "Stay back or the kid dies."

"Lana," I begged, hands out, palms up, "do anything to me, but let the kid go. His mother was murdered."

"Auntie Bella," Chris pleaded, his eyes like blue saucers, "please don't let me die."

35

Was it my imagination or did the gun waver?

"Chris, you're not going to die," I said with all the conviction I could muster. My eyes tagged Lana. "This is just plain silly. You can't kill everyone in town. Even if you do inherit the Mercado land, everyone will know you're the killer."

As Lana opened her mouth to reply, her raincoat pocket chirped like an angry bird. She ignored the cell phone's chatter and motioned with the gun. "Get back. Over there, away from the door." She shoved Chris toward me and pointed the gun at the chairs on either side of my knitting basket. "Sit," she commanded, as though we were dogs.

When she backed toward the chair under Emily's portrait, I noticed a slight limp. Chris saw it too. We traded glances.

She perched on the edge of the chair with the gun leveled at us, her left leg out in front resting on the heel, weight on the ball of the other foot.

"What's wrong with your leg?" I asked. I wanted her to know that I'd seen her weakness.

She shifted her weight, barely suppressed a wince of pain. "Twisted my ankle. Not a big deal." Never taking her eyes off us, she pulled the cell out of her pocket, punched a button and held the phone to her ear.

"Yeah, you done yet?"

Brief pause, then, "What's the problem?"

Another pause. "Well, kill the little fucker and get over here. Can't do the burn until you do."

Burn? Chris and I exchanged another glance. Poor kid. He looked terrified. Apparently Lana was going to kill us and torch the house to destroy evidence. Which might not be that easy, with today's forensics. What good would that do Chris and me? We'd be dead.

Who was this partner? Stan? Not likely, from what she said. Rik and/or Raymond? Some unknown person?

Silently I called on all the faith I'd ever had and some I didn't know I had. If I could keep her talking, something unexpected would happen. It would.

Lana glanced at her watch. "Getting late. Now where were we?"

Where were we? Did she really intend to tell us her story? Mike had told me about this phenomenon; criminals who wanted people to know what they'd done and how they'd done it.

As though enlightening a two-year-old, I repeated slowly, "You can't kill the whole town to get the land. Everyone will know you're the killer."

She gave me a small, plastic smile. "Oh that. I don't give a shit about the land. Or the god damned sewer plant. That's totally irrelevant."

"It's not irrelevant at all. Los Lobos needs a sewer. It's just the location that's the issue."

Listen to yourself, Bella. Like she needs a lecture on the sewer now, of all times.

Lana shook her head like I wasn't quite bright. "You don't get it. I want the money."

"The money?"

She scratched her head with the business end of the gun. Not too bright herself. "Yeah, the money, the dough, the moola, the do-re-mi."

"What money?" Chris croaked.

She tossed him a disdainful look. "The ransom money that was never used because I was supposedly killed. Our dear father brought it back from Mexico and hid it in the house."

"I wonder why he didn't give it to charity or the Church," I said, wondering how she knew.

Lana took a ragged breath. "Maybe he thought they'd come after Connie and he'd need it. Who knows what went through the fucker's mind? He cared more about her than he did about me."

"Lana, that's unfair," I said. "From all I've ever heard, Manny and Margaret-Rose were devastated by your kidnap and murder—that is, supposed murder."

Her eyes shot dark sparks. "I don't think so. They had two more kids and came back here, didn't they?"

"They probably had more kids to ease the pain of losing you. That's not unusual. And they only came back here after your body was found. At least what they thought was your body."

A brief silence settled over the room. I was surprised to see tears on her cheeks. "No, if they loved me, they would never, never have given up the search. Surely my mother knew I was alive. A good mother would know that in her heart." She drew another ragged breath. "They abandoned me, left me in that shit hole."

For the first time I felt a pinch of sympathy for this troubled woman. "Do you remember any of it?"

She sniffed noisily. "Of course not. I was less than two. After

I was snatched, the kidnapper took me home to his wife. They didn't have any kids—"

"Rare in a Catholic country," I interrupted.

"Whatever. After Manny refused to pay the ransom, she wouldn't let her husband kill me." With her free hand, she scrubbed at the tears on her cheeks. "I think by that time he kinda liked me too."

"Do you know why Manny refused to pay?"

"I think the police convinced him they'd have a better chance to get me back if he didn't."

"These kidnappers raised you?" She nodded. "Sounds like they were caring people, at least toward you."

"Failed kidnappers," she snorted. "Failed at everything else, too. Meanwhile, my real family was living like a bunch of little rich bitches."

"But you didn't know that at the time."

"Of course not."

"How did you find out?"

"Same way most kids find out about family skeletons. I overheard my supposed parents talking about it when I was about seven."

"Did you know your real name?" Chris asked, jumping in. He glanced at me for approval. Maybe he realized we needed to keep her talking. I just hoped he wouldn't ask questions that would set her off.

"I didn't know I was a Mercado until later."

"Do you know whose body was found?" I asked

She rolled her eyes. "Like that's important? I have no idea."

"What about forensics? Surely the authorities knew the corpse was not Corrina Mercado."

"From what I heard, it was a whole year later and the body was badly decomposed. Most likely the authorities just wanted the case closed so the *Americanos* would go back home and get off their backs."

I considered. "You're probably right about that. By the way, you speak excellent English."

"Thank you," she said simply.

"I would never have guessed your first language was Spanish."

A wry smile. "After I found out I was an American, I spent all my time learning English so I could come to America after I grew up and meet my real family."

"When did you learn your family name?"

"My parents told me after the plane crash. They saw it on TV. I crossed the border the next day."

"So you're here illegally?"

A shrug.

"Does Stan know you're undocumented?"

"No, by the time I met him I had papers."

"Papers?"

"Sure. Birth certificate, driver's license, school records, the whole enchilada." She smiled at her own pun. "They showed I'd lived in San Diego my whole life. Fake, but no one questioned them because I spoke English like a native."

"So let me get this straight. After you got your papers, you moved to the Central Coast and met Stan—"

"I registered for one of his classes." She tossed back her chin-length platinum hair to show how special she was. "The rest was easy."

"But why go through all that? Why not just reveal yourself to the family? They would have welcomed you with open arms."

"Connie would have, maybe." She snorted. "Do you really think brother Raymond would have accepted me? As for Rik—"

"You could be right," I agreed. "As Lana, did you reveal your true identity to Connie?"

"What! You think I'm stupid? As a loving auntie I was in a better position to learn their secrets. And talk they did. It was like a game that I always won. " She laughed. "They're such fools."

"How did you find out about the money?" Chris asked.

Good question. I'd been thinking about that too.

"The oldest way in the world. Connie got drunk one night—"

"Connie got drunk?" Amy *had* mentioned that Connie drank.

She smirked. "Her dirty little secret. Raymond was on her case about it all the time."

Silence for a long moment while I considered the implications of Connie divulging secrets while three sheets to the wind.

"Hello, anyone home in there?" Lana said, waving the gun in my face.

That got my attention. "What?"

"You're not paying attention to me," Lana said like a petulant child.

"Sorry, I got distracted for a moment."

"Well," she huffed, "as I was saying, apparently our dear, departed mother was also a lush."

"Like mother, like daughter," I commented.

"You got it. Anyway, Connie told me about the hidden ransom money. She was so wasted I doubt if she remembered the next day. Our parents let her in on the secret, but not Raymond or Rik. She was their little pet. She planned to take her share of the proceeds—and the ransom money—and leave the country after the land sale. Greedy little bitch, huh?"

Takes one to know one. "Did she tell you where the money was hidden?"

"No, but she said it was in the house."

"When did you decide to kill her?"

36

Lana paused. "Right from the get-go."

"Really?" That was cold.

"Connie had so much and I had squat. And now she was going to get the ransom money that, had our dear father paid it, would have given me the same childhood as the rest of them." She sniffed and wiped away a tear.

"Go on," I said quietly.

"Well, first it was just a daydream. After I started to make real plans, I knew I'd need a professional to do the actual killing."

"A hired killer?" I asked and she nodded. "How did you arrange that?"

She gave me an owlish look. "I was *raised* by criminals. One of their friends connected me to a person who works for the Vegas mob."

"Really?" I would never be surprised by anything again. Chris gawked at her like he'd been dropped into an episode of *The Sopranos*. It was almost funny.

"Yes indeed," she said with chilling authority. "The Vegas mob doesn't work only in Vegas."

"I'm not surprised." I glanced at Chris and realized his mouth hung open because he was gulping air. "Chris, take slow, steady breaths."

"Trying Auntie Bella." He looked like a goldfish who'd flopped out of his bowl.

"Put your head down."

Lana ignored Chris who now had his head between his legs. "Yes. By coincidence, she'd just been hired by the mob to teach another member of my illustrious family a lesson about paying his debts."

"Rik." It was not a question.

She gave me a twisted smile. "He deserves it."

"Maybe, maybe not," I said. "But this is insanity. How did you set up Connie's death?"

"Easy. As Corrina, I sent her an e-mail and we agreed to meet at the bluffs."

"Did you say you were her long-lost sister?"

"I didn't have to. She got it right away. On our walk we were going to make plans for telling the family. It was to be a big surprise." The same chilling smile. "Connie was surprised all right."

"You didn't show up, but your partner did."

"I was there all right to see that she did the job, but Connie never saw me."

She? "Wait a minute. Your partner is a woman?"

She grinned. "Yup. I guess that makes me an equal opportunity employer. One of her jobs has been to keep an eye on you."

"But why?"

"In case you saw something you shouldn't have at the bluffs that morning and talked to the wrong people." Her grin turned pure evil. "She mistook you for Connie at first. Turned out to be your lucky day."

Wow. "But, but, the person in the Hummer who tried to run me off the road was a man. He had a shaved head."

She smirked. "She shaves it when it suits her. You're as clueless as the rest of them. Let me give you a hint. Think red hair."

I gave her a hard look. Oh dear Lord. The connection had been there all along, if only I'd seen it. The man with the shaved head and the woman in a red wig were one and the same. How obvious could it be? They both drove Hummers, actually the same Hummer. "You mean—?"

"Of course. Wigs are handy in her profession." She smoothed her own blonde locks. "I may have to get me one after I expand my operation."

That all made sense, sort of, but there was still a missing link. If I was going to die anyway, I might as well depart this world knowing the whole story. "Okay, I understand she was watching me at the CRUD meeting and last Thursday at the funeral. What about that day in the restaurant parking lot? She was already inside when I parked next to her. She couldn't know I'd be there."

Lana waved the gun in a dismissive manner. "She didn't. That was pure coincidence. Believe me, she wasn't happy about it either. Especially as it tied her to the Hummer."

"A Hummer is not exactly a low-profile surveillance vehicle," she continued. "But it comes in handy for other things."

"Like pushing a car into the ocean."

"Exactly."

"What about the fire at Mercado Construction? Did you set that or did your partner?" If we lived through this, all the information would be important.

This question seemed to please her. "My partner is a woman of many talents. I wanted to send a message to my dear brother that he could be next."

"And that was *it*?" She nodded. Another piece of the puzzle clunked into place. The woman was completely insane. She'd hired a cold-blooded killer to carry out a vendetta against the family that had deserted her. I thought of another piece that still didn't fit. "What about Charles Cantor?"

She took her time. "What about him? I didn't realize he'd seen me out there that morning. It looked suspicious as hell after Connie turned up dead. Charles made noises about shutting his trap if I gave him money, but the more I talked to him the more I realized he'd settle for some good nookie. Told him to meet me at the cemetery Friday night and I'd arrange a threesome to die for." She was the only one who laughed.

"He never suspected?"

"Maybe. But he was thinking with his dick." She glanced at the Fedora now on the floor. "Got me a hat for a souvenir."

Now that was cold. "Okay, so with Connie dead, do you know where the money's hidden?"

"Not yet, but you do."

I was afraid she'd say that. "I do?"

She sat back in the chair and made herself comfortable. "You have the journals and the key to the money is in them. Has to be."

I remembered the map in Connie's last journal. Maybe if I just gave her the damn thing she'd go away. Maybe not.

"Auntie Bella, I can't breathe."

"Put your head back down!"

"Can't." Chris's eyes were starting to roll back.

"Lana, my nephew is hyperventilating. Can I get a paper bag for him to breathe into?"

"Not until I get the journals." Lana settled back in the chair. "We have all night."

We didn't, because a freight train hit the house. Actually it turned out to be thunder, but that took at least three heartbeats. Lightning skittered across the sky. The wind kicked up again, blowing through the open door, scattering papers with abandon. The lights flickered, died and came back on. More thunder shook the foundation and bounced off the wall behind her.

Lana turned toward the sound and I inched my chair closer to the knitting basket.

Once again the lights went out. A flash of lightning lit up Emily's portrait. It tilted sideways at a crazy angle. A gust of wind shook it loose. In slow motion it slid down the wall, scoring a direct hit on Lana's platinum noggin.

She grunted and tried to get to her feet, then sat back down, stunned by the blow.

This was my chance! I rummaged in the knitting basket. My hands shook so I could barely stuff the slender bamboo needle, point first, up my left sleeve. Quickly I moved to stand with my back to the open doors.

The lights flickered on and I glimpsed Chris slumped sideways in the chair. No time to check on him. Lana stood, a bit wobbly, but still with gun in hand. She limped toward me.

She was close enough for me to see the whites of her eyes. As she raised the gun, I both felt and smelled her breath, cold and foul as the grave.

Now or never. With my right hand I yanked the needle from my other sleeve and drove it upward into her eye. The sensation felt strangely satisfying, like spearing a grape with a fork. She howled and began to flail around. The gun slithered to the deck.

I grabbed the gun, planted my feet and trained it on her using both hands, like they do on TV. Bad mistake. Lana advanced like someone with nothing left to lose.

I should shoot her now. I should.

Hesitated a second too long. She karate-kicked my stomach.

A glancing blow, but I dropped the gun. She moved toward the sound, but I got there first and kicked the gun out the door. It slid under the railing and dropped to the ground below.

Blood streamed from her wounded eye. She veered left, then right, then straight toward me, hands out in front, a demented sleepwalker. "I can't see, damn it, I can't see. Help me."

She kept coming, and I let her. At the last possible second I twisted sideways.

With a soft grunt, she fell headlong into the loose section of railing. It broke apart with a single sharp crack, like a felled tree. Unable to stop her forward momentum, she screamed until she hit the rocks of Emily's prayer garden.

I edged forward and peered over the broken railing, seeing her prone form below. Horrified and yet attracted, I edged closer to the black hole left by the missing railing.

I should have been relieved; instead, waves of despair washed over me. I'd let someone die. I had been a nun, someone dedicated to making people's lives better, and now another human being was dead because of me. Why hadn't I grabbed her? Bea's long-ago voice drifted above the storm sounds. "Jump, Bella. You did a bad thing."

Had I?

"Sure you did. Go ahead, Bella, jump. It won't hurt."

I took a step toward the edge, and another, then stopped.

What was I doing?

I stepped back from the edge. "Stop it right now, Bea," I shouted into the night, "I'll carry your secret to the grave but I won't listen to you. Someone has to care for the kid you left behind."

I stood there for I don't know how long until I heard behind me, "Auntie Bella, what just happened?"

37

I stepped inside the familiar room, reached for Chris and all but buried him in a hug. "You hyperventilated. Feel okay?" He nodded "yes" against my shoulder. "Something terrible happened. Lana fell through the railing."

"Wow." He pulled back with a puzzled expression. "Why is that so terrible? She was going to kill us."

While I struggled for an answer, Chris moved outside and peered over the railing, scrubbing the rain from his face with both hands. "Sure she's dead?"

Good question. "Guess we better check, huh?" Something was noodling at me, something I needed to remember.

"Let's call 911 first." Chris ran inside, reached for the desk phone, listened and put it down. "Dead." He thought a moment. "What about her cell? She was talking on it."

"It went down with her."

Oh my God. That was it. "Chris," I said, moving to my knitting basket, "let me grab the journals. Then we need to go. She talked to her partner and the partner was coming here."

"Crap, you're right." He headed for the door. "Where's the car? I didn't see it when Miranda dropped—"

"In the barn. My cell's on the console. Go! Go!"

38

Chris and I scrambled downstairs, through the house and out the front door. We crossed the yard, rain driving into our faces. I hugged the journals to my chest, trying to keep them dry.

We approached the barn. "Chris, do you see Sam?" I asked.

"What? Can't hear you," Chris yelled.

"Sam, do you seen him? He was in the barn, but I don't see how he could stay there through all this." If Lana's partner decided to follow Plan A and burn the property, he might be trapped.

"No," he shouted, walking backward, his eyes scanning side to side. "He's probably still there."

"I hope so."

If the road was still open, we planned to head for the sheriff's substation. Chris could call as I drove. He cracked open the barn door and I squeezed through to pull the tarp off the Subaru while he slid the door all the way open. I looked around. Sam was nowhere to be seen.

"He'll be okay, Auntie Bella," Chris said, taking the tarp from me.

I forced myself to nod. "We have to leave now."

We scrambled into the front seat and let out sighs of relief. Perhaps we weren't really safe within the cocoon of the car, but it felt safer. The journals sat at Chris's feet.

I eyed my cell. "Call 911," I said, starting the car. I whipped out of the barn, not stopping to close the door, and hit the driveway with gravel spewing around the tires.

"No service." Chris held up the phone.

I swore under my breath. "Okay, try again after we get to the highway." I'd been too busy to be scared before; now my legs began to shake. We approached the gate. I wiped clammy palms, one at a time, on my jeans and gripped the wheel. "Bella, you can do this. It's only a couple of blocks to town and the road's straight as a stick."

"What did you say?" Chris asked.

"Nothing. Just talking to myself."

"You do that a lot." Silence broken only by the wind. Then. "Stop!"

I hit the brake. "What's wrong?"

"Something on the ground." He shot out of the car, and

dived toward a lump just inside the gate. It looked like a bunched-up yellow blanket. Trying to swallow down a huge lump in my throat, I followed Chris.

He leaned over and touched the lump. "It's Sam." Tears and rain mixed on this face.

"Oh no." Sam lay quietly on his side. Too quietly. There was blood on his head. He'd been hit with something. The butt end of a gun most likely. I dropped to one knee and placed one hand on his ribs. Impossible to tell for sure, but I thought I felt a faint heartbeat.

"Is he alive?" Chris asked.

"I think so. Let's get him to the car."

Between us we lugged the unconscious dog to the Subaru.

"I'll sit in back," Chris said, "to keep him warm."

His kindness brought out the tears that I'd kept inside since this crazy night began. I scrubbed them away; we weren't done yet. "Thank you, Chris. All settled back there?"

"You bet. Let's get the fuck out of here." Then, "Sorry for the cuss word."

"That's okay. You're allowed this time."

Next to the open gate, the Divina Mill sign swung crazily in the wind. "Emily, you've had a busy night," I said to myself, grateful to her or God or whoever, or whatever, caused the portrait to fall. Without that fortuitous event, we'd be dead now. I shivered and turned the car heater on high. The warmth would be good for all of us, especially Sam.

We entered the short access road that led to the highway. Passing the thicket where I'd seen the shiny patch from the widow's walk, I peered into the trees. Nothing but wet leaves and tree trunks. Perhaps my imagination had played tricks on me before. There was nothing to worry about.

Time to try 911 again. A glance in the rearview mirror showed Chris propped on one elbow, his upper body protecting Sam. Gripping the wheel with one hand, I flipped open the phone.

"No Service." Maybe we should consider another provider.

A flash of gray appeared in the side mirror. Oh dear Lord. I looked again. The Hummer. Lana's partner must have been hiding there all this time.

Pop, pop.

"What was that?" Chris said.

"Shots! Get on the floor!"

"But Sam—"

"Get down!"

I kept a death grip on the wheel and floored the gas pedal. The old Subaru fishtailed dangerously. Just when I thought it was going to spin out of the control, the tires engaged, spewed mud and water, and we lurched forward. If we could make it to Los Lobos Road, there'd be other cars, maybe the neighbors.

As we approached the highway, the Hummer careened around me and pulled ahead. What the—?

Should I turn around? Go back? No, she'd follow.

A hundred feet from the road I slowed. What was her plan?

"What's happening?" Chris asked from the back floorboard.

"She's turning left toward downtown."

"Maybe she'll just keep going to Tolosa and the freeway."

"Yeah, we might get lucky," I said.

We didn't. Just beyond the intersection she pulled into the center of the double yellow line and stopped. A risky maneuver on this high-speed stretch of road in this storm. Maybe not. There was no traffic.

I paused at the intersection and quickly weighed my options.

"What are you doing, Auntie Bella?"

"Shh, I'm trying to think."

I wanted to go east the short distance to the sheriff's substation in Los Lobos. To do that I needed to get around the Hummer. But if I turned left and tried to pass her, she'd shoot us.

Wait a minute. I knew something she didn't. Just past the S-curves on the road to the bluffs, a nasty little detour doubled back to town.

With no good options, I turned right and headed west. Maybe we'd get lucky and be able to flag down another car before the S-curves.

"You're turning the wrong way!" Chris yelled.

"There's a detour," I replied. "Stay on the floor."

"Okay."

It took her at least thirty seconds to figure out what I was doing and I put as much distance between us as possible. Tried the phone again; still "No service."

I checked the rearview mirror. Despite a heroic effort by the old Subaru, the Hummer gained on us. Ahead loomed the Mercado estate. The gate stood open, but if I turned in and the Hummer followed, we'd be trapped like rats. I veered left onto the narrow road that led to the bluffs and the detour.

The Hummer advanced relentlessly, and soon sat right on my tail. I gripped the wheel in the 10 and 2 position, and braced for gunshots. No time for even a Hail Mary.

Pop, pop.

I shook, Chris moaned, Sam whined.

Sam whined!

"Auntie Bella, Sam's awake."

Dimly my mind registered that this was something to be grateful for.

Glancing in the rearview mirror, I took a corner too fast, and over-corrected. The car rocked dangerously.

Pop, pop.

She missed. Good thing she couldn't shoot straight.

We approached the S-curves and the steep drop to the ocean below. I willed my legs to stop shaking so I could control the clutch and brake pedal.

More gunshots. Once again I gripped the wheel. Where was that detour? Almost impossible to find in the dark with rain out-gunning the wipers. Then I saw the intersection. Could I make it?

Did I have a choice?

I jerked the wheel hard to the left, careened across the on-coming lane and landed somewhere in the vicinity of the narrow, dirt road. But I couldn't stabilize the car. It rocked as though it was going to turn over, righted itself, then began to fishtail. All I could do was hang on.

Oh no. Suddenly I saw the "Road Closed" sign ahead. We were going to hit! I jerked the wheel to the left away from the steep drop-off on the right. The wheel twisted in my hands, send-ing waves of pain through my palms, wrists, and arms. To let go meant certain death. We skittered across the road faster and faster and finally, thankfully, ground to a halt in a ditch on the other side.

The Hummer wasn't so lucky. With a clatter and bang that sounded like the end of the world, it blasted through the sign and fell into the abyss of the drop-off, leaving behind only an orange flash in the night sky.

39

Chris and I sat there stunned and silent. Finally, I summoned the will to unhook my seat belt. Even that simple act hurt my bruised hands and left me winded and exhausted. Chris sputtered and complained from the back floorboard. Some part of me realized he wasn't hurt, but it was at least a minute before I could turn around.

Amazingly, Sam was still on the seat. "How are you doing, boy?" He raised his head and thumped his tail once.

Chris huddled on the floor. "Are you okay, Chris?"

"Think so," he said, sitting up. "What happened?"

"We landed in a ditch, but…but the Hummer drove through the barricade and went over the cliff."

"Wow."

For a moment all I heard was the downpour, then, "Better try 911 again." Groaning, he hoisted himself onto the seat next to Sam and folded his arms around the dog's neck.

I groped for the phone but it had disappeared. I asked Chris to crawl into the front seat and rummage for it while I stared into the void.

"Auntie Bella, I can't find the damned thing. We need to go back."

"Chris, I don't think I can get the car out of the ditch." I rested my forehead on the wheel. "I'll just rest a bit."

"No, we need to go back *now*. Let me try."

"Think you can?"

"Sure, had lots of practice. Some Dad and Janet didn't know about." I heard a faint chuckle; it may have been my imagination.

"Okay, I guess that'll work. How do we change seats?" Even that seemed an enormous effort.

"Easy." Chris cracked open the passenger door, letting in wind and rain. Sam whined softly. "Ditch doesn't look that deep." Before I could protest, he stepped into it, sloshed around to my side and tugged at the door. "Crawl over into the passenger seat."

I did as I was told.

"I'll bet you could use a cigarette," I said after he'd expertly maneuvered out of the shallow ditch, turned around and headed the car toward town.

He shifted the four-wheel-drive into low. "That's so over."

"Really." One more thing to be grateful for. I warmed my injured hands between my knees, rested my head against the seat back and closed my eyes, welcoming a return to sanity.

I must have dozed off. All of a sudden I heard Chris say, "Oh, gross!"

My eyes popped open. It took me a second to realize we were back on Los Lobos Road, near the turnoff for my house.

Chris slowed and pointed toward the shoulder. A man stood naked in the glow of the headlights. He was trying to flag us down with one hand and shield his private parts with the other.

Rik.

40

Late Sunday evening:

We presented a strange sight at the sheriff's substation: a bloodied dog, a teenager bare from the waist up, an hysterical woman clutching five notebooks, plus the man wearing only a damp Grateful Dead T-shirt.

Actually, that's not quite accurate. Rik and Sam stayed in the car while Chris and I stumbled through the entrance, wondering how we could explain the unexplainable. Turned out the deputies knew much of it already. A worried Detective Scully had taken himself out of a sick bed to check up on me. He'd stumbled upon Lana in the prayer garden.

Miranda and Amy stood together by the counter, Miranda in a man's windbreaker that hung almost to her knees, Amy in a pair of lime green strappy sandals with four-inch gold heels. Never had a pair of senseless shoes looked so good.

"What are you two doing here?" At the sight of them, looking so concerned, and well, just so normal, I burst into tears. Gigantic sobs started in my toes and worked their way up my whole body.

Amy all but buried me in a big-hair, Obsession-filled hug, while Miranda peeled off the windbreaker and wrapped it around a shivering Chris. They had come separately to the substation, Amy because she began to worry after our hospital conversation, Miranda because something didn't seem right when she dropped

Chris off at home. Good instincts at work in both cases.

While Chris and I battled the storm and the wrath of Hummer Woman, Detective Scully had stood in the rain and once again called the EMT. Lana died on the way to the hospital. Pleading imminent pneumonia, the detective then took to his bed.

At the substation, an almost-hysterical Rik told his story, relating how the hired killer stripped him to make sure he wasn't wearing a wire. Just as she put a gun to his head, Chris and I drove by. She decided we were more important targets.

I told Rik he owed us big time. He looked at me like he didn't know what I was talking about.

Now I peered over Amy's shoulder, past a pouf of teased hair, to see Deputy Marquez approaching. "Mrs. Kowalski," he said, "we've sent deputies to investigate the accident on the detour off the bluffs road.

"Good," was all I could manage.

Marquez studied his clip board, then looked at me. "Your home's a crime scene and you can't go back there for a few days. Is there a friend you and the boy here," he nodded at Chris, "could stay with?"

"They're both coming home with me," Amy said. "Don't call Detective Scully until we get out of here. Mrs. Kowalski can give her statement in the morning and the detective can stay in bed."

Deputy Marquez nodded like this might be the first sensible thing anyone had suggested all evening. He turned to Rik, who now stood in trousers borrowed from a deputy's locker. The cuffs made khaki puddles around his hairy toes. "And you, sir? Can we call someone for you?"

"Raymond Mercado," he croaked, "my brother. Or Stan, my uncle."

Amy was herding us toward the door. I stopped dead. I'd forgotten about Stan.

I tugged Amy's hand away from my elbow. "You'd better send deputies and the EMT to Stan Mercado's house in Tolosa. Lana said he had mushroom poisoning."

Shaking his head, Deputy Marquez acted on this latest pronouncement. Amy once again nudged me towards the door. "Come on, you've given them enough marching orders for one night. You and Chris need to get out of those wet clothes and into hot showers. Bella, I'll even give you my last Lunesta."

My mind had begun to function again. "Amy, I have to stop by the hospital and tell Mike."

Amy's plump hands flew to her ample hips. "And tell him what? Your home was invaded, you and Chris were held hostage and two people are dead? Let the man have a good night's sleep before his tests tomorrow, for God's sake. It's probably the last sleep the poor man will get until all this is settled." She glanced at the wall clock. "Besides, it's almost midnight and I need to get out of these heels."

"What about Sam?" Chris asked. The Lab lay on a blanket in one corner of the substation, eyeing all of us like the bunch of crazies we were.

Miranda put her hand on Chris's arm. "Go with them. I'll take Sam to Doctor Choy's Emergency Care. If there's anything seriously wrong, I'll call your cell."

As I said, the girl has good instincts.

41

Monday morning:

Slowly I emerged from my cocoon of sleep. Something was wrong, something I didn't want to face. Then I remembered. Last night. I groaned, flipped onto my stomach and pulled the pillow over my head. Maybe if I faked illness, they'd let me stay in bed 'til Christmas.

Even with my head buried, I heard Amy on the phone in the

next room. Her place was spacious for a condo, three bedrooms, but the walls were so thin I wondered what, besides Laura Ashley wallpaper, held them up. I couldn't hear the exact words, but I knew she must be talking to the sheriff's office, her office, TV people.

I sat up and looked at the clock. 11 A.M. I'd never slept that late in my life. I flexed my hands, one finger at a time. Stiff and bruised, but all in all, not too bad.

Last night's tragedies were the biggest thing that ever happened in Los Lobos, perhaps in all of Tolosa County. Amy needed to put out the newspaper and here she was, stuck babysitting us. I hopped out of bed, almost losing the bottoms of my borrowed, queen-sized pajamas in the process.

A tentative knock. I hitched up my britches, sat down and hastily pulled the blanket around me. "Come in."

"Hey, Auntie Bella." Chris poked his head around the door. He wore a sad smile and a generic white T-shirt, the latter no doubt also donated by Amy. "Can I fix you some tea?"

"Sh...sure." Tears sprang to my eyes, making even that difficult to spit out. The kid was so thoughtful. How come Janet and Ed couldn't see that side of him?

"Chris, we need to call your parents. They'll see it on TV. Be prepared for the worst. They'll probably insist you come straight home."

He flopped in a chair next to the bed, stretched out skinny legs clad in last night's grungy jeans, and folded his hands over his stomach. "Already did that. Figured I'd better get it over with."

"And...?"

He looked down and contemplated his thumbs. "And, well, can I like, stay here for the rest of the summer?"

Did I hear right? "I, I guess so. Did you tell them the whole story?"

"Sure."

"So why aren't you on the next plane?"

A small laugh. "Well, Janet made noises like this was so fuc..., sorry, *terrible*, that California was the land of the devil, blah-de-blah, blah-de-blah, but…"

"But what?"

He gave a sad shrug. "Truth is,… they don't really want me. I mess up their neat little lives."

The poor kid. "What did your dad say?"

"Not much." He locked his thumbs together and held them up. "You know how he always goes along with Janet. That way he doesn't have to make decisions."

"So what did *she* say?"

"Well, she said she prayed over it—"

"Not long apparently, if you just called this morning."

He looked up and smiled. "Yeah, she got a quick answer. Anyway, she wants you to call her, but basically she says I should stay here and help you guys out of this mess. That it's the right thing to do."

"Chris, she's right."

He cocked his head like that was a new idea. "What do you think Uncle Mike will say?"

Mike. I stared at Chris, suddenly remembering Mike's tests this morning. So many things happening at once. I started to get up then realized I couldn't because of the PJs. "Look, I can't really speak for him, but I know he'll need extra help. And Chris—" I knew I was going too far, but couldn't stop myself.

His eyes drilled into mine. "What?"

"Maybe…maybe you can stay forever."

He gave me a dazzling Christopher Jensen smile, then slowly shook his head. "Thanks, Auntie Bella, but I need to get back by September. It's my senior year. I've been with my friends since kindergarten and we've been stoked about graduation for three years. Does that make sense?" He looked at me from under his thatch of yellow hair.

The kid was so wise. How did he get that smart in just seventeen years? "Perfect sense. You're making the right decision, but…" Dare I mention this now? "There's something else."

"What Auntie Bella?" I could see that my words worried him.

"Well, this may not be the right time to bring it up, but last night was awful. So awful it probably hasn't sunk in for either of us yet. You're bound to feel the effects, and I suspect sooner rather than later. Kind of like soldiers back from the war? Do you understand what I'm trying to say?"

He nodded. "That's what Miranda said too. One of her uncles is a grief counselor for the schools. She said like, maybe I could talk to him."

"Well," I smiled, not able to manage a laugh, "you two seem to have made a good start. You can talk to me too, if you want. Talk is good. Can't have too much talk in a situation like this."

He nodded and unfolded himself from the chair. "Got it. Let me fix tea while you shower. Maybe I'll have some too."

"That would be gangster," I said.

He shook his head at my attempt to be cool, then grew quiet and pensive, almost shy. "Uh, when you see Uncle Mike, tell him I said like, 'hi.'"

"Will do. Now get."

Chris ambled toward to the door, then turned. "Auntie Bella?"

"Yes?"

"Your driving last night? Now *that* was gangster." He gave me two thumbs up.

* * *

When I arrived at the hospital an hour later, an aide was attempting to take Mike downstairs for his tests, which luckily had been delayed. First he would have an MRI, then short-term sedation for the angiogram.

"Hell no, I'm not getting in that wheelchair. I can walk." Mike glowered in the bed, arms folded across his chest.

The aide, a Queen Latifah type, drummed French-manicured nails on the chair handles. "You're not walkin'. You fall on the floor, you sue the ass off the hospital and me too. Then where I be?"

Mike silently appealed to me for help. After I gave him a you're-on-your-own shrug, he turned back to her. "Give us a minute." Seeing that didn't go over so well, he added, "Please?"

"Talk fast, big boy." She vanished into the hall.

He buried me in a bear hug, a lot like Amy's last night, except instead of Obsession, I smelled Eau de Hospital. And he definitely needed a shave. I disengaged, rubbed my burned cheek, and straightened the neck of his gown. "Nice shirt."

He grunted, "Ain't it though?" and reached for me again. "Heard you had yourself quite a night. You okay?"

I gulped, nodded.

"Chris?"

"He's amazing." Tears sprang from a well I thought had gone dry. Damn those waterworks at unexpected times. I scrubbed my eyes.

"I'm still a little vague on the details. We'll talk about it later, after I get these goddamned tests over with."

I gulped. "Okay."

"Say, would you do something for me?"

"Sure, anything."

"Would you call Detective Scully and tell him I said thanks for his help in getting the EMTs so quick?"

I smoothed the bed sheet. "Mike, we need to thank him for more than that. He got out of a sick bed last night to check on me."

Mike blinked. "He did?"

"Yup, he was a little late, Chris and I were already gone, but what he did was above and beyond. I think he'd appreciate hearing from us, and the sooner the better. You call and I'll make him some cookies when things settle down."

Silence while he considered. Then surprisingly, "Okay, you're right. Fence mending is definitely in order." He grinned and gave my hand a decisive pat, once again the cop in charge.

Maybe not.

Queen Latifah appeared in the doorway. "You ready for the chair?"

"Yes, Warden," Mike said.

42

While I waited for Mike to come back upstairs, I picked up the latest issue of *People*. The aroma of chicken-something floated from a nearby cart piled with lunch trays. My stomach rumbled like the hold of a ship. At Amy's I'd been able to manage only the tea Chris fixed.

Wishing for another cup now, I opened the magazine, trying to bury my anxiety about Mike in the latest misadventures of that Axis of Absurdity, Britney, Paris and Lindsay. Half an hour later, a shoulder tap jerked me back to the real world.

"Bella?"

I turned my head and saw a pale arm, the short sleeve of a beige shirt, and finally, a face that looked like it had been run over by a semi. "Stan?"

I jumped up, swung around and gave him a hug, then pulled back. It was like hugging an ironing board. "Nice to see you, Stan," I said, and realized how dumb that sounded.

Good one, Bella. There could be nothing nice about this day for Stan.

The veins in his neck twitched as he said, "I'm just finishing up with…with Lana."

"I'm so sorry." I wondered for the umpteenth time, could I have saved her if Chris and I hadn't run for our lives? Some things are just unknowable. That question would haunt me for a long time, maybe forever.

"I identified the body last night, but…but…" His whole body trembled.

I put my hand on his arm. "Easy, Stan."

"I…I had to come back this morning to sign more papers." He pointed his chin down the hall toward Mike's room. "Thought I might find you down there with your husband, but they said you were here. Maybe we can talk?"

"Have a seat and we'll do that." He smiled his thanks and collapsed into the chair next to me. Fortunately we had the waiting area to ourselves.

Instead of talk, an uncomfortable silence stretched between us. Did he blame me for Lana's death? "Stan, I've been thinking about last night and…I wonder if I could have done more for Lana."

He stared at me open-mouthed. "Why would you think that?"

"Apparently she was still alive, but died on the way to the hospital. At least that's what the sheriff's deputy said."

He made a "tsking" sound. "Nonsense, you did exactly the right thing. The phones were out and you had to save yourself and the boy. Lana and her partner were on a collision course that could only end badly."

I took a slow, deep breath and relaxed into the chair. Stan didn't blame me after all. "I'm sure glad you're still around," I said. "Lana said you had mushroom poisoning."

He studied his folded hands. "She wished. I'd taken a nap and when the deputies screeched into the driveway, I was staring at Lana's empty closet. I thought she'd just taken off. After I saw the deputies, I was sure she'd had an auto accident. I didn't realize…" He clamped a fist over his mouth.

I reached over and patted his shoulder, the skin warm beneath the thin cotton shirt. "We don't have to talk about it."

"No, I want to, hell, I *need* to. That's why I looked you up. You're so easy to talk to."

"Thanks," I said quietly. Both Amy and Charles Cantor had said the same thing. I guess it was a good thing, but sometimes I heard things that made me sad and uncomfortable.

Stan shuddered. "God, I married my own niece, like a character in some bad soap opera. It would be funny if it weren't so creepy. I feel like a pervert."

"Stan, no one who knows you will think you're a pervert. Lana set you up. By the way, *why* did she think you had mushroom poisoning?"

He shrugged. "Earlier in the day I made my special mushroom medley with some wild ones I had in the freezer. I suspect she added a piece or two of *amanita phalloides* I also kept frozen."

"*Amanita* what?"

"Sorry, Death Cap mushroom. Wipe out your liver in no time flat. I keep *aminitas* separate and clearly labeled."

I shuddered. "Why even have them?"

"Some of my students are from south Asia, where they use a lot of wild mushrooms in cooking. Anyway, long story short, many Asians have been harvesting these by mistake and mushroom poisoning is way up. I planned to show them to my students so they could pass the word at home."

I gave him half a smile. "No good deed goes unpunished."

"Ain't that the truth? Fortunately, I didn't eat any of the medley. Hell, I lost my appetite after I saw she'd taken off."

"Good thing. Lana indicated that she and her partner—" Here I paused. "By the way, do you know her partner's name?" It seemed weird that she had no identity.

He shook his head. "No, but the car registration will tell them. I understand they found the Hummer smashed on the rocks. There was a red wig on the floor, but no body in the car."

"Really?" I said. "She was probably thrown clear. Her body will wash up in a day or two."

"If she doesn't become shark food," Stan answered.

I shuddered at the grisly image. "Lana and her partner were determined to find the money and leave the country. I guess they wanted to be in Mexico before *our* bodies were found."

"Like Thelma and Louise," he muttered.

"I guess."

"My own niece," he said, like he still couldn't believe it. "Connie's twin." He looked at me and his face seemed to sag. "I can't think of her as Corrina. To me, she'll always be Lana."

"I understand," I said, hoping that when the dust cleared, he'd have a few good memories of Lana.

"So she came to your house looking for Connie's journals?" he asked. "I've only gotten the story in bits and pieces. Why did she think you had them?"

"They found my credit card by the flower pot where the shop key was hidden."

"They?"

"Rik, Raymond and Lana."

A barely perceptible nod. "I guess they were going to clean out the shop."

"Yeah, and look for the journals. They each had reasons for wanting them."

"Do you think Rik and Raymond were in on this?" Stan asked, his eyes widening.

"No. After people die tragically, survivors get very nervous about things like diaries and journals. I think Raymond just didn't want them made public."

"As in 'what happens in the family stays in the family'?"

"Exactly. As for Rik, well…he was abusive toward Connie when they were young."

"Sexually?"

I shook my head. "Not that she said, but she claimed in the journal he drowned her cat."

Stan shot out of the chair, pounding one fist with the other. "The son-of-a-bitch. Connie was such a sensitive little thing. Something like that would scar her for life."

Apparently it had, I thought.

"I'll kill him with my bare hands."

I rose, put my arm around his waist and gently led him back to the chair. All the air had gone out of him, like a popped balloon. He had this hapless air that tugged at my heart. "Stan, don't compound the tragedy in your family." What's left of it, I added to myself. "I doubt that Rik can be prosecuted, but I assure you he will eventually get what he so richly deserves."

Last night was a promising start.

The magazine had slipped to the floor. I tossed it back on the end table. The Axis of Absurdity on the cover had nothing on the Mercado family. Hell, maybe they'd end up in *People*. Wouldn't readers love to find out that a famous rock star physically abused small animals as a child? (Not that they'd hear it from me.)

Stan looked up and caught my eye. "Bella, I still don't understand. Why did Lana want the journals and why did you take them?"

"It's complicated." I sat back down. "Lana was sure the information about where Manny hid the ransom money was in one of them. As for me, I had a hunch Connie's journals might provide a clue to her murder after I reread her obituary."

"Sounds like classic woman's intuition."

I decided not to call him on the sexist comment. He didn't mean any harm. "Originally, as you suggested, I thought the journals were in her house. I was going to use my credit card to pick the lock, also at your suggestion."

"I guess we all have criminal tendencies," he said with a ghost of a smile. "So how did the credit card end up by the flower pot?"

"Well, when I drove by"—I didn't tell him Chris was with me—"I saw Rik's car in the shop lot. I parked in front of Lockhart's bakery, crossed the street and peeked in the window. Rik was inside with a lantern. I figured he was looking for the journals and that he'd already checked the house. After he left empty-handed, I retrieved the key from under the flower pot. My credit card dropped out of my pocket. They all saw it on the ground, and Rik was tickled pink to bring it back to me."

"I'll bet. Had you read the journals by the time he arrived?"

I shook my head. "This all happened early Saturday morning. I worked the library sale during the day and when I came home Mike was ill. What with one thing and another I didn't get to them until late Sunday night."

"Last night," he corrected.

"Right." I stared at him. God, less than twenty-four hours since all this started to unravel. It seemed like eons.

"And in the journals you found out about Rik's abuse. What else?" he asked.

"Well, Lana, speaking as Corinna, had e-mailed Connie. They arranged to meet at the bluffs the day Connie was murdered."

His jaw dropped. "Lana set her up?"

"Looks like it."

He shook his head. "Bad enough she used me, but an innocent, pregnant woman…"

Why had I ever felt any sympathy for Lana? She certainly didn't deserve it. "Pretty bad, I agree."

"*Pretty bad?* Hell, that's the most evil thing I've ever heard." He passed a hand across his eyes. "If Connie had only said something to Raymond or me, she'd be alive today."

"True, but Lana/Corinna told her not to tell the family. It was supposed to be a surprise. Also, Connie played everything so close to the vest, even in her journals. She didn't write that Corinna was her twin, though according to Lana, Connie knew."

"That was our Connie," he acknowledged.

"There's something else you should know," I said.

"What's that?" he asked. "Does this get worse?"

"No, it might actually be good. There's a map in the last journal, Stan. Your brother hid money, a lot of it, in the house after the family came back from Mexico City."

"Money?" Stan asked, looking puzzled. "What money?"

"Apparently the ransom that was never paid. Connie knew about it, the parents told her, but interestingly, not Rik or Raymond. That's what Lana and her partner were after."

"How did Lana know about the map?"

"Lana said Connie got drunk one night and told her. She said Connie didn't remember the incident later."

Stan sighed. "I'm not surprised. She always drank too much, you know." I told him I'd heard that and he asked quietly, "Where are the journals now?"

"I turned them in at the sheriff's substation last night." I hesitated. "I guess I could be in real trouble."

"Real trouble? Did the deputies ask how you got them?"

"Actually, they didn't. But I did break into Connie's shop."

Stan reached for my hand. "If I'm not mistaken, Raymond or Rik would have to press charges for you to be prosecuted. And given what you've told me, that's not going to happen. If it comes to that, I'll go to bat for you."

I felt my eyes fill. "Thank you, Stan."

I wiped my cheeks with the clean handkerchief Stan provided and we talked some more. I gave him most of the details, leaving out how I stuck a knitting needle in Lana's eye. He'd find out in time. Or maybe not. As for me, I'd probably never pick up a knitting needle again.

"So what will happen to the money after they find it?" I asked.

"Rik and Raymond are the rightful heirs, hell, the only heirs, so I guess it will go to them. I guarantee you it won't go for anything useful."

"What a shame."

He shrugged. "Ain't it?"

"What will you do when this is all over?"

He stared out the window at the cars in the parking lot below. "I don't know. Probably leave town, maybe travel for a while. Try to shake the bad memories out of my head. I don't think the university will want a teacher who had an improper relationship with his niece."

"You told me the marriage was never consummated."

"It wasn't, but who's going to believe that? Hell, I knew before Connie died that my marriage wasn't going to work. Lana was never going to be a wife in the physical, or any other sense. I'd just about decided to cash in my 401(k), pay her to annul the marriage and take herself out of Dodge."

"She probably would have turned you down. She was after bigger fish than your 401(k). She wasn't going anywhere until she found that money."

"You're right. It seems so obvious now, how she sucked up to Connie right from the first."

"Connie was her own twin," I said. "I can't believe Lana put that out of her mind completely."

"She hired someone to kill her, didn't she?" he retorted.

"That's true." Lana was truly what she seemed, one heartless bitch. But then, she was insane. I had to keep that in mind.

"I wonder why the women decided to kill Connie before Lana got her mitts on the journal," Stan said. "Seems like they would have waited."

"Possibly Connie was suspicious."

"I doubt it, Bella. She always had this incredible naiveté. She trusted everyone."

"That's what everyone says. She didn't write about being suspicious in the journals. When you come right down to it, other than the stuff about Rik and the map, she didn't really write much about feelings, the way people normally do in journals."

"Typical of Connie not to let her hair down, even in her journals," he said. "She pretty much kept things inside."

"That's what Amy claimed," I said.

"I wish one thing," he said in a low voice, "I wish I'd said something to Connie about her drinking."

"Did her parents know she drank?" He nodded silently. "What did they think?"

"Well…" He hesitated. "Margaret-Rose liked her tipple. Raymond, Manny and I knew it, and it sounds sexist as hell, but we men thought 'the girls' had this little problem and it was no big deal."

"It killed Connie."

He studied the swirls in the gray tile under his feet. "It did indeed."

We sat awhile, the silence between us comfortable now. "Stan," I said. "I have one more question."

He turned to me. "What?"

"Why did you call the paper and leak the information about the land sale?"

His eyes widened. "You knew it was me?"

I gave him a half smile. "Even though you disguised your voice to sound like The Godfather, I figured it had to be you. We called you 'Deep Throat.'"

He actually grinned. "I wish."

"Why did you keep calling, and what did you hope to accomplish? You don't even live in Los Lobos."

He folded his hands and studied them. "I called to keep up the pressure and it worked. Got the deal out into the open and before the public so it could be discussed. That's what democracy is all about. All this under-the-table stuff in government has to stop."

"I agree. Hopefully things will be better after the dust settles on all this."

Before he could answer, Queen Latifah arrived. "Your husband's back in his room." She smiled and I took it as good news. "Doctor's with him."

43

The following Sunday morning:

"Still love me, Bella?"

I turned to Mike beside me on the sofa in the West Wing. He'd been home for six days. The coronary angiogram had revealed some blockage, but not enough for surgery or angioplasty. He was being treated for now with medication, diet and exercise. There'd be an evaluation in six months.

He didn't like any of it, but for once in his life he'd decided to follow orders. For that I was grateful. These simple thoughts were all I could seem to manage these days.

I reached up and ran my palm over my husband's pepper and salt buzz cut, enjoying the tickle on my skin. Prickly, I thought, like the man himself. "You know I still love you Mike, but…"

Mike grimaced. "You know what somebody said about that, don't you?"

My hand dropped. "That the real message comes after 'but'?"

"Exactly. I think you're trying to say you can't get past the fact that I provided the sperm for Connie's baby."

"Please don't put it that way." I gazed outside at the new section of railing on the widow's walk. It still needed a coat of paint. After the crime scene clean-up people left, Chris and Miranda had replanted Emily's prayer garden. Someone, possibly Chris, fixed the broken frame of her portrait. Good as new, she once again stood watch over us.

I sighed. Repairs to our home were progressing, but what about repairs to our spirits, to say nothing of our relationship? Who would fix them?

"Why can't you just say you were the baby's father in plain English?" I asked, picking up a half-finished blanket and then putting it down. I wasn't ready to start knitting again.

He squirmed. "Because that makes it seem like something it wasn't."

"Why don't you tell me what it was then?"

He drew a deep breath. "Well, I've tried to tell you, but you go off all half-cocked. I wasn't in love with Connie, felt nothing for her physically—"

"Nothing?"

At least he had the honesty to admit, "Well, almost nothing, but that's beside the point. She seemed so fragile—"

"Everyone keeps saying that."

"Because it's true. She wanted a child but couldn't seem to manage an adult relationship."

"Did she ever have one?"

"How the hell would I know? Anyway, once she made up her mind to get pregnant, she didn't want to just go to a sperm bank and take her chances. So she started looking around at the guys she knew—"

"I'll bet she did."

"Bella, will you quit?"

No, I wouldn't, couldn't quit. Even now, even after both Connie and her sister were dead. "So she chose you, just like that." I snapped my fingers.

"No, it wasn't that simple. She thought I had some good genes to pass on, besides of course, my good looks and scintillating personality."

"Too bad she didn't ask me about that one."

He had the grace to smile. "At first I said no, but then I reconsidered." Here he hesitated, running his fingers through his hair. "This is so hard, Bella, but I thought it might be like finding Ethan in some small way."

Of course. Why hadn't that occurred to me? I thought of the tiny school picture Mike kept on the kitchen message center. Because Ethan's body was never found, Mike had no closure for his son. Now there was another child he'd never know.

My hand trembled as I touched his. "Why didn't you ask me?"

"I was afraid you'd say no. Then where would we go? You know how people always say, it's easier to ask for forgiveness than permission?"

"That's not always true. If you'd come to me and asked, I would have said no initially. After I had time to think about it, I might have relented, especially if you'd told me what you just said about Ethan. Easy to say now," I allowed.

Mike spread his hands before him. They had a few of what my mother called "liver spots." Funny, I'd never noticed them before. "Too soon old, too late smart," he muttered, picking at one of the spots.

"Another old chestnut, not always true."

"So where *do* we go from here?"

His words hung in the air like tiny time bombs, each one with the potential to change our lives forever.

"I'm not sure," I said, stalling.

"Should I leave?" he asked into the silence.

"Do you want to?"

"No, you first," he said.

I couldn't believe it. The most important discussion of our lives and we were acting like strangers who'd reached a doorway at the same time.

"After you," I said. For some reason, I found this funny. The corners of my mouth twitched and then formed themselves into a smile. The smile became a chuckle, then grew to a sidesplitting shriek.

Mike gawked at me like I'd lost my mind, and turned his head away.

The laughter died stillborn. No sound in the room for I don't know how long. I watched a spider on the wall, heartsick I'd given the coup-de-grace to our relationship by seeming to mock it. Perhaps I could explain.

"*He-he.*"

"*He-he.*"

I turned my attention to my husband, thinking how much I still loved him. For a big guy he had this ridiculous little mouse squeak of a laugh that I found endearing.

"*He-he.*" His shoulders shook.

"Mike, look at me."

Tears streamed down his face. "*He-he.*" He held out his arms and gathered me into a hug. I felt his heart beating rock steady against my chest. Once again laughter started somewhere around my toes and moved upward until it engulfed me. We held each other and laughed at the absurdity of life and our own particular place in that life, until our stomach muscles screamed in agony.

"So I'll take that as a no, that you don't want me to move out," Mike deadpanned. That set us off again.

"At least we can share a good laugh," I wiped my eyes as we finally returned to sanity.

"I think I'd call that a promising start," Mike said.

I nodded. "It is, but it's not enough. I don't think we can do this on our own." I picked up my knitting and put it down again.

"So what are you saying?" Mike said, suddenly somber.

"That we should talk to someone."

"Talk to someone?"

"You know, like counseling."

He squirmed back to his side of the sofa and folded his arms across his plaid shirt. "No way. It's against the code."

Mike had what he called "the code," a set of rules he lived by. For example, he never paid for parking, even if it meant walking a mile in the rain. And he rarely, if ever, asked for help or advice.

"You don't understand," I said, "We need to learn to communicate."

Mike turned to me, his slate-gray eyes narrowed in silent rebuke. "My old Polish *babka* would have laughed her ass off. Pay someone to teach us how to *talk* to each other? We can borrow a book from the library for Christ's sake."

"No," I said. "There are subtleties to this that we just don't understand. It's not a do-it-yourself project that you learn from a book. You're an ex-cop of the old school and I'm an ex-nun, trained to ask God, and God only, for help. We need to get beyond that and I for one don't know how."

He chewed on that awhile, finally turning to me. "An ex-cop and an ex-nun having communication problems? Who could imagine such a thing?"

"Almost everyone we know."

"Hmm. Who would we go to, Father Rodriguez?"

"No, I don't think so, though he did ask me to take on Connie's homeless program."

"What'd you say?"

"That I'd think about it. But we're getting off-track. Miranda's uncle is a grief counselor. He'll be seeing Chris all summer."

"Good idea. The kid's been through hell."

"I agree. I'm sure the uncle can recommend someone."

"Another place to start," he said. "What if I hate the guy?" He stopped. "Or gal?"

"Woman, not gal, Mike."

"Sorry. Then we'll get another therapist. So that's a yes?" Mike's eyes misted over, surprising me and perhaps him as well.

"It's a yes."

"We need some way to seal the bargain."

"And what would that be?" I asked.

He scratched his chin, pretending to think. "Oh I suppose the time-honored way would do. Chris and Miranda are out until six, right?"

"That's what they said."

"Are you tired?" he asked.

"No, you?"

"Me neither, but we could take a Sunday nap anyway. Haven't had many of those lately." He gave me a goofy look that passed for a leer.

"Look," I said, "I'm not sure I'm ready."

"How about if we just lie down and hug, see what comes up?"

I smiled. "It's a start."

* * *

Five Months Later:

After an unprecedented show of faculty and student support, Stan Mercado was assured by the university of continued employment. He and Amy now meet for lunch once a week.

Further investigation into the plane crash that killed the senior Mercados found no evidence of foul play.

Back home in Cleveland Chris Jensen can't wait to finish his senior year. He plans to attend the University of Tolosa where Miranda is a freshman.

Lana's partner-in-crime is still missing and presumed dead. Bella found her little white dog wandering near Los Lobos Road and took him home. When Sam rebelled, Miranda adopted the canine orphan.

Rik Mercado has just been refused permanent residency status by the sub-Saharan nation of Gabon.

The ransom money was found in the Mercado home and disappeared into the brothers' bank accounts. The Land Conservancy has announced plans to purchase that property from the brothers and resume plans to build a Nature Center.

Raymond Mercado has offered to sell, not donate, his land east of Los Lobos to CRUD as the new site of the wastewater treatment plant. Typically, half the residents think that's a dandy idea, and half are dead set against it. This despite the specter of looming fines and the threat of Cease and Desist orders against individual homeowners.

Mike's heart problem continues to respond to medication and lowered stress. After discovering a mutual interest in racquetball, Mike and Detective Scully have become unlikely partners in twice-weekly games.

Under the guidance of a wise counselor, Mike and Bella's marriage now has more good days than bad. Bella is still obituary editor for the *Central Coast Chronicle* and writes occasional columns on knitting as therapy.

Bella doesn't know it yet, but she's about to become involved in two cases of murder, one cold, and one hot as tomorrow's headlines.